LIZZIE BORDEN, ZOMBIE HUNTER

C.A. Verstraete

~ White Wolf Books ~

LIZZIE BORDEN, ZOMBIE HUNTER

Thanks to the Kenosha Critiquers and friends, for feedback and support: Doris, Janet, Jean, Stephen S., Steve R., and Vicki.

Second Edition, White Wolf Books
www.cverstraete.com

Cover art and design: Juan Villar Padron,
www.talenthouse.com/jotapadron

ISBN: 978-1717351654

ISBN: 1717351654

Printed in the USA

Praise for
LIZZIE BORDEN, ZOMBIE HUNTER

"A good yarn told in a well written and engaging style."
—The Rotting Zombie, 7 of 10 zombie heads

"Historical fiction without ruining the original story or creating an entirely false world. ... A cool twist on an old mystery." —Melanie, FangFreakinTastic Reviews, 4 fangs

"I'd definitely have to recommend this book to any horror, history, or zombie lover. ... Very much worth the read." —Stormi, Boundless Book Reviews

Praise for
LIZZIE BORDEN, ZOMBIE HUNTER 2

"Lizzie Borden is back, and so are the zombies shambling their way through this fun and engaging book. Lizzie has lost none of her *bad-assitude!*" —Angela, Horror Maiden's Book Reviews

Praise for
THE HAUNTING OF DR. BOWEN

"The imagery in this book is brilliant... and creepy!"
—Rebbie Reviews

For Lizzie Borden fans who wonder, what really happened that day?
Now you know.

Table of Contents

Chapter One

August 4, 1892

Lizzie Borden drained the rest of her tea, set down her cup, and listened to the sound of furniture moving upstairs. *My, my, for only ten o'clock in the morning my stepmother is certainly energetic.* Housecleaning, already?

THUMP.

For a moment, Lizzie forgot her plans to go shopping downtown. THUMP. There it went again. It sounded like her stepmother was rearranging the whole room. She paused at the bottom stair, her concern growing, when she heard another thump and then, the oddest of sounds—a moan. Uh-oh. What was that? Did she hurt herself?

"Mrs. Borden?" Lizzie called. "Are you all right?"

No answer.

She wondered if her stepmother had taken ill, yet the shuffling, moving, and other unusual noises continued. Lizzie hurried up the stairs and paused outside the partially opened door. The strange moans coming from the room sent a shiver up her back.

When she pushed the door open wider, all she could do was stare. Mrs. Abby Durfee Borden stood in front of the bureau mirror clawing at her reflected image. And what a

1

horrid image it was! The sixty-seven-year-old woman's hair looked like it had never been combed and stuck out like porcupine quills. Her usually spotless housedress appeared wrinkled and torn. Yet, that wasn't the worst. Dark red spots—*blood*, Lizzie's mind whispered—dotted the floor and streaked the sides, of the older woman's dress and sleeves.

Lizzie gazed about the room in alarm. The tips of Father's slippers peeking out from beneath the bed also glistened with the same viscous red liquid. All that blood! What happened here? What happened?

She gasped, which got the attention of Mrs. Borden, who jerked her head and growled. Lizzie choked back a cry of alarm. Abby's square, plain face now appeared twisted and ashen gray. Her eyes, once bright with interest, stared from under a milky covering as if she had cataracts. She resembled a female version of *The Portrait of Dorian Gray*. Another growl and a moan, and the older woman lunged, arms rigid, her stubby hands held out like claws.

"Mrs. Borden, Abby!" Lizzie yelled and stumbled backward as fast as she could. "Abby, do you hear me?"

Her stepmother shuffled forward, her steps slow but steady. She showed no emotion or sense of recognition. The only utterances she made were those strange low moans.

Lizzie moved back even further, trying to keep out of reach of Mrs. Borden's grasping fingers. Then her foot hit something. Lizzie quickly glanced down at the silver hairbrush that had fallen to the floor. Too late, she realized her error.

"No!" Lizzie shivered at the feel of her stepmother's clammy, cold hand around her wrist. "Abby, what happened? What's wrong with you?"

Mrs. Borden said nothing and moved in closer. Her mouth opened and closed revealing bloodstained teeth.

"No! Stay away!" Lizzie yelled. "Stop!"

She didn't. Instead, Mrs. Borden scratched and clawed at her. Lizzie leaned back, barely escaping the snap of the madwoman's teeth at her neck.

"Mrs. Bor—Abby! No, no! Stop!"

Lizzie's slight advantage of being younger offered no protection against her stepmother's almost demonic, inhuman strength. The older woman bit and snapped like a rabid dog. Lizzie struggled to fight her off and shoved her away, yet Mrs. Borden attacked again and again, her hands grabbing, her teeth seeking the tender flesh covered by Lizzie's long, full sleeves.

The two of them grappled and wrestled, bumping into the bedposts and banging into furniture. Lizzie yelped each time her soft flesh hit something hard. She felt her strength wane as the crazed woman's gnarled hands clawed at her. How much more she could endure?

Her cries for help came out hoarse and weak. "Em-Emma!" She tried again. "Help! Help me!" Lizzie knew her sister had come in late last night from her trip out of town. *But if Emma already woke and went downstairs, will she even hear me?*

Lizzie reeled back in panic as her spine pressed against the fireplace. She pushed and fought in an attempt to keep this monster away, yet Mrs. Borden's ugly face and snapping teeth edged closer and closer.

Then Lizzie spotted it: the worn hatchet Father had left behind after he'd last brought in the newly chopped wood. *No, no!* Her mind filled with horror, but when her stepmother came at her again, Lizzie whispered a prayer for forgiveness and grabbed the handle. She lifted the hatchet high overhead and swung as hard as she could. It hit her stepmother's skull with a sickening thud.

As impossible as it seemed, Mrs. Borden snarled and continued her attack.

Lizzie hit her again and again and again. The blows raked her stepmother's face and scraped deep furrows into tender flesh. The metal hatchet head pounded her stepmother's shoulders and arms, the bones giving way with sickening crunches. Mrs. Borden's broken arms dangled, hanging limp and ugly at her sides… and yet, dear God, she continued her attack.

With her last bit of strength, Lizzie raised the hatchet again, bringing it down on Mrs. Borden's head. Only then did her stepmother crumple and fall into a pile at Lizzie's feet. It took a few minutes for Lizzie to comprehend the horrible scene. It didn't seem real, but it was.

With a cry, she threw the bloodied hatchet aside. She gagged as the weapon caught in the braided artificial hairpiece hanging from the back of Mrs. Borden's gore-encrusted scalp.

Retching, Lizzie ran to the other side of the bed, bent over, and vomited into the chamber pot. She crossed the room and leaned against the wall, her shoulders shaking with each heart-rending sob.

Her hands trembled so hard she could barely hold them still, but she managed to cover her eyes in a feeble attempt to block out the carnage. It didn't stop the horrific images that flashed in her mind, or the many questions. And it certainly did nothing for the soul-crushing guilt that filled her.

"Why?" she cried. "Why?" *Dear God, what have I done? What have I done?*

Chapter Two

Q. What time did you come downstairs?
A. As near as I can remember, it was a few minutes before nine.
　　　　　—Lizzie Borden at inquest, August 9-11, 1892

Lizzie staggered to the bureau mirror and stared. A wild-eyed woman gazed back. Mousy brown hair stuck out around her head in a disheveled halo. Spots of blood and gore dotted her clothes and face. She broke from her trance and looked up in alarm when someone called from downstairs. Oh, no, Emma! She couldn't let her sister come up here!

"Lizzie? Is everything all right?" her older sister called. "What's Abby doing up there?"

"It's nothing." Lizzie forced herself to sound cheery. She acted like nothing was wrong. "No need to worry. I'm helping Mrs. Borden pick up a box she spilled while cleaning. I'll be down in a minute."

Lizzie hurriedly ran back into the room, grabbed a cotton gown, and dipped it in the jug of water on the bureau. She rubbed the bloody streaks from her face, hair, and hands. Her blue morning dress was too soiled and stained to fix. It would have to be discarded. For now, she put on the old pink wrapper Mrs. Borden had left hanging in the closet and tied it around her waist.

She inspected herself again for any errant spots, and seeing none, rushed from the room. It was only when she got halfway down the stairs that she saw the red blotches on her shoes. Oh, no! She looked around and seeing nothing of use, pulled down her plain white petticoat and thoroughly wiped the tops of both of her sturdy black shoes. She breathed hard, fearing Emma's appearance any minute. The bloodied undergarment tucked out of sight under her voluminous skirt, she almost got down the stairs when she remembered—the hatchet!

Every nerve on edge, she rushed back upstairs and peered into the room. Mrs. Borden's body lay slumped on her knees beside the bed, like she'd been praying. Choking back tears, Lizzie pulled the hatchet free from where it had hooked her stepmother's raggedy hairpiece and let the blood-drenched braid drop to the floor. A jagged Z remained on the back of the dead woman's scalp, a gruesome memento of her fate.

A horrific image of a gory Mrs. Borden flashed in Lizzie's mind. "No, please, no," Lizzie muttered. She pressed her temple. "I can't think of that now. I can't."

Forcing herself to stay focused, she wiped and wrapped the hatchet in a towel before hiding it between the folds of her skirt. With each step, her heart hammered in her chest. All she had to do was make it downstairs without Emma paying attention.

To her relief, she managed to slip into the kitchen unnoticed while Emma dug around in the icebox. It gave her a scant few minutes to shove the hatchet out of sight behind the containers of lard Maggie had failed to put away.

Emma still paid no mind, instead rummaging around for who- knew-what, given they'd breakfasted not more than an hour ago. *No wonder she's getting a tad pudgy*, Lizzie thought. She took another deep, cleansing breath, and struggled to calm herself. She couldn't let Emma know what was going on! She had to act like everything was normal.

"Emma? What are you looking for? Mrs. Borden said she felt a cold coming on so we should all fortify ourselves. Care for a cup of tea and honey?"

Emma ended her rooting around and bit into an apple with a shrug. "Maybe a few sips. I am feeling a bit sluggish. It's so hot. Where's Maggie?"

"Still sleeping, I suppose. She mentioned feeling sick after washing the windows in this heat."

"I'm surprised Abby isn't yelling for her to get out of bed. You know how she feels about sloth."

Lizzie merely nodded, and bit back a retort about her sister's own habits, when a noise in the adjacent sitting room caught her ear. Was Father back from the bank? She glanced quickly at Emma, who paid no attention to the sound of furniture moving in the other room. But then she heard something that sent a shiver up her back—a low moan.

The sound even got Emma to stop munching her apple and look up. "What was that? Is Father sick?" She took a step toward the kitchen door. "Maybe I should see—"

"No, wait," Lizzie warned, trying to rein in her panic. "You sit and have your tea before it gets cold. I'll check on Father and bring a cup in to him."

To Lizzie's relief, Emma agreed and plopped into a kitchen chair. Lizzie hurriedly grabbed the tea kettle, poured hot water in the cups, and added some sliced lemon. She paused as the gruesome image of Mrs. Borden came to mind. What if something was wrong with Father, too? She had to keep Emma here until she could check if everything was all right! But how?

Lizzie went to the pantry and grabbed the jar of honey when she spotted the answer—a small bottle of Laudanum tucked behind the baking soda and jars of spices. Father must have left it there for use when he couldn't sleep. Much less than the usual dose should do the trick, she guessed. All she wanted was to keep Emma out of the way for a while.

After putting a drop in one of the three cups, she quickly put the bottle back and finished her preparations, being sure to add a pinch of cinnamon and a good dollop of honey to mask the bitterness. The room filled with the crisp scent of lemon and the spiciness of the cinnamon as she let the tea steep.

Everything ready, she set the tray on the table and gave Emma her tea before sipping from her own cup—undoctored, of course. "Mmm, this new English Breakfast tea with cinnamon has a very nice flavor to it, don't you agree?"

Emma took two unladylike slurps before nodding. "Hmm, it's not bad. I like the honey in it, but it has a bitter aftertaste I think."

Lizzie stirred hers and took another taste. "Maybe there's too much cinnamon, or it could be the lemon. I think that can make it a trifle bitter at times, but you know Father likes his strong. I'll take his cup—"

Hearing another sound in the sitting room, Lizzie nearly dropped her spoon in alarm. This time, her sister didn't seem to notice. Her eyelids drooping, Emma slurred her last few words, "Getting kind of *shleepy*," and with that, she dropped her head on her arms.

Lizzie pushed the chair in a bit closer to the table to be sure her sister wouldn't fall to the floor. Emma remained slumped at the table, her soft snores filling the room. Lizzie moved quickly. She took the hatchet in hand and stuffed the bloodied towel inside a bag of refuse that had to be burned.

A quick peek through the doorway told her Father had returned home, or maybe as she suspected, he might not have ever left. How odd to find him still sprawled across the old black settee this late in the morning. She tiptoed into the room and set the hatchet by the fireplace before approaching him.

"Father? Are you ill?"

He moaned in response. Lizzie moved closer. Her heart beat like a marching band in her chest. Her nose twitched at the odd smell in the room, like something foul, or meat going bad. "Father? Are you—?"

She gasped as he turned enough for her to see the ghastly grin on his face. Horrified, she stumbled away from him as fast as she could. Dear God! Whatever could cause such an awful change?

Her father's face, never handsome yet commanding just the same, resembled an image from one of her childhood nightmares. His open mouth revealed rows of yellowing teeth that chomped at the empty air. His eyes had rolled back, showing the whites. Lines of red-tinged drool dribbled down his chin and spotted the brilliant white of his Lincolnesque beard.

Usually a fine dresser who took pride in his appearance, his once pristine vest beneath his black coat now looked like he had worn it on a battlefield. The shiny, yellow-gold fabric was crinkled and splotched with spots of what she recognized as blood. She crept a few steps nearer and stared, trying to understand what had happened to him. Did he, too, become ill with whatever Mrs. Borden had?

A nervous quiver began in Lizzie's legs and worked its way up her body as she studied him. Her stomach roiled. Her stepmother's appearance had been terrible, but her father looked much worse. Blood framed his mouth. It smeared his chin. The sight made her turn aside and begin to heave. How had he become so beaten and bloody? Was it an accident? A fight? Or worse—had he also been attacked? Would the horrors never end?

Once the nausea abated, she sighed and struggled with what to do. *Maybe I should try to get his attention, let him know I'm here to help.* She moved closer and took his hand in hers.

Just as quick, she dropped it and shivered. Brrr! His hand was so cold! Even the gold ring she'd given him years ago, which he still wore, felt like it had been dropped in a snow bank. She shook her head. But how was that even possible in the heat of summer?

She moved back in alarm and waved her hand to see how he would react. She gasped as he turned his odd white eyes in her direction and moaned. Like her stepmother, her father showed no real signs of recognition. He paid no mind to his surroundings. It was like he'd just stepped from a meat locker, or had been holding a block of ice, or...

The words failed her. He, too, felt as cold as death.

She gulped, hesitant to even consider such a sacrilegious improbability. Her stomach roiled at the thought. No, it's impossible. As she watched, he attempted to pull himself upright, his movements as awkward as a fresh-caught fish flopping around on the deck. Her mind reeled. *I don't understand this. I don't.* His condition was simply unfathomable.

The thought that maybe he'd been wounded, or had some other malady, prompted her to lean in closer. Suddenly, he gave a deep-throated growl and lunged. His cold fingers tightened around her arms. She struggled to free herself to no avail. It was like trying to shake free from a pair of iron manacles.

Despite his inability to get up, and the flabbiness he kept camouflaged under expensive, well-fit suits, her seventy-year-old father was a strong man. His belief in hard work, or maybe it was his stinginess, had led him to continue chopping wood and doing other back- breaking chores he could have left to hired help, or someone much younger.

Lizzie screamed as he pulled her closer. His yellowed teeth clacked together; his fetid breath blew in her face.

Whatever this disease that had affected him, it was worse than anything she'd ever encountered.

She cringed at his gut-wrenching moans. *Oh, God, I don't know how much more I can take! It's awful. I have to get away from him, I have to!*

"Oww!" Lizzie yelped as he pulled her toward his gaping maw. It felt like her arms were being yanked from their sockets, but she kept fighting. *I have to get away from him!* She kicked and pushed with all her might. She struggled against him until finally, her bid for freedom worked.

She tumbled to the floor with a hard, bruising thump, but as Lizzie struggled to her feet, her father somehow rolled over. He fell onto his back, flopping around like an upside down crab. His arms and legs beat the air until he suddenly reached out, grasping her arm with his claw-like fingers.

Lizzie screamed, no longer caring who heard, as her father's well-muscled arms pulled her toward his gnashing teeth. "Someone, please, someone help me!"

Every muscle quivering, Lizzie fought with everything she had to keep his mouth away from her body and limbs. Her strength waning, she hoped to fight for as long as possible when Emma yelled from the doorway.

"Father!" Emma screamed. "Lizzie, what are you doing? You're hurting him!"

A quick glance told Lizzie her sister was still not herself. Lizzie struggled to talk while she fought to keep her father at arm's length.

"Emma, help." She panted with the effort. "Please, help. He's sick, he's gone insane. Help me."

Emma finally blinked and stared like she was seeing everything for the first time. "Lizzie! What should I do?"

"The hatchet!" Lizzie pleaded. "Get the hatchet. Hurry, please hurry! I can't hold out much longer."

Chapter Three

Q. Was he (your father) asleep?
A. No, sir.
Q. Was he reading?
A. No, sir.
—Lizzie Borden at inquest, August 9-11, 1892

L izzie's hopes for getting free rose as her sister rushed to the fireplace and grabbed the heavy, worn hatchet Father usually left there after he chopped wood. Emma took several steps but paused, unsure, her face sweaty and pale.

Don't go into shock now, Lizzie prayed. She tried to remain calm and encouraged her sister. "Emma, hurry. Hit him. Hit his arm so I can get loose!"

Father moaned and twitched, the trembling going up Lizzie's arm as he tightened his grip. She began to hyperventilate, not sure how she could keep him from getting even closer.

"Emma," Lizzie whimpered. Her sister stood in the same spot, her eyes watery with unshed tears. "Emma, please," Lizzie begged. "Please, do it. Hurry!"

Emma raised the hatchet and hesitated, her face frozen in fear. "Lizzzzie! I-I can't do this. I can't!" She began to cry. "Why are you making me do this, why?"

Lizzie tried again to pull away, and failed. Father's teeth clacked together like castanets. If nothing happened, she feared there wasn't much time left to escape. "EMMA, please, he's moving. Please, he's hurting me. HELP ME! Emma, do it. DO IT NOW!"

12

Lizzie's yells shocked her sister into action. Emma raised the hatchet and swung. Uttering a cry, she looked away as the hatchet head struck Father's back. Dark, black blood soaked through his coat and stained the sides of his vest.

It wasn't enough. He growled and bit and clawed at Lizzie like a wild animal.

"Father, no, no!" Lizzie yelled. "Emma, again, please!" Her cries joined Emma's heartbroken sobs. "Hurry. Oh, God, please hurry! DO IT NOW!"

With a cry, Emma lifted the hatchet high. She swung again. This time, it glanced off Father's arm and caused him to release his hold on Lizzie's one arm. With a moan, he jerked his head in Emma's direction, but maintained his death grip on Lizzie's other arm.

Lizzie leaned back, kicking as hard as she could. The growing pain in her leg, and the gruesome crack of his fingers breaking chilled her. Yet, she dared not stop. She ignored Emma's screams and kicked out again, over and over.

His grip finally loosened. His arm went slack. Lizzie scooted away from him and glanced at her sister, who stood in stunned silence, her face almost as pale as Father's. "Emma! Quick, slide the hatchet to me. Hurry!"

The hatchet slid across the floor, spinning like a child's top. Unfortunately, it stopped just out of reach of Lizzie's left hand. Unladylike as it was, she scooted across the floor and wrapped her fingers around the hatchet just as Father flipped over.

"Lizzie, he's getting up!" Emma skittered back to the doorway in fear.

The sight of him leaning clumsily on one knee, attempting to rise, was the only impetus Lizzie needed.

"Don't look," she yelled at Emma. "Turn your head. Close your eyes."

After the first hit, Lizzie closed her eyes, too, but kept swinging the hatchet. WHACK. WHACK. WHACK.

She swung and sobbed, hitting and hitting until Father's body fell with a big, house-shaking thud. With a gasp, she dropped the bloody hatchet when the tool head split apart from the battered wooden handle. Only then did she dare look around the room, nearly dropping to the floor in a faint. Blood had splattered everywhere. It streaked the worn, wooden floor, splashed the faded flowers of the wallpaper, and dotted the worn fabric of the settee Father had favored for his after-dinner nap.

The cloying metallic scent and the faint odor of rot filled the room. The sight and smell made her stomach roil. Even worse, Father's head had been bashed like a rotten pumpkin run over by a wagon. Lizzie tried not to pass out.

She felt like a monster, but Lizzie knew she'd had no other choice. The real monster lay at her feet. *I had to do it. I had to.*

There wasn't time, however, to think about what had changed both him and Abby so. She had to get Emma past what she'd witnessed. They needed to clean everything and themselves before the crime was reported. A glance at Emma, who leaned against the doorway, her eyes vacant, told Lizzie it might not be easy to do.

"Emma, dear, I know how shocking all this has been," Lizzie said, her voice soft and soothing. "Take a deep breath. Yes, that's good. Listen to me. You were taking a nap as you were tired from your trip. When you came downstairs, you saw Father. You're stunned by it all, which is true. Understand?"

Her sister's weak answer made Lizzie think Emma was still too shocked to truly comprehend everything. Emma stood and twisted her hands, her face haunted like the war-torn men Lizzie sometimes saw begging downtown.

Let her keep hold of her sanity, Lizzie prayed silently. Moving slow and easy, she approached her sister and gingerly touched her arm. Emma looked up at her with a start.

"Emma, I need your help. We have to put Father on the settee. Help me lift him, would you?"

Her sister stared at her, then down at him again, before she nodded.

"All right, you take his feet." Lizzie went to lift his head, fighting to keep the vertigo at bay as she gazed at the bloody mess of her father's face. His eyeball had been split in two and hung out of the socket. She turned aside and gagged.

Lizzie removed her torn, blood-spotted petticoat, wrapped Father's head and shoulders with it, and carefully hoisted his upper body. Sweat dripped down her face with the effort as she and Emma struggled to move his heavy bulk. They barely made it the few feet, with both of them dragging him much of the way. After several tries, she and Emma finally managed to lift him partway onto the settee.

Finished, she put an arm around her sister's shoulder and gently led her into the kitchen. Grabbing a wet cloth, she quickly wiped her face and hands before urging Emma to sit and do the same. "Yes, wipe your hands," she suggested. "Take another sip of your tea."

Emma went through the motions, her eyes blank. She picked up the cooled tea and took several sips until Lizzie whisked the cup away. Emma needed to be relaxed, but not too groggy or inebriated.

"Now, take a deep breath. Better?"

Emma gave a wan smile and another slow nod.

"Good. I think you should lie down for a while. I can take care of the rest, all right?"

"But-but what about Abby? Where is she?"

"Never mind, I'll see to Mrs. Borden." She put an arm around Emma's shoulder as they walked through the sitting room to the front hall staircase. She couldn't have her sister going up the back stairs and looking in on their stepmother.

"Now remember, when the police ask, you were upstairs. You know nothing about what happened. Understand?"

Emma's bottom lip quivered as she began to cry. "I-I can't lie. They'll know I'm not telling the truth. Fa-a-ther!"

They were wasting time.

With a sigh, Lizzie took Emma by the arm and pulled her back into the sitting room. "Look at him. Take a good look. There is something incredibly wrong in how he attacked us. He tried to bite us! He was NOT himself. He didn't even know us. Do you want to see more?"

Lizzie tightened her grip in an attempt to pull her sister further into the room, but Emma resisted and backed up.

"Nooo," she protested. "I-I can't bear it."

"Very well." Lizzie let go of her sister's arm. "Remember, this is important. You saw or heard nothing. Somehow, Father contracted this strange illness. Maybe he's not the only one. We need to find someone who knows about such sickness and can help us. Now, let me handle everything, all right? Emma, please, this is important. You have to trust me."

To Lizzie's relief, Emma gave a final, sad sigh as she made her way upstairs, dragging her feet like she'd been through a war. She had. They both had.

The stress of all the rushing around squeezed Lizzie's chest until she could barely breathe. Panicked, she mopped the floor and wiped away the errant blood spots she saw on the walls before pulling off her bloodied dress and wrapper. Those things, plus her ruined petticoat and spotted stockings, went into the stove. She stared at the dress, her waste-not instinct prompting her to think maybe she could clean it. Acting like someone not thinking properly, she pulled the dress out, instead deciding to shove it in the front closet until later.

Goosebumps broke out on her arms as she hurried back into the kitchen to tidy up, and not just because she stood there scandalously clad only in her undergarments. Her mind worked furiously as she washed the cups and put the tea items away. *Did I convince Emma that something had been terribly, horribly wrong with Father? Did I calm her enough so she won't share the whole awful truth of what happened?*

The washing done, Lizzie dug in the back of the pantry for the nearly full bottle of whiskey Father kept hidden there. She pulled it out, and with a deep breath, opened it. Every inch of her temperance supporting self recoiled as the strong scent of the alcohol wafted over her, but she tamped down any feelings of guilt. *Yes, I've already done worse.*

Her fingers shaking, she raised the bottle to her lips and gulped. The liquor burned her throat like hellfire as it went down. A second later, she leaned over the sink, choking and gasping as the horrible liquid came back up. Tears trickled down her face as she took another drink, fought to swallow, and choked again before she finally succeeded in keeping it down.

She wiped her eyes and sighed deeply. *Well. Now I'm both a murderess and a drinker.*

Disgusted, she capped the bottle and shoved it back in the pantry, out of sight. She did a final check, and satisfied nothing was out of place, rushed upstairs to dress. Hopefully, she wouldn't forget anything. *Face and arms washed? Yes. Nails scrubbed and brushes cleaned? Done. Hair*

17

combed and wiped? Done. Clothing destroyed… Oh, the dress. She hesitated. *Never mind. I'll tend to it later.*

A quick rinse of peppermint water erased any remaining traces of alcohol on her breath. Everything looked to be in order. Still, she paused and fretted. Finally, she donned a blue dress similar to the one she'd worn earlier and tiptoed back down to the sitting room. A glance at the clock on the mantel showed it was a quarter of eleven.

She glanced around the room and gasped. Wait—no! The hatchet! She checked the floor once more, then grabbed an old towel and cleaned the bloodied hatchet head and handle. She tested holding the wrapped bundle at her side, making sure she could hide it within the folds of her dress. Once her grip felt comfortable, she paused and listened. The house remained quiet. Good, Emma must've fallen asleep.

Her heart pounding, she snuck out the kitchen door, rushing across the yard to the barn. Once inside, she blinked several times to adjust her eyes to the dimness. A moldy smell and the rank odor of animal dung filled her nostrils. The hay! Yes! She dropped the hatchet handle and kicked the piles around, the dampness and animal smells filling her nostrils.

Her panic grew as she ran back inside, a muttered prayer on her lips that she hadn't been seen, and then rushed to the cellar. She dumped the hatchet head in a pile of other rusty, old, forgotten tools, hoping no one found it.

It took every ounce of determination she had to stand still. She leaned against the scarred wooden door, closed her eyes, and tried to calm herself. Her deep breathing filled the silence. *Breathe in, out.* Finally, she opened her eyes. *Very well. I'm ready.*

18

Once upstairs, she stood in the front hall listening to the sounds above her... someone walking around, doors closing. She braced herself for the chaos to come.

Holding tight to the staircase post, she took a deep breath, then let out a loud scream. "Emma, Maggie! Come down quick, Father's dead! Somebody came in and killed him!"

Chapter Four

SHOCKING CRIME.
A Venerable Citizen and His Aged Wife Hacked to Pieces.
—Headline, *The Fall River Herald*, August 4, 1892

W hen the police arrived, Lizzie took care to appear calm and controlled, though she was far from it. Her insides quivered like she'd been locked outside on a cold night for hours without a proper coat or cloak. She felt like a clumsy, quaking mess, but knew to show no emotion or reveal that she'd had any prior knowledge of what had happened.

Emma, bless her soul, turned out to be more help than Lizzie could have anticipated now that she'd gotten past her initial shock. Emma answered the police inquiries in a straightforward manner, her testimony about not knowing what was going on strengthened by the information that she'd just returned from a two-day visit out of town. Verification of her trip gave credence to her report. Their maid, Bridget Sullivan, whom they called Maggie, had been asleep upstairs and remained blissfully unaware. *Probably from overindulging in her 'medicine,'* Lizzie thought.

"Sleepin' in my room, I was, until I heard Miss Lizzie callin'," Maggie said in her thick brogue. "I got tired and wasna feelin' well after washin' the windows, so hot it's been."

There was a lot of questioning, which Lizzie endured with grace until she finally asked Emma to bring her something to drink. "I feel a touch sick to my stomach," she admitted, her voice low. She sat in the dining room, hands

20

in her lap, willing herself to stay focused and calm. She had to pay attention. It was hard, but she pinched her palm as a reminder to stay alert. The whole event disturbed her greatly.

All too soon, even the supportive presence of their neighbor, Adelaide Churchill, became cloying, though Lizzie did her best to act appreciative.

Mrs. Churchill set the lukewarm cup on the table. "Have some tea."

Lizzie gritted her teeth behind a smile of thanks, preferring the glass of juice Emma brought her instead. She ignored her neighbor, who insisted on sitting next to her, her eyes scanning every move anyone made with interest. Frankly, the woman unnerved her. *She's like the Cheshire Cat, all smiles and feigned kindness while she's ready to pounce*, Lizzie thought. *Hypocrite!*

Lizzie concentrated on keeping her thoughts and emotions steady while she put some distance between herself and her neighbor. *I can't fall apart now. I can't. Not now! I have to think of Emma.* She gave her sister a sad smile before Emma left the room.

True to character, it took only a minute or two before Mrs. Churchill displayed her usual nosiness. Lizzie's annoyance turned to alarm when the woman got up and left as well. Only minutes later, she came running back, with Emma right behind her.

"Oh, my! Heaven help us!" cried Mrs. Churchill. "Abby's upstairs!"

"Lizzie! Abby's dead!" Emma gave a wide-eyed stare, and her best shocked expression, both true reactions since she'd had no idea what had happened earlier.

Lizzie jumped to her feet as Emma swooned. She managed to get her sister into a chair with the help of one of the policemen. Mrs. Churchill fanned Emma while Lizzie ran to the kitchen. She hurried back with a glass of water, a cup of warm tea doctored with a little whisky and honey, and a cold, wet rag to wipe her sister's pale face.

Moments later, Emma began to whimper. "Lizzie, Lizzie, it's awful," she muttered. "Awful."

Lizzie set the tea down and tried to comfort Emma, who continued to cry silently. Finally, she got her sister to take a sip of water. While Lizzie knew what had happened, the announcement still brought the horror of it rushing back.

"It can't be!" Lizzie cried out and clapped a hand to her breast. "I thought Abby went out. I was certain of it! What happened?"

Chaos swirled around her. Emma's crying, Mrs. Churchill's paranoia, and the police pounding up the hall stairs to the guest bedroom set Lizzie's nerves on edge. She held in the urge to scream while Maggie stood there, her face white as chalk.

"Oh, it's jes' terrible." The maid wiped her tear-stained face and wrung her hands. "I dinna know how anyone could be doin' such a horrid thing. It's awful."

When Maggie swayed, Lizzie yelled and reached to steady her. A questioning glance from one of the officials, his shrewd eyes studying her as Mrs. Churchill helped Maggie, made Lizzie pause.

Emma and the other women sobbed in near hysterics. Lizzie remained calm. She wiped her hand across her eyes, her weariness real, as she reasoned it out. She'd never been much for female hysteria. *Someone has to stay in control*, she thought. If she fell apart now, like Humpty Dumpty she'd probably never be whole again.

The histrionics ended with Maggie seated, more in control of herself again. Lizzie handed her the cup of tea and watched how Maggie greedily gulped it down, which made her wonder how much the maid enjoyed her spirits in her off-hours. *Not that I should be one to judge*, Lizzie thought, having overcome her earlier abhorrence. She had forced herself to take her own discreet sip before setting the bottle aside. She needed it. They all did.

A bit of color once again on Maggie's shocked face, Lizzie wandered to the doorway and tried to hear what the officials had to say.

"Looks to have been dead a while," one said.

"He's as cold as that one there, I'd say."

"Somebody strong did this, or someone mighty angry, I gather…"

Her cheeks warmed as she listened. That childhood advice about not eavesdropping for fear of what you might hear came to mind, but Lizzie dismissed it. This time she needed to know, no matter what was said. She turned away and tried to control the surge of anger. She'd best get accustomed to the questions and scrutiny.

Despite her Uncle John being seen near the house, and the unknown man she'd overhead Father arguing with at the door a few nights ago, she suspected the police would focus on who was home at the time of the murders. They'll look at Maggie, who was asleep, and Emma who was upstairs in her room, having just returned from a visit out of town. *That makes me the best suspect.*

Lizzie's thoughts raced. She reasoned that some of their recent financial dealings, like Father buying back the house he'd given her and Emma to rent out, might make her look bad as well. Maybe they should've waited to ask Father to pass on some of their inheritance. But wait for what? *How could I have known what would happen?*

Then there was her occasionally uncomfortable, sometimes strained relationship with her stepmother. Lizzie sighed. Families and personal relationships were so

23

complicated. She braced for the worst. Then she heard a couple of the investigators talking amongst themselves about the deaths.

"Looks like she'd been dead at least an hour before he was killed," one said.

"He's not been dead long," another said. "Trace of warmth yet in the body."

Warmth? She stumbled and quickly pulled herself out of sight, back into the kitchen. How could that be? The memory of how chilling her father's touch had been made her shiver. She couldn't think of any real explanation for it. Of course, most of what had happened this day made no sense, no matter how she looked at it. It simply couldn't be fathomed. But what would she tell the police? What could she tell anyone who asked what had happened?

Lizzie knew she had best obtain the services of an attorney for herself and Emma. Would it really go that far? She couldn't be naïve. She had no real explanation for what had gone on while she was at home.

She knew of several good attorneys through Father's solid business position in the community, his presence on several bank boards, and the B.M.C Durfee Safe Deposit and Trust Company board. Of them all, one name came to mind and topped the list—Mr. Andrew Jennings. He had a kind demeanor, but always struck her as a thorough, no-nonsense man: the perfect attorney.

After finding the number in one of Father's ledgers, Emma obligingly went to one of the neighbors to make a discreet telephone call to Mr. Jennings' firm. The irony made Lizzie shake her head, given Father's aversion to having one of the "newfangled" devices, as he called it, here at home. "Bad enough they're encroaching on our space everywhere else," he often complained.

Emma returned several minutes later. She sidled close to share Mr. Jennings' response with Lizzie so no one could overhear.

"Did anyone know who you were talking to?" Lizzie asked, a trifle nervous.

"No, they gave me my privacy," Emma assured her. "He said he'll gladly represent you and me both, if needed. He also insisted you say nothing further without him being present."

The conversation pleased Lizzie, who squeezed her sister's hand. "Thank you, Emma. That is reassuring."

Mr. Jennings need not have worried. Any further questioning went on hold as officials from the marshal's office finished up their cataloguing of both rooms where the bodies had been found. Lizzie grabbed Emma's hand and held it tight as they watched the medical examiner and his assistant transport Father's and Mrs. Borden's bodies out to the waiting wagon. Both she and Emma bit back sobs, but remained stoic.

His work done, the official in charge suggested it might be best if she, Emma, and Maggie stayed elsewhere. "Is it a requirement?" Lizzie asked. The official shook his head. "Then we'll stay here, in our own home," she insisted.

The actual places of the murders—the sitting room and the guest bedroom—remained off-limits, though Lizzie figured it couldn't make much difference. There had been enough visitors traipsing throughout the house earlier. She also suspected that no one in the household wanted another look at the gruesome scenes. She, for one, had had quite enough. She wanted to be alone.

Lizzie went to her room and changed into her sleeping gown to rest, though she didn't expect she'd get any sleep. She mulled over the events of the day even if she was no closer to understanding the details now than before. It still bothered her immensely. What could have made Father and Mrs. Borden act so? Why did this happen to them? Why?

Her bewilderment soon turned to grief. She spent several minutes hiding deep, gulping sobs behind her hands. Finally, her emotions spent, she wet a cloth from the cool water in the pitcher on her bureau, wiped her face, and tucked into bed. She hated laying there, her mind rehashing every bloody moment. Sheer exhaustion finally put her in a deep, albeit disturbed, sleep.

In her dreams, she ran and ran, pursued by a mob of horrid, bloodied creatures. They closed in, their fetid breath fouling the air, claw-like hands reaching for her, when… THUMP. A loud noise startled her from her nightmare. She gave a frightened cry.

Lizzie sat up, heart pounding, taking deep breaths, when she heard it again. THUMP. THUMP. She listened, afraid to move. Wait, the sounds… Someone was knocking downstairs. The clock in the hall chimed eight. Is it that late? Who could be bothering them at this hour?

She fumbled around in her attempt to light the oil lamp on her bedside table, her hands shaking like she had palsy. She threw on her wrapper and opened her door just as Emma opened hers.

"Somebody is downstairs," Emma whispered. "Have the police come back?"

Lizzie went to the window and stared out at the street bathed in the moonlight. "No, nothing is out there. Please, don't worry. Go back to bed. I'll take care of it. Go on now."

Grabbing the lamp, she went into the hall and rushed down the stairs as another knock sounded. "Coming," she called out, keeping her voice as low as possible. "Give me a moment, please. Who is it?"

Usually, she didn't hesitate to open the door. After all, she knew her neighbors. She'd never been afraid. But now... An unexpected fear inched down her back. She pulled the wrapper tighter around her.

Her mouth went dry. She felt her heart thud in her chest as she gripped the banister so hard her fingers went white. Her sweaty palms slid along the polished wood. She had plenty of reasons to be afraid after the day's events. Who could be out there? Did someone want to do them further harm?

She breathed harder with each step, yet she kept going, if only to tell whoever was out there that the police had been alerted. Even if it wasn't true, she didn't know what else to do.

But what if whoever brought this sickness to her family had returned to finish what they started?

Chapter Five

Could it be that the murderer was concealed inside the dwelling and had awaited a favorable moment to carry out his nefarious plans?
—*The Fall River Herald*, August 5, 1892

L izzie continued down the stairs, heart pounding. A most unladylike curse slid from her lips. Why, oh why, has a telephone never been installed here at home? She knew why, of course, but one of them should have insisted on it! The strong, burning smell of the lamp made her cough. She realized that with everything else on her mind, she'd forgotten to clean it.

Whoever was outside pounded on the heavy oak door again. Lizzie hesitated in the entry hall's doorway, especially when a deep male voice called out. "Miss Borden? Please, I need to talk to you!"

Breathing deep, she focused on keeping herself calm. She quickly grabbed one of Father's umbrellas from the hall stand. At least it offered some kind of protection. Her steps slow, she tried to keep the lamp steady lest she drop it.

"Who-who is it?" Lizzie tiptoed into the parlor and peered hesitantly through the lacy curtain in the front window. The sliver of brightness from the moon gave her a glimpse of a tall man at the door, his face shadowed. She jumped back in alarm, dropping the umbrella onto the floor. "What do you want? Leave us alone! I've already contacted the police!"

The man took a step back and apologized. "Miss Borden, please forgive me. I never intended to frighten you. Your attorney, Mr. Jennings, sent me."

"How do you know him?" she questioned. "Is it an emergency? How do I know you're telling the truth?"

"Here." He fumbled with something in his hand and bent down. "I'll slide my card under the door. Do you have it?"

She went to the hall and watched the small white card appear under the crack in the door before picking it up. "Yes, yes, I see it."

The card read, Mr. John Charles Fremont, Attorney-at-Law. Mr. Andrew J. Jennings, Attorney-at-Law. Firm of…

"All right, it-it seems to be in order." She straightened, her irritation growing. "This is really inconsiderate to bother us so late. We are a house in mourning. What do you want?"

"Miss Borden, please. It's urgent I talk with you. Will you open the door?"

She swallowed the last of her misgivings about him being a masher, or someone nefarious, and opened the heavy oak door a crack. Her light offered a surprising glimpse of a tall, attractive man with a serious face and startling blue eyes. His good looks tempered her irritation, but only for a moment.

"Well?" Lizzie blustered, her patience wearing thin. "Are the police coming to arrest me?"

Her visitor's eyebrows rose at the question, but Lizzie had to know. Why else would he be here now?

Mr. Fremont shook his head. "No, not yet." He leaned closer and whispered, bringing with him the scent of mint. "Please, I don't want to alarm you. Look, I know what you did. I know what really happened today."

His words made her leap back in alarm and try to slam the door. She would have if he hadn't stuck his well-shined shoe in the jamb like some ill-bred salesman.

"Please, leave," she ordered. "Now. The police should be here soon."

"Wait, Miss Borden, please, hear me out. I don't mean to frighten you. Mr. Jennings sent me because of my work on, um, cases with special circumstances. No need to worry, anything you say is protected by attorney-client privilege."

"You are NOT my attorney. I hired Mr. Jennings, not you."

"In a way you already did since I am connected with his firm. You'll need my help and that of the others working with me."

Maybe it was the earnestness of his appeal or the guileless look on his face that got through to her, but an inner instinct told her to trust him. "Very well, Mr. Fremont. I'll listen to what you have to say. If I find you are trying to take advantage of me, I will contact the authorities again."

"Fair enough. Now, please, you need to change into street clothes. I need to show you something of importance."

That did make her suspicious. She stepped away from the door in concern. "Now? At this hour? Maybe I should contact Mr. Jennings for further verification."

He took a deep breath. "Miss Borden, there isn't much time. I can explain everything on the way, but you have to see it yourself. Then you'll know I'm telling the truth."

Still, Lizzie hesitated, which caused him to utter a mumbled curse.

"Look, I suspect you found your stepmother acting strangely, not like herself at all," he blurted, his voice urgent. "She neither recognized you, nor paid attention to you calling her name. She tried to attack you, even to bite you, as did your father. You hit them several times, but found it had no effect. All they did was growl, and they felt ice cold

30

to the touch. Neither of them stopped until you hit them in the head. Am I right?"

Lizzie staggered as the horror of it became clear. When he reached out and touched her arm, she let him. His touch was steady, comforting. "How-how did you know?" she whispered.

"That's what I need to show you. Please, we need to leave right away."

She studied him a moment. It might be foolish, but she decided it should be fine. After all, no one but Emma knew about the call to Mr. Jennings, so she really needn't worry. Besides, he has such nice blue eyes and dimples. A masher or anyone with bad intentions surely wouldn't have such a nice-looking face or be so polite, would they?

"All right. Give me a moment, please. Wait here."

As luck would have it, she'd left one of her day dresses in the hall closet instead of putting it back in her bedroom armoire. Rather than go upstairs, she set down the lamp and slipped on the wrinkled garment behind the kitchen door. *I'd better get my riding coat*, she thought, *since it's turned cooler.*

"Miss Borden? We must leave."

On a whim, she grabbed the gray silk scarf to cover her hair, surprised to hear a crinkling sound. She pulled at the scarf, almost able to feel her visitor's impatient breath on her neck.

"Yes, just a minute, please."

She worked to un-snag the scarf and found it had caught on the edge of a small, white paper package stuck in the pocket of Father's favorite black coat. It occurred to her that he'd mentioned going to pick up something on his way to the bank. But she suspected with it being warm early in the day, he certainly wouldn't have needed his heavier coat. Or maybe he'd put it on first and changed into the lighter coat instead? Her mind worked. *Did this have anything to do with the mysterious man I heard him arguing with some days ago?*

After finally loosening the scarf, she wrapped it around her head. The package went into her own coat pocket until she could study it further.

"Miss Borden? Please, can we go?" her visitor asked again.

The door shut and locked, Lizzie hastened her steps to keep up with her visitor, who nearly bolted down the street. "Mr. Fremont, what's the hurry?" she whispered at his back.

"Miss Borden, we have no time for formalities. Call me John." He stopped for a moment beside her and took her elbow. "I don't mean to be forward, but the others are waiting." He began to walk, his pace quicker. "We must hurry."

"Mr. Fre—John. Oh, I suppose you might as well call me Lizbeth or Lizzie if you want, though I do prefer Liz."

She allowed him to help her into a well-kept carriage pulled by a handsome black horse. The moonlight glowed on the carriage's shiny painted surface. "Others? Who are we meeting?"

A smile lit his face as he hopped in the other side of the carriage and clucked to the horse. "All right, Lizzie, I mean Liz. Hang on, we should be there shortly."

Her hands gripped the front padding of the carriage tight as the horse trotted down the empty street. "But where are we going?"

"Oak Grove Cemetery."

Lizzie sputtered and choked on the words. "Oak Grove? My father and stepmother are going to be buried there in two days time! Why are we going there of all places?"

The horse's iron shoes made a rhythmic clickety-click against the street's worn red bricks as they sped to their destination. The trees hung eerily over the roadway, the dim glow of the kerosene street lighting doing little to lighten the desolate atmosphere. At this time of night it felt slightly ominous, but the route was as familiar to her as the road to her own front door. The short ride would've been pleasant, under other conditions, of course.

"John, what—"

His voice stopped her questioning. "Let me explain since we'll be there shortly. I know that you noticed something odd about your parents. They—"

"Mrs. Borden was my stepmother," she interrupted.

"That doesn't matter right now." He flicked the reins at the horse, which began to trot faster. "As I was saying, I'm sure you saw they didn't hear or really see you, and how cold they felt."

Lizzie nodded. "They felt so cold and clammy, like-like…" Her thoughts whirled. She lowered her voice. "Both my father and stepmother felt almost someone already deceased. But that cannot be, can it? The dead do not move or walk."

"As preposterous as it sounds," he explained, "I'm afraid they're doing just that, and more. All we know is that a kind of sickness, some disease, has infiltrated the area, making the dead come back and commit terrible deeds. Those of us who are members of the Saint Alphonsus Society have pledged to protect our city. We're working with the officials to make sure this stays quiet, and is contained and controlled."

Her head spun. *Dead… Quiet… Contained?*

"It makes me think of Miss Shelley's *Frankenstein* come to life," Lizzie murmured.

He shook his head. "More like Mr. Stevenson's *Jekyll and Hyde*. I think there is something diabolical, some madman, behind all this."

33

The carriage stopped several steps away from the Gothic stone arch guarding the entrance to the park-like final resting place of the city's former residents, and of the important and well-to-do in the community. Clumps of ivy covered most of the aged surface, revealing only a few letters of the words etched in the stone above. Not sure why, but feeling a sense of comfort, Lizzie silently mouthed the familiar saying like a talisman, *The Shadows Have Fallen and They Want for the Day.* She prayed those particular shadows remained far away.

John alighted and gave the outer area a quick inspection before coming to her side of the carriage. "The horse will be fine here since they have been contained, and stopped, out by the gravesites."

"They?" she asked.

He helped her from the carriage and gently held her arm. "I must warn you. What you're going to see is jarring, like nothing you've ever seen. It will be absolutely horrifying. The Society members must do whatever they can to stop this scourge. It's an ugly, ugly sight. Now, stay close. Whatever you do, do not run or leave my side under any circumstances, or I can't protect you."

She nodded, still puzzled at his warning. "I won't."

Lizzie never considered herself one who frightened easily. Run away? She thought not. But as they slowly made their way to the cemetery entrance, her mind imagined all manner of awful things. Still, none could be more ghastly than the scene she had left behind at home.

Her mood darkened as Emma left the room. The awkwardness between them bothered Lizzie. She had hoped the party would have helped draw Emma out. She'd thought it could even provide a way for her sister to get to know Pierre better. She'd been wrong on both counts.

I was too wrapped up in talking with the other guests to see if Emma felt comfortable. She hoped Emma would get back to her old self soon, especially since they still had a lot of information to look into yet.

Looking out the window, she spotted two unwelcome visitors shuffling down the center of the street. Lizzie grunted in frustration, even if she had nothing else to do. Grabbing her weapons bag, she pulled out the small handheld axe and went outside. The monstrous duo quickened their shambling steps once they sensed her waiting at the end of the walkway in front of the house.

As they lunged, she took out her frustrations with each bite of the axe.

WHACK. WHACK. WHACK.

Lizzie's hope was that she and Emma could somehow make peace with each other, the past, and especially, with what their lives had become.

Chapter Twenty-Nine

News: Following the trial, *Fall River Daily Globe* reporter Edwin H. Porter shares the "real story" of Lizzie Borden in his new book, *The Fall River Tragedy: A History of the Borden Murders.*

"**E**mma?"

No answer.

Lizzie went downstairs after rising much later than usual and found the house quiet, her sister already departed to the train depot for the visit to her friends. Emma's sudden departure without saying goodbye filled Lizzie with sadness. She also felt bewildered at this most unexpected turn of events.

Maybe a few days or so apart will be good for both of us, she decided. It would give her time to think and make a game plan. She had a strong feeling, though, that her behavior had probably been the main impetus in Emma's decision.

She realized too late that her thinking had been totally wrong. Emma was right. She never should've thought of parties, or such frivolities, with all the terrible things happening. Given the past year, she'd simply wanted to ignore it all for a while. All she'd wanted was to put everything behind them for one night and have a little fun. No wonder Emma got angry. Her sister felt the mounting pressures and looked at things with a clearer insight. Lizzie knew she sometimes acted like Nero fiddling while Rome burned.

Ever since Emma's near attack, Lizzie had seen a marked difference in the sheer number of creatures appearing on the streets and roadways. When she went out for her quick daily walk, she found herself passing groups of neighbors who had witnessed the changes, too, and stood nervously talking together about the growing horrors. Many clutched hunting rifles, or had other weapons in hand. They still ignored her, but she overheard some of them making plans to leave.

Already she had seen a number of nearby families rushing to load their possessions and children into carriages for a trip out of town. She saw other families being driven down the road, wagons and carriages packed to the hilt. They weren't going to the seashore.

Peering out the window, Lizzie watched police officials set up a patrol at the other end of the road closest to the main thoroughfare. This time, she felt no unease at their presence. Of course, their refusal to set up any roadblocks closer to her home only confirmed John's warnings about the official stance toward her.

She knew the neighbors blamed her for the lack of protection. As a result, she'd seen some of the men patrolling outside their homes on their own. More than once she heard shots and watched them take aim at an approaching creature.

Her heart heavy, she went downstairs to sharpen her knives and axe, and check that all her weapons were ready. She thought of Emma. *I hope she doesn't stay away too long.* With each swipe of the blades against the sharpening stone, Lizzie realized she had some decisions to make—whether to let the disagreement go on and wait for Emma to sort it out, or be the one to approach her sister. Then there was Pierre, who hadn't yet shown anything but a respectful, brotherly interest in Emma. Lizzie suspected he could be the real reason behind Emma's unexpressed anger, which also left her with a dilemma of her own. *Do I let him know my feelings toward him have changed?*

As she pondered the idea, her mind drifted again to their last kiss, which truth be told, was never far from her thoughts. She'd tried to forget, to push it away, but so far it had proved irresistible—and left her wanting more. The feelings kept coming back with a vengeance, like the yearning for a big, equally forbidden piece of chocolate cake.

The chime of the front doorbell broke Lizzie out of her daydreaming. Brushing back her hair, she went upstairs to answer. Peeking out the window, she was surprised to find none other than John on the doorstep. He looked frazzled as she welcomed him in.

"John, what're you doing here?"

"Liz, I'm absolutely stunned. Have you seen this?" He thrust a dog- eared copy of *The Boston Globe* at her.

"No, I'm behind in my reading. Why? What happened?"

Unfolding the paper, she eyed the front page and gasped. There, in giant black letters, stood the headline she'd hoped to never see. DOES LIZZIE BORDEN PLAY A PART IN RECENT ATTACKS?

The story went on to delve again into the other axe murder. It listed several incidents where people had been nearly attacked, had died mysteriously, or simply disappeared. The writer hinted at an influx of "diseased" individuals in the region, but left out the true background and the Society's involvement, focusing instead on finding a way to get her name in the report.

"This-this is ridiculous," she stammered, her outrage growing. "This makes no sense at all. All they did was rehash old facts and scramble the rest so they could use my name to sell papers. I may contact Mr. Jennings and have him lodge a complaint. At least they left out any mention of the Society."

"Yes, though the reporter hints about our involvement, and I quote, 'several people who escaped harm reported certain unidentified individuals taking charge of the attackers.' Meaning us." He cleared his throat before continuing. "This whole report leaves us with a dilemma. I'm sorry to say this, I truly am, but it may make it harder for us if you're involved."

All she could do was stare at him, his comment catching her totally by surprise. If she'd been thinking ahead as to the real reason behind his visit, maybe she wouldn't be so shocked. She should've guessed he was up to something. She shook her head in disgust, both at him and at herself.

"Is this a formal request for me to stay away from the group? Or is this merely a suggestion?"

He nervously cleared his throat again. "None of us can tell you what to do. If you want to keep on with what you're doing, neither I nor anyone else can stop you. I just wanted you to know that it may be harder for you to remain unnoticed."

Her patience at an end, she showed him the door. "This is news? The trial is over, but my sentence continues. From day one, I have been hounded and watched. Nothing has changed in that respect. Absolutely nothing. Thank you for coming by. Let this be your last visit."

He went out and stood a moment on the doorstep, looking as if he wanted to say more, but thought better of it. Instead, he turned and walked away. She slammed the door, her anger boiling. *So be it.*

As if to rub salt in her wounds, she stood by the window and watched a couple neighbors shooting at a group of undead creatures shambling around the corner. Several Society members appeared on the scene to help, recognizable by the distinctive new red armbands marked with the initials SAS for Saint Alphonsus Society. Apparently, the need for secrecy no longer applied. As she closed the curtain, Lizzie felt a twinge of envy and disappointment that no one had bothered to offer one to her.

"Huh, well, they can keep their armbands." She decided to keep on with her own plans and personal patrols. Maybe Emma would be back soon to help, she hoped.

The other bad, or at least unexpected news of the day, came later when someone from the building department telephoned saying her request to put in a new section of fencing would be delayed. It wasn't earth-shattering news, of course, but another unwelcome annoyance. John had also mentioned that many projects and business dealings seemed to be put off or lost these days, especially when it involved anything or anyone connected to the Society. It made her wonder if in truth, the city— namely some high-ranking official—wasn't keeping tabs on her and anyone she was even remotely associated with. Maybe that was the real reason for John's cryptic warning.

Without Emma around, Lizzie felt lost. The house seemed too empty. She dared consider the unthinkable: *if Emma decides to not come back home, will I be able to stand it? Could I live totally alone?*

Lizzie didn't think their argument that serious, or was it? Could their estrangement go that far? But she suspected Emma had been more upset than it appeared. Maybe the pressure of living under constant scrutiny, plus having to always watch out for those creatures had finally got to her. *Or could it be Emma finally had had enough of me and the whole situation?*

Lizzie dreaded having to consider the possibility and wondered—was it all enough to push Emma to move away,

208

or possibly stay in Fairhaven? It seemed impossible, but if Emma did that Lizzie knew there was nothing she could do about it.

The thought soured her mood, making even the tea taste bitter. Loath to sit idle, she set her cup aside and began a renewed search through Father's papers, hoping to spot anything she might have missed. When nothing new came to light, she shoved the pile aside in frustration. Then it dawned on her. *Wait a minute!* She mulled over Emma's comment—the grinding stones. If Father bought them, then where were they? What did he need them for?

Her mind worked. What could be the key to the puzzle fell into place. Lizzie groaned, wondering why none of them had thought of that before! She must be losing her mental faculties. Here they had searched both warehouses, but no one had done the obvious—looked around Father's pride and joy, the handsome, red brick A. J. Borden building he'd had constructed on Main Street.

Excitement filled her as she found the letter listing the other supplies Father had ordered. *Will I find anything there besides caskets? Will I finally learn what Father needed with all those supplies?* What about those creatures chained in the warehouse?

She had a hard time containing her anticipation. Gathering up her tools and bag, she double-checked she had everything of use and went to change into a regular, less attention-getting day dress. As much as she enjoyed wearing the more practical, and much more comfortable, bloomers she'd had made, the garment had to be confined to her fighting, or training around the house. She almost decided to forgo convention totally and wear it when she went shopping, but she still didn't relish bringing more attention to herself if she could help it.

That left one other problem: finding someone to chauffeur her. With John no longer available, and considering his latest comments, she felt uncomfortable asking any of the other Society members for assistance. Nor did she want to be in the position of her request being turned down if they held to the same notions as him. She hesitated but a moment and finally decided to call Pierre, who gladly—almost too gladly, she might add—welcomed the chance to see Father's business. He said he'd welcome helping her get to the bottom of the mystery.

The clank of the mailbox announcing the arrival of today's post proved a welcome diversion while she waited. She took the handful of mail inside, quickly flicking through the envelopes since the majority had Emma's name, when she saw an envelope lying on the floor.

I must've dropped it, she thought. Emma, she suspected, had scrawled her name and address on the front in a firm hand. Her sister's handwriting had never been good. Writing in haste only made it worse.

"She must've slipped the letter into the mailbox as she left," Lizzie muttered. "I'm glad she reached out. I really am."

She opened the letter, feeling more hopeful that any rift between them would soon be corrected. The crisp white linen sheet crinkled in her hands as she unfolded it. She stared in confusion at the hastily scribbled message. It read, *Meet me at Father's business. Two o'clock. Come alone.* It was signed with a big initial 'E'.

That was all it said. A quick glance at the delicate gold watch pinned on her blouse told her it was just past one. How odd that Emma would decide to go to the very place she'd planned to visit! Her sister must have come to the same conclusion she had.

Lizzie looked again at the letter, front and back, but had no doubt her sister wrote it. If Emma wanted to meet her there so they could both investigate and air their disagreements without anyone else round, Lizzie certainly would honor the request. It seemed like a good idea for a number of reasons.

Too impatient to wait for Pierre, she instead ran to telephone a couple of her previous chauffeurs. Luckily one of the young men agreed to take her downtown. Hurrying, she set the letter on the table, grabbed her weapons bag, and adjusting her hat, went to stand in the front doorway to wait.

As luck would have it, the young man pulled the carriage up in front of the house sooner than she expected. She nodded to him in greeting as he hurried out to help her into her seat.

"Where to, Miss Borden?"

"If you can take me to Mr. Borden's business on Main Street, please, then you can leave as I have some things to attend to there."

He dipped his head and flicked the reins at the sleek, black horse. "Very well, Miss."

211

Chapter Thirty

FREE FROM GUILT.
—Headline, *The Morning Call*, San Francisco, June 21, 1893

T he A.J. Borden building stood modern and solemn in the midday sun, a sturdy reminder and fitting memorial of Father's standing in the business community. With spacious offices, plenty of interior storage, and large, attractive storefront windows at the street level, Lizzie suspected the building would be in use for many years to come. It certainly showed Father's foresight.

With a sigh she thanked the young man who helped her out of the carriage, and made her way to the back door, glad to see no one about. She didn't want to talk with anyone who happened by. As she fit the key in the lock, the door creaked partly open, a sign Emma must have arrived already.

Lizzie slipped inside and closed the door, waiting for her eyes to adjust to the dimness. Dust motes danced like Dracula's minions in the stream of sunlight filtering in from the top windows. She shivered, wishing some other reference had come to mind.

"Emma?"

No answer.

Her shoes shushed on the polished wood floor, the only sound in the stillness. Lizzie edged her way carefully down the hall, wondering if Emma had decided to wait in Father's office. A skittering sound made her gasp and wheel about. For what felt like minutes instead of seconds, she stood, listening, her heartbeat pounding in her ears, but all remained quiet. How silly of her. Of course a building like this surely had mice and other rodents.

"Get hold of yourself," she whispered.

The offices she passed sat empty. A lone gray hat hung on a wall hook. A tired black umbrella rested in a corner, the only clues that anyone had been there at all. For the most part, the offices looked well-ordered and efficient. She smiled at the sight of the piles of typewritten pages sitting on many of the desks—and not a typewriting machine in sight. It looked like Father held to his attitude against the machines, even here.

She continued down the hall and stopped at the largest office door at the end, which she rightly assumed, was Father's office. She waited a second, and hearing nothing, pushed the door open. "Emma?"

To her disappointment, the room stood empty though she spotted what looked like her sister's black and brown tapestry bag on the floor. While she waited for Emma's return, she took the time to peruse the room. An impressive walnut desk topped with various writing accessories, folders, and a light sprinkling of dust commanded attention in the center of the room. A dark brown leather chair sat behind it like a throne.

The walnut paneling gave the space a serious, business-like air, but also made it dark. She flicked the key on the wall gas light and quickly scanned the rows of gold-stamped leather volumes on the bookshelves behind the desk. Another large leather chair and a smaller chair in front of the desk, along with a tall walnut coat stand in the corner, completed the furnishings.

Lizzie checked the clock again. One-thirty. She had plenty of time. She wondered about Pierre. *Is he waiting for me at the house? Did he get angry or disappointed that I wasn't there and leave?*

213

Sighing, she tapped her fingers impatiently on the polished wood of the desk. Where in the world was Emma? Lizzie set her bag down, plopped herself in the large chair behind the desk, and flipped through the correspondence, bills, and letters. A series of numbers scribbled on a small scrap caught her eye. *Hmm, I wonder...*

She gazed around the room before going to stand in front of a rather bland painting of a farmhouse set amid a golden field of wheat. The artwork hung on the wall in an ornately carved gold frame. Curious, she lifted the edge of the picture and stuck her hand under it, feeling around on the wall. Certain she was on the right path, she lifted the art off the wall, set it aside, and peered at the small metal safe the painting had hidden.

Her first attempt at the dial failed. She tried the numbers again, this time turning the small knob in the opposite direction. The click after the last number told her it had worked. She popped the door open and pulled out a batch of papers. As she flicked through them, her heart fell at the contents. One page listed the names of many influential people who had financed several shipments from—the Caribbean? What could Father have gotten from there?

She folded the page and slipped it into a pocket in her skirt. The rest of the papers on the desk proved less interesting until a familiar logo caught her eye. She held the paper closer, noting the elegant lettering, but it was the actual name that got her heart pounding.

There on the top of the page was the same description as the sign she'd seen on that wagon outside the house: *A.B. and C. Tonics.* She groaned as the initials became clear. *Why didn't I see this before?* A. B. stood, of course, for Andrew Borden, but who, or what, did the C. stand for? Or was it only a clever way to use the alphabet-style symbol as a trademark?

Now more pieces of the puzzle fell into place—the logo, Father's supposed role, and the connection to ingredients like Licorice Root that she and Emma had found earlier. Emma had been right, she mused. The list had been items in a kind of recipe, a tonic, of all things.

It made her wonder. She would've thought Father had enough business concerns to keep him busy, what with the mortuary supplies, selling caskets, his time on the bank boards, plus his civic duties. The unknown concerned her the most. She never expected him to be in the tonic and patent medicine business, too.

She chuckled, realizing her folly. Why should she be surprised? If there was money to be made, Father naturally found a way to get in on the venture.

THUMP. She jumped at the unexpected noise and went to the door. "Emma? It's about time you got back!" Lizzie complained. "You were so specific about the time, and now you leave me sitting and waiting for you." She paused. "Emma?"

She peered out at an empty hall. Nothing moved or made a sound.

Lizzie's impatience flared when more pounding sounded from further down the hall. "Emma? Where are you? Whatever are you doing? Will you please answer!"

She tried to tamp down her anger as she followed the sound. She went down more long hallways and passed other offices until she reached a pair of double doors. One of the doors opened easily. She sniffed, surprised at the strong aroma of cloves, coupled with the sweet, spicy scent of cinnamon. Underneath, she detected a slight musty scent.

The casket showroom. Several types of caskets, ranging from plain burnished wood to gleaming mahogany and walnut, filled the large room. Gold and silver handles glistened. Scented candle holders hung on the walls. A sense of calm filled her as she surveyed the solemn, decorous atmosphere.

Lizzie went into the next room in search of her sister, but instead found herself in what looked like an apothecary. The mid-sized room had been fitted on one wall with shelves, now stocked full. Various boxed ingredients and large containers lined another wall. A long wooden bench and a large worktable completed the furnishings. She picked up a small bottle, not surprised to see the now-familiar tonic label. The scent of licorice and cinnamon tickled her nose.

Looking up, she noticed a long metal chute extending down through a hole in the ceiling. The chute, which served as a kind of funnel, had been pushed aside, giving the workers more room to move around as they assembled ingredients.

On closer inspection she saw a light coating of something on the metal surface. It wasn't dust, she realized. Dipping her finger in it caused light puffs to rise from the powder. Her nose tickled. *Achoo!* She rubbed her powder-coated fingers together, noting the gritty texture.

Lizzie hesitated a moment before she held her fingers to her nose, sniffed, and let out another big sneeze. There seemed to be no detectable scent, but it did irritate her nose. Puzzled as to the source, she wiped the unknown ingredient off her hands. She made for the hall, wondering if she could find the beginning of the chute and see what it was used for.

As she stood in the cavernous space, she felt vibrations under her feet. Something was moving, or being pushed around; something big. All thoughts of that fled when she noticed something white lying on the stone floor near the stairs. She dashed across the room, her inner alarms jangling.

"Emma!" Lizzie picked up the white, lacy handkerchief, every nerve in her body jangling. "Emma!" Lizzie raced back and forth, growing more frantic. "Emma, where are you? Please, answer me!"

Her heart pounded so hard Lizzie felt faint as she eyed the worn, wooden staircase. Seeing nowhere else to go, she carefully made her way to the upper level, her hand trailing against the cool stone wall beside her for support. She went up the rickety steps, cringing with each creak of the wood, yet determined to find her sister.

As she got to the top and stopped before a heavy wood door, she heard what sounded like yells. It was hard to hear with the increasingly louder thuds, like something heavy was being moved. Her mouth dry, she wrapped a sweaty hand around the doorknob and pulled it open.

"NOOOO!" She screamed at the sight before her. "Oh, no, dear Lord, no!"

Chapter Thirty-One

Suppose that a man should tell as many different stories as Lizzie had done.

—*United Press, Semi-Weekly Gazette and Bulletin,*
Pennsylvania, 1892

"No, no! Who did this?" Lizzie cried. "NO!"

Her heart in her throat, she stared at the frail figure bound and tied in front of her. Dear God, what kind of fiend would do such a thing?

She stumbled into the cavernous, mostly empty space, barely able to hear above the pounding of the giant grinding stones as they shifted in the center of the room. A quick glance told her the slabs, each weighing at least a hundred pounds and wider than two large men, had been positioned and lowered by the heavy chains and winch above. The stones turned on a center rod and ground the material placed under them, which then fell into a kind of sieve. The material, she suspected, then traveled down to that chute she'd seen in the workroom below.

In the middle of the mechanism stood a quivering Emma, gagged and confined to a small wooden platform constructed above the stones. Emma shifted and squirmed, trying to loosen the ties fastened around her limbs. The wooden boards she stood on swayed and rocked in response to her every move. She jerked her head and yelled, her cries muffled by the cloth covering her mouth and wrapped around her head.

Lizzie gasped. Emma's position looked far from stable. "Emma, wait, stay still!" Lizzie yelled. "Don't move! DO NOT MOVE!"

She tried to see if there was a way to get up on the platform with her sister without jostling it more, when the door banged open and startled her. She jumped back with a cry.

A deep voice uttered a falsely cheery greeting. "Would you look at who it is? Well, we meet again!"

The man stood in the shadows by the door, making it near impossible for her to determine his features. Then he moved into the light, a wicked grin on his face. Lizzie wobbled, her knees growing weak, as she recognized none other than the mayor's companion, the man who had threatened her at the trial.

He gave a low, sinister laugh, his mouth twisted in an ugly smirk. "There, is that better? I expect you now know who I am?"

Lizzie grabbed at her waist, realizing too late that she again had foolishly left her bag behind, this time in the office. She glared at him. "You! What are you doing here? What do you want? Did you do this to my sister? If you—"

"If I what?" He laughed louder. "What do you intend to do—lay me out like you did your parents?"

Lizzie felt her face grow red and hot with anger, which only prompted him to laugh harder.

"Listen, you don't fool me. You pretendin' to be all respectable when you're nothin' but a lone duck. You keep your mouth shut if you want to be keepin' your sister over there safe."

As if to make his point, he glanced up at something she'd paid no attention to when she first came in—a worn gallery circling most of the room. The wood looked battered, broken, and ready to fall apart. That wasn't what made her mouth go dry. She eyed the door at each end. What was behind those two doors worried her the most. She gazed again at her tormentor, willing herself to show no fear as he gave an evil chuckle.

"Bet you're wonderin' what's goin' on, aren't you?" He leered at her in sinister delight. "Well, I'm only the messenger. I'll let somebody else do the talkin'."

With that, he stepped aside. A feeling of dread filled her as a rotund, well-dressed man, his face stern, an unlit cigar hanging from his mouth, stepped into the room. None other than Mayor Coughlin glared at her, his face even more judgmental and hateful than before.

"Too bad the court let you go, but I won't see you ruining everything we worked so hard for," he warned. "Things were going well until your father got himself infected. A shame, since he was the real brains behind the business. Brilliant idea he had, just brilliant."

Lizzie's eyebrows rose as she wondered what he was talking about. "You—you're mad. You have no—"

"Be quiet." He motioned to the other man, who pulled a long leather strap from his pocket. "Keep your mouth shut, or he can take care of you, or maybe that sister of yours."

The man took a menacing step toward the sobbing form of Emma.

"No, no, don't," Lizzie yelled. "Please, leave her alone!"

The mayor waved his accomplice back before he continued his monologue. "Now, as I was saying, it's such a shame your father got himself sick, but I see it as nothing but a little bump in the plan. One of the ships Andrew invested in came back from the Caribbean with spices, and a crew infected with a strange illness. Several of the men were locked in the cabin below deck, and what do we find? Why, they were not dead as we'd been told! Unfortunately, some of the crew got too close and were attacked. A horrid sight, but we knew then what these creatures needed to survive, so we knew how we could control them."

"Disgusting," Lizzie spat. "You won't get away with this!"

The mayor's face turned dark. His eyes squinty, he pointed the unlit cigar at her. "Who's going to stop me? You?"

Lizzie hated the feeling of being unable to do anything. "Someone will be here to rescue us. Then I'll let the authorities and others in the business community know what you're doing!"

"Oh? Why, maybe you should ask Samuel for help," the mayor chuckled. "Yes, you know who Samuel Smith is, of course. He was a great help to us and to your father, keeping those creatures over at the warehouse. Too bad he's no longer around, what with that workplace accident and all."

He paused to let his words sink in. Lizzie gasped and realized that Samuel was one of the men who'd been attacked! "What happened to being a man of honor in your office?"

Her words only made him cackle more. "Honor? Oh, I have honor. I'm providing the public with a service. I'm freeing the streets of this plague your father brought upon us. I suspect my colleagues will realize my great service when I tell them how I tried to expose your father's plan at great risk to myself."

Lizzie grimaced, her stomach sour. She glanced at Emma, who squirmed and continued her muffled protests. Lizzie's mind worked as she tried to figure a way out. *I have to get Emma free before this crazed man does anything worse. But how?*

"I wouldn't worry your pretty head too much," the mayor warned and stuck the unlit cigar in his pocket. "Don't think you're leaving anytime soon. If the jury had done their job, this discussion wouldn't even be necessary."

The way he stared, his eyes as cold as the creatures he was harboring, made Lizzie fear even more what he might do. Somewhere along the way he'd crossed the line from light to darkness, from sanity to insanity. The real question was—how far would he go to keep his evil plan working?

"So." He shuffled back and forth, tapping the tips of his fingers against each other. "You're an intelligent woman. Surely, you have an inkling of the perfect solution?"

His big-toothed grin made her think of a giant copperhead snake ready to strike. Lizzie glared and folded her arms. She refused to give him the satisfaction of an answer. It made no difference, of course, but made her feel a tad better.

"What's wrong? Cat—or should I say, zombie—got your tongue?" He began to cackle again. "Not yet, not yet. You must see that those creatures are the perfect workers. They need absolutely nothing—no food, no water, no payment of any kind. All we had to do was keep them confined so they couldn't fulfill their bloodlust. And once they served their usefulness, well, they still had value. You saw the workroom below?"

A dizzy feeling hit her as he pulled a hand from his pocket and held out a small bottle. Even from a distance she knew what the label said. Her mind worked at an explanation for his cryptic comment. The workroom... the bottles...

Lizzie glanced at the stones still moving, churning, and grinding beneath the platform where Emma was tied. She remembered the look and feel of that mysterious gritty powder...

Oh, no. Wait! Oh, dear God, no! Lizzie gagged and held a hand over her mouth. *What horror is this? Was he telling a tale—or could it indeed be the horrible, gruesome truth?*

The mayor's ugly smile grew wider. "Ahhh, so you do see! What better way to preserve life, my dear, and offer the promise of health than to use the flesh of those who may never die?"

"No, no, this is wrong! "Lizzie cried. "This is absurd! Father had nothing to do with such madness. You dare pass the blame to him for your evil deeds? Loose my sister! I'll see you in jail for this, I will!"

The mayor's wild laughter filled the room as he stepped back to the doorway after waving a hand at his intimidating cohort. The other man slipped out to who knew where. The mayor paused, giving one last directive: "I know I can't find as neat a solution for getting you out of the way as I did with those creatures, but I think this may be as fitting. And if you do manage to escape, well, with all the wild and varied stories you've already told, do you think anyone will believe you? I heard you've become quite as skilled a killer as you are a liar. I suggest you use those skills wisely."

Emma's muffled screams intensified as the mayor disappeared into the hall. The door slammed behind him. The clank of the lock being thrown let Lizzie know they'd be stuck here for a while, but hopefully not for long. She prayed Pierre, or someone, found Emma's note on the table at home.

Trying to remain calm, she glanced around the room for a window they could escape through, or maybe they could go out one of the old doors on the upper gallery. But to her horror, as she watched, the first door opened. Then the second thudded open, making it clear that was no longer an option.

Emma's cries of alarm drew Lizzie's attention. She glanced at her sister and when she looked upward again, she knew they had far worse things to worry about. The creatures' long, deep moans filled the room and echoed off the walls. Her eyes watered at the stench of sewer rot, and the putrid odor of decay that wafted down from above.

"Emma, hold on!" Lizzie yelled.

She coughed and covered her nose. Taking a deep breath, she leaped onto the rickety wooden platform next to her sister. The two of them clung to the chains as the platform swayed and creaked, making Lizzie's heart pound in fear with each arc. She prayed the platform held and didn't fling them downward to be horribly maimed, or worse.

"Hang on tight, Emma! Hold on!" She took the gag from Emma's mouth and then worked at her sister's bonds, her fingers shaking as she pulled on the knots in the restraints. Finally, they came loose. Emma grabbed her in a hug and then hung on as tight as she could to the platform.

As the first of the undead creatures shuffled out of the door onto the worn, creaking gallery above, Lizzie leaped off the platform and ran to the door. She grabbed an old rusted metal pole she'd seen lying on the floor. Using every ounce of her strength, she pulled, pried, and banged on the door. Tears streamed down her face as she tried somehow, in any way possible, to ram or wedge the door open.

Emma's screams urged her on. Lizzie's hope surged as she almost got the pole wedged into the tiny gap between the door and the wall.

"Hurry, oh, God, please, help us," Emma sobbed. "Lizzie, please hurry!"

"I'm trying Emma, I'm trying!"

Even as she uttered the words and attempted to wedge the pole into what looked like an impossibly small space, Lizzie's optimism faded. She knew it would fail.

Still, unwilling and unable to give up, she worked on as the moans of the steadily burgeoning group of creatures above them grew louder and hungrier.

Chapter Thirty-Two

The difficulty is, she is not an ordinary woman, she is a puzzle…
—Joe Howard, *The Boston Globe*, June 20, 1893

The sound of the wood creaking above them grew louder as the horrific group of ghouls became larger. Ten soon became twenty, then thirty, and then fifty until Lizzie estimated that the group had ballooned to at least seventy creatures. The gruesome scene had her praying as never before that the gallery would hold until Pierre, or someone, came to rescue them.

Taking another good look around at their surroundings for a possible escape, Lizzie hesitated to express her worst fears: that they might not make it. As she looked at her sister across the way, she knew nothing needed to be said anyway. Emma understood. Still, no matter what, she could not—and would not—stand here and give in without a fight. Lizzie vowed to protect Emma, regardless of the personal cost.

The seconds and minutes passed. The door didn't budge. Lizzie knew then the moment had come. She stopped her pushing and pulling. To her credit, a calm Emma nodded without Lizzie having to make any explanation.

As Lizzie made her way back to where Emma stood on the platform, she eyed the upper level. The creatures jostled each other as they neared the edge of the gallery, their gray, decayed arms and hands reaching over the railing. Their moans echoed off the walls in an eerie wail she knew would haunt her for the rest of her life.

Lizzie gasped as one neared the gallery edge and reached out, its foot hanging over, and then rocked backward in a clumsy two-step. If too many of them pushed forward at once, she feared the flimsy railing would break. It would send all the creatures crashing down on them. If that happened, would any of them survive the fall? Most of the creatures would probably end up too crippled to move. But as she'd seen before, somehow even those with the most badly mangled bodies managed to drag themselves along in pursuit of their prey.

"Emma, can you get down?" Lizzie asked. "Help me find anything we can use for weapons. Stupidly, I left my bag in the office. I thought I'd find you first before I went back there."

"I'm sorry," Emma whimpered. "I thought the note asking me to come here was from you. If I hadn't let that man…"

Lizzie wished she could give Emma a much-needed hug. "No, it's not your fault. Someone sent me the same note. We both must be strong and fight those things off. Put whatever you find in a pile here."

Her face sad, Emma glanced upward, but finally nodded in agreement. "Yes, I can do it." With that she carefully held the hem of her skirt up, moved back and ran, managing to jump across the open expanse surrounding the grinding stones. She began gathering items into a pile.

"The only thing I can figure is we need to stay here, behind the stones," Lizzie said. "If those creatures fall, and are still mobile, we have to lure them here so they fall into the pit under the stones."

Emma voiced her approval. "That's a good idea."

It was Lizzie's only good one, since the gathered pile of tools and items looked far less promising—a handful of nails, a hammer and a couple other hand tools, some

227

discarded pieces of clothing, plus other pretty much useless odds and ends.

"It's not much. Maybe we can take those shirts and clothes, tie them together, and see how far they stretch. That would give us a little—"

The rest of Lizzie's words were drowned out by loud thumps and what sounded like someone yelling on the other side of the door. The creatures moaned and became increasingly agitated, making the gallery sway even more.

Uneasy, Lizzie ran to the door and held her ear to the wood. "Pierre? Is that you?"

His voice sounded muffled and hard to make out, but never more welcome. "Trying—break—but…"

His words kept fading out, replaced by thuds and muffled groans as he attacked the door and the lock from his side. Lizzie's uneasiness grew as the more he pounded, and the more noise he made, the more agitated the ghoulish group above them became. She ran back to Emma and helped her move their small cache of items closer to the door, and to the rear of the stones.

"If that floor gives way, they'll probably fall down on both sides there and there." She pointed to the open space below each section of the gallery. "Some may be able to move and get close, so you need to get them out of the way."

She handed Emma the metal rod she'd used unsuccessfully on the door. "I'd rather you use this. Keep them as far away from you as possible, all right?"

"But-but what'll you use?" Emma looked at her and down at the few hand tools among the clothing piled on the floor, her eyes wide in alarm.

It was a good question. Lizzie glanced at the increasingly active group above. Some of the creatures had begun moving back and forth in a demented dance as their hunger and desperation grew. Teeth gnashing and jaws chomping, they grabbed at the railing, their moans intensifying at being out of biting distance. She didn't expect them to stay up there for long.

"Never mind. Give me time, I'll think of something. Just remember, you get one chance. Make it count. Jab at them. Stab them hard. Don't let them get close to you."

With that, she grabbed Emma in a tight squeeze. Kissing the side of her face, Lizzie wished her well. "Be safe. I'll protect you as best I can. If it's too much, jump back on the platform where they can't reach you. At least from there you can shove them into the pit. All right?"

Emma returned Lizzie's hug, blinking away her tears. "I-I will. I'll try, I promise. I can do it. I know I can."

Lizzie felt somewhat reassured that Emma would do her best. She should be fine. Glancing at the swaying gallery above and its horrid occupants, she prayed her words wouldn't come back to haunt her.

A minute later the door crashed open, sending Pierre stumbling in. He handed over her bag. His eyebrows rose in question, but he kept his admonishments to himself. An ear- splitting creak sounded from above.

UNNNNHHHHH!

The creatures moaned and reached out as one, sending the gallery into a deadly swing. It swayed and pitched wildly back and forth. The creatures shuffled from side to side. Lizzie hurriedly grabbed a mid-sized sword from her bag and thrust the hilt at Emma. "Here, take this. Get in position! Go!"

The room became a cacophony of sound—wails of the undead, Emma's screams, and the ear-piercing sound of cracking wood. A second later the railing gave way sending the undead bodies to the stone floor below. They hit with a sickening thud and the crack of bones.

229

"Get over—"

Pierre's orders got lost in the deafening moans of the crippled creatures now writhing on the floor mere steps away. With a cry, he jumped to the right, slashing and stabbing and cutting at the fallen creatures before they became aware enough to untangle themselves from the broken pieces of wood.

"Wait!" Lizzie waved at her sister to stay in position and ran forward on the left side. "Emma, stay there!"

Emma gave a nod of encouragement as Lizzie jumped, pointing her own sword toward the stunned group. Some of the creatures looked dazed and slightly confused as they lay tangled in the mess. She put a quick end to them.

The others, already aware of her presence, growled and snarled like feral cats. The red veiny lines crisscrossing the whites of their eyes had no effect on their ability to pinpoint her location. As one, their ugly heads swiveled in Lizzie's direction. Their sightless eyes locked on her.

The creatures opened mouths filled with stubby pieces of their remaining teeth, or released deep, hungry moans from partial mouths, their jaws hanging or snapped off in the fall. The blunt end of her sword knocked off the rest as she plunged the point into the pulpy mass of their diseased brains. The sword released with a wet slurp.

Lizzie steeled herself, resolving not to go faint at the revolting sights and sounds. She moved on, plunging the sword into the next one and the next after that as fast as she could while her arm strength held.

Despite their Herculean efforts, it wasn't enough.

The mass of mangled creatures—some near whole, some broken—shouldn't be able to go anywhere, yet dear God, they still wriggled and squirmed. A quick glance told Lizzie Pierre had made a little progress but he, too, couldn't stop all of them.

They jabbed and stabbed, trying to finish off the group. Then the nightmare escalated. While most of the creatures fell when the railing broke, the gallery itself had held. As the first group toppled off the edge, the others had somehow pushed to the sides and away from the open edges. Now they stood and watched from sightless eyes. To her horror Lizzie noticed something she hadn't seen before in any of the other monsters they'd already encountered: true cunning.

Several of the ghouls moved forward with a snarl, reached out, and then slunk back from the edge before trying it again. This methodic, ghoulish dance kept on for several minutes. With a loud growl, one flung itself off the edge. It landed on top of the slithering, wriggling pile on the right side of the room and slowly stumbled to an upright position atop the moving mass. Amazingly, it continued to stand on its crumpled feet, the broken toes splayed sideways as it shambled its way off the pile with a loud moan.

"Pierre!"

"Got it," he cried.

ROWR! URRRRRRHHHH!

The room filled with ugly roars and growls as the creatures began to topple and fall one after the other, the broken ghouls below serving as their ghastly cushion.

To Lizzie, it felt like hell had opened its mouth and spewed out its contents.

Chapter Thirty-Three

$12,000,000 Blaze at Fall River.
Started in Abandoned Mill.
—Headline, *The New London Day*,
New London, Connecticut

"**E**mma!" Lizzie yelled.

All she could do was glance quickly in her sister's direction before the creatures required all her attention. To her dismay, the remaining twenty ghouls that had been stranded on the gallery now stood on wobbling but unbroken legs and feet atop the pile of other ghouls.

The ghouls gazed at them with evil faces. Their mouths chomping and biting, they moved forward almost as one. *Crack. Crunch. Crash.* The cracking and breaking of the skulls and bones of the other monsters beneath them sent the hairs on Lizzie's neck shooting up like spring grass. Goosebumps covered her arms.

She grabbed the revolver from her bag, hurriedly cocked it, and aimed. CRACK! The first went down with began shooting. She repeated her actions, again and again, hitting other monsters. Thank goodness her aim and preparation time had improved. All too soon, though, she found herself out of bullets, which in her haste and stupidity she hadn't replenished.

Tossing the gun aside, she pulled out her sword and swung. THWACK. It hit bone. She swung again, cutting through the spinal cord like rope. She struck several others, but a problem soon became apparent. Even as she and Pierre vanquished many of the ghouls, some still managed to slink behind the front group. They shuffled off to the side where her sister offered a more attractive target standing on that platform.

Emma bravely stabbed the metal pole at the snarling creatures reaching for her across the several-foot chasm. Lizzie gasped as a couple overeager creatures leaned in too far. They fell like spinning tops, and with a final moan, got sucked inch by horrible inch down the hole under the moving stones. She turned aside, sickened, as the creatures continued to moan and claw at them even as their bodies were ground into a pulpy, gooey mess. Pockets of awful gray dust floated in the air and made her sneeze.

Lizzie's alarm grew at the sight of yet more creatures focusing on Emma. *Uh-oh.* It made her think of David versus Goliath, though this fight couldn't be more unfair. Holding both the sword and her bat high, she ran, waving her arms at the group gathered on the left side of the pit.

"Emma! Move to your right. Get them to come closer to me!"

Emma went sideways, sending the gruesome group shuffling to the right with low, plaintive moans.

Taking a deep breath and trying to block out the wretched scent of decay, Lizzie gathered speed and ran, both weapons at the ready. She swung and hit the creatures at the rear of the group closest to her their focus yet on Emma. Pulpy brains and black gook sprayed the walls, her face, and everywhere else. Lizzie choked at the rotten stench and wiped her face with a grimace. The bloody image of her father flashed in her mind. *No, don't think of that. Ignore it.*

Emma's scream broke Lizzie out of the bad memory fast. "Liz-Lizzie, HELP!"

A loud clatter and an ear-piercing screech of metal on stone made her wince. Lizzie's eyes widened at sight of the most heart-rending scene she would ever witness: Emma backed against the platform, the metal pole stuck in the chasm where it had dropped. From the edge of the now-stopped grinding stones, several sets of diseased, mangled hands reached out and grabbed for her.

"Pierre, help Emma, get to Emma!"

Lizzie screamed and ran toward the monsters, picking up and throwing anything she could get her hands on. Her efforts proved useless, of course. They ignored her, but her bat proved more deadly as she yelled and swung. "Argggh!" The skull of the ghoul nearest to her cracked and exploded. Fragments and nasty-smelling remains scattered everywhere like an anarchist's bomb exploding in a graveyard.

"Emma, watch out! Use my sword!" Lizzie threw the weapon onto the floor of the platform. Emma grabbed it and swung at the other creature, but missed.

"Emma, don't stop. Jab! Keep swinging!"

The creatures' heads swiveled in Lizzie's direction for an instant, but Emma's proximity was too enticing. They waved mangled arms at her. Black ooze covered the stones as the ghouls' hands scraped against the edges of the rock. With each movement, the remaining soft, decayed tissue scraped off, turning the ends of the ghouls' arms into gory stumps. Yet that didn't stop them.

Then, as if the worst hadn't already happened, it did: more creatures shuffled in her direction, giving Lizzie no choice but to leave Emma and go after them. She turned, but not before witnessing something that made her even more panicked—a plume of smoke rising from beneath the stones.

"Fire!" Emma yelled and stepped back, while she swung the sword at the ghouls surrounding the platform. "I see flames. Lizzie, Pierre, help me! Please! Get me out of here!"

Chapter Thirty-Four

Heat Wave and Drought in Europe.
Malaria Everywhere in Wisconsin.
A Terrible Famine... Dead Bodies Devoured.
—Assorted headlines, 1893

Lizzie's adrenaline shifted into high alert as she ran and bashed the creatures however she could. Several went down, and a few fell yet continued to chomp and scrabble across the stone floor like demented crabs. Another swing of her bat ended their demonic progress. She had no time to worry about them, though, as she plunged into the rapidly burgeoning smoke.

"Emma? Emma, can you see me?"

"No, no, it's too smoky."

"Are any of them still near you?" She coughed again. "Emma?"

In the few minutes since the flames had shot up from the floor below, the fire had grown in size and strength. Lizzie coughed and covered her mouth with the hem of her dress as she waved at the billowing clouds of smoke. She whispered a prayer that neither she nor any of those creatures got too close to each other in the haze.

"Emma! Pierre, do you see her?"

Lizzie's heart pounded like a drum as she stumbled through the smoke. She put one foot carefully in front of the other and felt her way since the smoky barrier had totally confounded her sense of direction. "Emma, I can't see anything at all. I need you to keep talking to me. Pierre?"

Emma's voice came to her as if from a distance. "Lizzie, I-I don't see you, where are you? Liz-Lizzie!"

"Here, I see you," Pierre called. "I can see the pole by the stones. I'm reaching—" His words broke off. "Holy—" he yelled again and cursed.

Lizzie moved forward at a snail's pace, feeling around with her foot first so she didn't end up too close to the pit and fall in by mistake. Pierre's grunts, and the guttural sounds of one of the creatures, told her the two had met unexpectedly in the smoke. A shiver went down her back as she thought how wrong that situation could have gone.

Something fell to her left with a thump and disappeared, letting her know where the pit was. "Emma, are you all right? Pierre?"

"Y-yes, I'm fine." Emma's voice wavered. "Please, hurry."

A second later, Lizzie broke through the smoke. She spotted Pierre, who was trying his best to ward off two stronger creatures that had managed to stay on the attack. She gave a huge cry and rushed forward as one of the monsters turned its ghastly, bashed-in face in her direction.

Using every ounce of strength she had, Lizzie swung the bat at the black hole on top of the creature's open skull. The bat struck dead-on, crushing the skull and diseased brain mass like a hard-shelled nut.

"Ugh." Lizzie grimaced and pulled the bat free as the ghoul fell truly dead at her feet like a discarded rag doll. "Emma?"

"I have her," Pierre called out. "I see you. Go a few steps forward. Stay away from your left side."

Lizzie broke through the smoke, getting a heart-wrenching glimpse of Emma huddled against the back of the platform. All she could do was hold her breath as her sister attempted to leap from the platform.

Instead, Emma came to an abrupt halt and backed up. She shook her head and sobbed.

"No, no, I-I can't," Emma cried. "I can't do it. I won't make it across. My legs are too wobbly."

All of them had the same wide-eyed stare, the blackened face, and the damaged clothing of people who'd been in war. However, Lizzie thought Emma looked more worn out from her battle. Her hair stood out in a messy halo around her head. The hem and sleeves of her dress hung in shreds. Black gook spotted her face. Giant patches of blood and gore streaked her arms.

As Emma struggled to get her footing, Pierre leaped across to the platform. "Liz, your sword!" He picked up the weapon and threw it to her while he encouraged Emma. Lizzie screamed and urged Emma to move when flames burst into view from beneath the platform. "Go, Emma, jump, jump! You have to get out of there!"

As if to make the point, an odd sound at the doorway caught her ear. Lizzie glanced up in alarm at the sight of several undead creatures shambling in from the outer hall. Then a few more snarling, ugly specimens followed in after them. Their moans filled the air.

"Emma, you have to jump. NOW! We have to go!"

The smoke suddenly billowed up as a flame burst through the open hole in the pit and urged Pierre to action. He took Emma by the arm.

"Together. We go on the count of three. One, two, three!"

Emma screamed as they leaped and Pierre pulled her across the chasm. They landed in a pile, Pierre rolling and holding her, trying to absorb most of the fall. He jumped to his feet and helped Emma up while Lizzie tried to head off the group of creatures shuffling faster in their direction. She swung the bat, sending the two closest to her tumbling like dice, but the others kept coming.

Quick as a flash, Pierre wrapped his hands with a piece of cloth and yanked the metal pole from where it had stuck in the pit, the end sizzling from the flames below like a freshly cooked steak. Lizzie had to grimace as he jabbed the heated end through one of the creature's eye sockets, literally frying its diseased brains with a disgusting snap, crackle, and pop.

He jabbed the still-sizzling pole at another one, filling the room with the acrid, sickening odor of charred flesh. "Go, get out of here!" He yelled and waved them on. "I'll catch up. Go before more come in!"

Lizzie grabbed her sister by the arm. They ran a few steps when, to Lizzie's horror, Emma stumbled and fell. "Owww! My ankle! I twisted it! Lizzie, help!"

Pierre's warning came too late. With no other choice, Lizzie flung the bat to Emma and started whacking at the ugly creatures stumbling through the door with her sword. She swung and stabbed, cut and whacked. Heads rolled, rotted flesh fell to the floor in gory piles. Lizzie felt the fatigue and war-weariness creep into her arms with each strike.

She wished it would end.

Finally, the room cleared of zombies, she took a breath and rubbed her aching arms only to see Emma slump over in a faint. To make things worse, another creature had slipped into the room undetected. It now shambled unimpeded in Emma's direction. Lizzie gasped as it shambled forward, intent on its prey, black drool dripping from its mouth.

"NOOOOO!" Lizzie screamed and ran, sword pointed, hoping those few seconds were enough time for her to reach her sister. Luckily, Pierre got there first. With a yell, he whacked off the head of the approaching creature seconds before Lizzie reached it.

"Go ahead, hurry, I have her," Pierre yelled. "Let's get out of here!"

He picked Emma up from the floor and into his arms. She groaned, but remained unconscious as the two of them ran out the door and down the labyrinth-like hall. Billows of smoke had them coughing, but hadn't fully filled the building yet. They pounded down the stairs and ran past the workroom, the mortuary, and more creatures shambling around, lost in the various rooms.

They banged out the door and leaned against the wall outside, sucking in the fresh air. Thankfully, Lizzie saw Pierre had been more insightful than she'd been and had closed the courtyard gates behind him. Several of the creatures clawed at the bars as the horse whinnied and nervously pawed the ground. They had no time for celebration, however, as they spotted several ghouls inside shuffling in their direction.

"Liz, hurry, shut the door." He gently placed Emma into the carriage's backseat. "It may not keep them in, but at least it will slow them down."

Seeing that another creature had now joined the other two at the gates, Lizzie doubted they could escape without drawing the attention of more. But again, Pierre demonstrated his ability to think fast and plan ahead, something she failed to do. In that respect, he and Emma were a lot alike.

He laid out his plan. "Our only chance is to rush out of here full-speed. The horse is already panicked, but we have to do it. Go unhook the gate. Once it swings open, jump in the carriage. We should run down any of them that get in the way. Ready?"

She wasn't as sure as he was, but agreed since they had few choices. She took a deep breath and unhooked the gate. The monsters outside lunged, snarled, and pushed the gate open. Lizzie ran back in a panic, and as Pierre kept a tight hold on the horse's reins, she leaped in beside Emma, holding her close as two of the ghouls stumbled toward them.

"YAA!" Pierre flicked the reins. "YAA!"

The horse screamed and lunged, rushing the gate at a gallop. Lizzie tightened her hold on her sister as the carriage swung wildly. It ran over the creatures, and bounced her and Emma to the opposite end of the bench. Emma mumbled something as the horse screamed and charged.

The carriage spun around the corner in a wide arc as the horse galloped onto Main Street.

Pierre strained and pulled at the reins, admonishing the horse, "Whoa, there, whoa," until finally it slowed its frantic pace. He managed to slow the horse to a trot before stopping at the side of the road. No one said a word.

Lizzie took in their surroundings. Tears filled her eyes at the sight of what had happened during the hours they had been trapped inside.

All around them was utter chaos. It looked like the end of the world.

Chapter Thirty-Five

I am far from my home, and I'm weary after whiles, for the longed for home-bringing, and my Father's welcome smiles...
—From "My Ain Countrie," Lizzie's favorite hymn

All around them, overturned wagons littered the street, their goods spilled all over the roadway. Loose horses trotted around the debris, or ran around in a panic, their reins or harnesses tangled. People helped each other from their carriages and worked to help free the injured. Flames flared from the broken windows of several store buildings. In the distance, dark plumes of smoke rose in the air, signaling the fires had spread closer to the mills and to the warehouses by the riverfront.

Lizzie knew they had no time to stay, or ponder the events, as screams rent the air. More ghouls had arrived. Wherever Lizzie looked she saw them, a true nightmare come to life. The creatures shambled onto the street, sending people fleeing. Those who paid no attention found themselves overtaken by the creatures as evidenced by the increasing screams.

Pierre urged the horse forward. "We'd better get out of here."

He swung the carriage around just as one of the ghouls stumbled into view and made its way, growling and moaning, toward a neatly- coiffed older woman and her well-dressed husband. The elderly couple stood beside their carriage in shock, arm in arm, too frightened to move.

"Wait, wait!" Lizzie jumped out and pulled the stunned couple toward the carriage. The woman whimpered as Lizzie pushed her inside. The man, dapper in brushed gray pants, a matching jacket and matching gray hat, nervously rubbed his silvery mustache and bobbed his head timidly in thanks.

Luckily, they took off before the ghastly group got within reach. Pierre managed to snake the carriage around the fallen wagons and evade the debris. Lizzie leaned out the window and cracked the whip as hard as she could to keep the ghouls away as they went by. If one came too close, she swung her bat, succeeding in getting most away from their carriage. The horse whinnied in terror and would've bolted, sending them careening out of control, if not for Pierre's calming voice and strong grip on the reins.

Everywhere they went Lizzie saw nothing but destruction, chaos, and horror. She held the hand of the poor dear next to her, who sobbed softly, and patted her face with a lacy handkerchief. Her husband shook his head, muttering a continuous litany of "my, my, my."

Block after block, street after street, the horse clip-clopped past scenes Lizzie knew would haunt her for weeks and months to come. Yet, despite the awfulness, in her heart she couldn't blame Father for any of this. As she saw it, the only ones at fault were the mayor, and his companions. She vowed to make sure they were brought to justice once reason, order, and peace returned.

The carriage zigged and zagged past pockets of horror, the scene of creatures gorging on the bloody remains of some poor unwitting citizen they had overtaken so foul, so gruesome and ghastly, that the woman beside her screamed. She fell back in a dead faint, which was for the best, perhaps. Her husband looked down and covered his face with his hat, but not before Lizzie saw his tear-filled eyes and quivering lip.

Lizzie's heart hurt for them. She truly wished they didn't have to witness such horrors. That she didn't even flinch

242

once made her wonder at her own state of mind, and how hardened she'd become because of it.

Such self-analysis had to wait. Thankfully, more groups of police fighting off the undead mobs came into view. Flashes of red SAS armbands on the arms of those assisting no longer bothered her. She applauded their efforts in stopping this madness.

They rounded the corner onto Third Street, her nerves on edge at the thought of the creatures that could be hiding among the leafy branches of the trees in the lovely pear orchard near her old home. The memory of her and Emma sharing one of the freshly picked pears as children made the loss of such innocent moments hurt even more. To her relief, the carriage continued on with no trouble.

Finally, their elderly passenger motioned for Pierre to stop in front of a charming little house fronted with neat bushes, the lawn nicely trimmed.

"This is our home," the man whispered as he helped wake his wife. Lizzie cautioned Pierre to stay in his seat. "I'll help them to the door and do a quick check so you can watch Emma."

Fortunately, a quick inspection uncovered no foul intruders. Lizzie wished the couple well and waited until they got safely inside. She hoped they remained safe as she climbed back into the carriage, and they continued on. The welcome sight of the sturdy stone edifice of St. Mary's Church as the carriage turned onto Second Street gave her a sense of peace. As the horse trotted down the road, she saw several local hunters, along with many neighbors patrolling the streets, rifles at the ready.

Lizzie leaned forward as they drove up to the Hill, anxious to get a glimpse of home. She prayed her beloved Maplecroft still stood proud, tall, and undisturbed. Her anticipation grew. It felt like days since she'd left instead of only hours.

"Look, Emma, we're almost home!" She patted her sister's shoulder.

Emma mumbled again, saying something that sounded like she was leaving, which made no sense.

"Emma, what did you say?" Lizzie's excitement faded as she gazed at her sister's pale face. "Emma? Emma, wake up."

She softly shook her sister's shoulder, yet Emma remained unconscious. Her skin felt hot and clammy. Tiny beads of perspiration dotted her cheeks and forehead. "Pierre, hurry. We need to call the doctor. Emma isn't waking!"

Her joy at finding the house undisturbed with no undead visitors shambling about felt insignificant in the face of Emma's downward spiral. Lizzie hurried to open the door as Pierre carried her sister in.

"Here, take her to the bath. Never mind her clothing. I need to get her cooled down. Hold her up so I can get some cold water over her."

Emma's skin felt as hot as a poker taken from the fire. Her face looked pale. After removing her sister's shoes, Lizzie filled the tub with cold water. As she looked Emma over again, she saw nothing wrong: no scratches, marks, or visible gouges on her skin. She had seemed tired and frail before, but nothing as bad as this.

The cold bath seemed to help. Emma's skin finally felt cooler to the touch. Pierre helped lift her from the tub and into a chair, then waited outside while Lizzie removed her sister's wet clothes. Once she was decently covered in a heavy chenille robe, she called Pierre back in.

"If you could take her into the parlor and put her on the settee," she suggested. "I can watch her more easily from there."

Emma's breathing appeared steady, but the continued lack of response worried Lizzie. As she said goodbye to Pierre and welcomed in the doctor, he had little to recommend other than crushed aspirin once Emma could swallow it, and an alcohol bath to keep the fever down. "It appears to be some kind of fever," he said. "There is really nothing I can do for her."

His diagnosis only angered Lizzie. She did as he suggested, wiping her sister down with rubbing alcohol, and getting her to ingest a small spoonful of aspirin diluted in water, but Emma still lay quiet and unmoving.

Lizzie sat and held her sister's cool hand. Tears filled her eyes as she gazed at the dark circles around Emma's closed eyelids, and the pale, sickly hue of her face. "Oh, Emma, I am so sorry, so sorry. You tried your best. You acted so bravely. I'm so, so proud of you."

As she lifted Emma's near lifeless hand to her cheek, Lizzie tried to hold back the tears so as not to turn into a blubbering mess. Worry filled her as she went to change into a dressing gown and set a pot of tea on the table, prepared to stay up all night if necessary.

That done, she pulled the blanket over Emma and settled into the chair, wanting to be near in case her sister needed her, or if there were any changes. She braced herself for the long haul as whether for good or bad, Emma's condition remained yet unchanged.

Chapter Thirty-Six

The Scourge is Over! Mayor Held for Heinous Crimes.
—Headlines, *The Fall River Herald*

"Emma, they did it, they did it! The mayor was arrested!"

Lizzie bounded down the stairs to the sitting room, a fresh, crisp edition of the newspaper in hand. The paper crinkled as she spread it out on the table. "Emma, this is wonderful news. The newspaper says: REIGN OF TERROR ENDED! FALL RIVER MAYOR ARRESTED! MURDER PLOT UNCOVERED!"

She smoothed out the front page of *The Fall River Herald*, glad to share this moment with her sister, whom she was sure felt the same sense of satisfaction she had that the fiends would be brought to justice.

"This is indeed great news," Lizzie remarked. "Of course they brought up our name again, and Father's building, but the real focus is the mayor and his role in this whole fiasco, as it should be. It appears he had others involved in Boston, as well. I'm so glad they caught him. Now we can all put this terrible episode behind us and get on with our lives."

Of course, she knew it would take a while for everyone to get over such a disaster. In the ensuing days, order gradually returned to the city, though the damage was extensive. The downtown and the business district resembled a war zone. The burned warehouses on the riverfront were now charred, empty shells.

However, between the efforts of the police, the citizens, and the Society members, the monsters had all been caught and vanquished. Citizens felt some reassurance that no further public infection had been located. The immediate danger had ended. It would, of course, take years to rebuild and bring their fine city back to its former condition.

Lizzie also gave her full consent for police officials to confiscate the ghastly materials at the Borden building. She hired workmen to repair the damage, as well. Getting everything from those awful experiments gone for good couldn't happen soon enough. She and Emma both wanted it to be over.

The only change she was certain Emma disliked had been her decision to get a dog. "Emma, I know how you feel about dogs, but I decided to bring the most darling Boston Terrier home. I promise to keep him out of your way upstairs."

Oddly enough, once the actual danger passed, and those who had left in the height of the attacks began returning home, Lizzie soon learned that her former status as the local pariah hadn't changed a whit.

When she took the dog for a morning walk down the street, any neighbors who appeared outside at the same time pretended to not see her. They turned their backs, or hurried inside. It hurt, she had to admit. Soon she confined her outdoor excursions to her own gardens. She and the dog had to be content in their own backyard.

Past friends and family members continued to shun her as well. It soon became too uncomfortable for everyone when any of Emma's few acquaintances called to ask about her. Rather than go into a lengthy explanation about Emma's ill health, and endure the accompanying awkward silence from the caller, Lizzie simply told them Emma had gone to Fairhaven to recuperate. Soon those calls ended, too.

The break that hurt the most, though, came on the day when she finally decided to say goodbye to Pierre. "I can never, ever, thank you enough for all you' done for me, and for Emma," she said when he called to check on her sister. "I'm so glad it's over. We'll never forget what you did for us. We both wish you well."

The gentleman that he was, Lizzie knew Pierre understood what she meant without her having to explain further. He graciously didn't make it harder on her by protesting.

She settled in at home, prepared to lead a quiet life surrounded by her books, her favorite music, and the companionship of her dog, and her sister. After the trial and then all the chaos, fighting, and the horrors of those monsters, both of them had had enough upset and raucousness in their lives to last a lifetime.

Occasionally a driver came to take her shopping, but Lizzie found it easier to rely on deliveries. A couple of kindhearted women helped her by providing light meals, and cleaned the upstairs rooms when needed. Life became slower, simpler.

Since too much togetherness could be detrimental, she chose to spend a lot of time by herself on the sun porch reading, or watching the comings and goings on the street, the dog at her side. She usually joined Emma in the sitting room for lunch since her sister preferred the coolness downstairs.

Their lives went on at an even keel, day after day, until Lizzie grabbed the paper one morning. She saw the headline, and ran downstairs in a panic to share it with Emma. "Emma! Emma! Oh, this is horrible! I thought they caught them all. The mayor's accomplice. He's still out there!"

Lizzie stared at her sister, unwilling, unable, to grasp what this meant. She and Emma had been living quietly, content that the worst was behind them. And now this! She fretted and wrung her hands. *Did this mean everything could start up again? Will Emma and I have to live the rest of our lives looking over our shoulders?*

The unexpected blare of the telephone upstairs made her jump. "Oh, what a morning! Emma, I'll be back in a minute."

Pulling up her dress hem to avoid tripping, she rushed upstairs to the parlor and answered the telephone. "Hello. What? Speak up, I can't hear you." The earpiece shook in her hand. "What did you say? Who is this? Hello, hello?"

The phone went dead.

A chill hit her. What was going on? She tried to process the whispered message when the doorbell rang. Panic fluttered in her chest; her breath caught as she peered through the lacy curtain before opening the door.

"Pierre, what're you doing here? Come in. Is something wrong?

He came in and held out a newspaper. "I had to talk to you. Did you see this?"

She nodded. "I did. Worse, I think he just called me."

He reached out and grasped her shoulders. "What do you mean?"

"Someone was on the telephone a minute ago. The man spoke so low I could barely hear him."

"What did he say?"

Lizzie took a breath before she answered. "I'm sure it was him. It sounded like he said almost the same thing he told me at the end of my trial except in less polite words. 'Watch yourself. This isn't over.'"

She tried to take comfort in the way Pierre held her hands in his. In his eyes she saw concern, and if she was not mistaken, something more. *Maybe his feelings for me haven't changed*, she thought, but knew this was not the time to think about that, or about herself.

He cleared his throat and released her. "What do you want to do? Should we call the marshal?"

She thought about the pros and cons, pondering their next move. Her choice was clear, if not welcome.

"No, not yet. I never wanted to go there again, but we have to go back to Father's business. The officials cleared it out, but I suspect there are some places they never searched. As you know, Father had many secret hiding places."

"I'm free if you need my help. Your sister..." He paused.

"She'll be fine. This is her rest time. I would appreciate your going with me."

"I'll take you wherever you want to go."

She remained silent on the way to the Borden building. Pierre probably wanted to talk about her decision to push him out of her life, and about Emma. She now felt maybe she'd been too hasty.

"Liz, I wanted to tell you how glad I am to see you again. I confess I'm still not sure why you felt we should break off communication."

"I'm glad to see you, too. I fear I was hasty, but it's not something I want to discuss now, if you don't mind."

He pulled the carriage to the back of the building. "We'll talk later. I'll lock the gate while you unlock the door."

It took a few minutes of fighting with the lock before she got the door open. Stale air rushed out. She could still smell the unmistakable lingering odor of rot and shivered. She'd intended to never come back here. If not for this morning's news, she would've rented out the building, or at some point even sold it without ever stepping foot on the premises again.

Pierre came up behind her and interrupted her musing. "All set?"

"Yes, I just want to get this over with."

He lit two lanterns and handed her one as they crept silently down the labyrinth of hallways. Lizzie's heart felt like it would explode as the memories rushed in with each turn—the creatures stalking them … the feeling of being trapped … the fear on Emma's face … the sight of her sister crumpled on the floor. She gasped and touched the wall, as if she could push it all away.

Pierre set down his lantern and wrapped her in his arms. He held her close as her shoulders shook with sobs. "It's all right, Liz, I know how hard it is. They'll get him, they will. You and Emma will be fine."

She took a deep breath. "I know. It's a little overwhelming. I never expected to see this place again, but I'll do whatever I can. I intend to see Emma remains safe, and that fiend punished. I appreciate your coming with me. All right, I'm ready."

They continued down the hall where Lizzie noted the turned-out desk drawers and overturned boxes in the adjacent rooms. Streaks of soot from the fire blackened the walls. It appeared the police had done a thorough search, but she kept going. Once in the main section of the building, she eyed the stairs leading to the upper level a moment before she pointed to a doorway behind the staircase. "We have to go to the cellar."

The lanterns cast an eerie glow across the aged stone steps leading to the lower level. Once they got to the bottom, the refuse tossed about told her this had been searched, too.

"Looks like the police found everything," Pierre said.

Lizzie shook her head as she felt along the cold, stone walls. "Maybe not."

"What're you looking for?"

She knelt on the packed earth floor and rubbed her hand horizontally across the surface. "This. I saw it mentioned in some of Father's papers."

She stopped at a section of hewn rock that felt jagged to the touch, but wouldn't draw anyone's attention if they didn't know about it. Ignoring the sharp edges, she pounded the center with her fist. On the second try, the rock section slid out with a scrape of stone against stone. Inside sat a few torn scraps of paper, and nothing else.

"Oh, no." She stood to her feet and wrung her hands together. "It looks like he found it. The mayor's accomplice probably knew where this was long before I came across it in the papers I was putting away."

"What was in there?"

"Father's note said he hid a copy of the tonic formula, along with details about the experiment and the undead creatures, in what he called a 'wall safe' in the cellar."

"That may not help anyone else, or maybe those papers were taken long before," he said.

"Yes, or it could be a way to resurrect this whole ghastly business if someone evil enough like the mayor's accomplice had a mind to do it," she agreed. "It wouldn't take a lot for them to start over."

They went back upstairs where she locked the door for what was hopefully the last time. After taking one last glance, she got in the carriage with a wish it all was over.

Pierre squeezed Lizzie's hand as he guided the horse down the road. "Don't worry. We'll find him. We will. No matter how long it takes."

She had no answer.

After saying goodbye, she went inside the house, her heart heavy. "Emma? I'm home. I'm going to feed the dog. I'll bring lunch down in a minute."

She placed an assortment of fresh chicken livers, hearts, and gizzards, along with some choice beef bits, in a bowl. She had to put the horror of this recent development behind her. There was nothing she could do but be vigilant until the fiend showed his face or, Lord help them, another outbreak occurred.

That said, Lizzie knew it was important to keep her spirits up, for both her sake, and Emma's. She had much to be thankful for—both of them did. They had a fine home. They wanted for nothing. The re-appearance of Pierre in her life had been an unexpected bonus. She decided to ask for his help in adding more safety reinforcements around the house. It would make her feel much better.

Lizzie relayed the day's events to her sister as she carried the tray carefully down the stairs. "I know neither of us wanted to go to Father's business again, but Pierre was quite helpful. Actually, it was nice to see him."

She decided to not mention her decision to see Pierre again, pushing down the feelings of guilt over her lie of omission. She felt it as necessary as her need not to tell Pierre the whole truth about Emma's condition. They would face that later.

The bowl of bloody beef pieces and raw chicken parts clanged against the bars of the specially-built cage that had been installed as a precaution when they first moved in. It had seemed a wise move to make for protection at the time. She'd never envisioned how much it would be needed later.

Lizzie turned away, raising her voice to block out the grunts, groans, and obnoxious noises the undead Emma made as she crammed the raw food into her mouth. The twice-daily meals appeased Emma and kept her quiet, which allowed Lizzie to keep her sister hidden and safely confined.

As far as anyone knew, Emma had recovered from her illness and moved away, something Lizzie realized would never happen—not once she'd found the gouge on Emma's back.

Once it became clear Emma would never recover, Lizzie had wrapped her in a blanket and managed to drag her still-unconscious sister downstairs. There, she'd tried to make her as comfortable as possible in her new surroundings.

Despite Emma's transformation, Lizzie could not—and would never—see her as one of *them*, one of those horrible, bloodthirsty creatures who preyed upon others. Not Emma. Not the sister who had stood by her through all her trials. No, Emma wasn't like that, and never would be.

Lizzie resolved to make their home a haven, a place of peace, where she would care for Emma as her sister had cared for her. She would do that no matter what, and for as long as Emma needed her.

~* ~* ~*~

If you enjoyed this book, I hope you'll write and post a short review. Even a short line or two is appreciated and helpful to other readers. If you do post a review, I'd love to hear about it. I also may share part of it on my blog and/or website. I love hearing what readers think!

Be sure to sign up for my occasional newsletter (at top center column) at my website. Thank you!

—C.A. Verstraete, chris@cverstraete.com

Message from the Author

Dear Reader,

I was always taken with Lizzie Borden's story and the never-ending debate of whether she was innocent or guilty.

To this day, the Borden murders continue to be an intriguing crime, one that may never be fully solved—until now. After taking another look at the ghastly crime scene photos of Lizzie's father and stepmother, I knew why the crime occurred—at least in an alternate, fictional sense.

This book is the result of my musings. I think once you've read the story you'll see that it is entirely plausible

Thank you for coming along on my journey and getting to know the "real" Lizzie Borden.—*Christine Verstraete*

The Real Life Crime

To this day, there is no clear consensus as to who actually committed the double murders of Andrew J. Borden and his wife Abby Durfee Borden at 92 Second Street in Fall River, Massachusetts, on a hot August morning in 1892.

While many believe former Sunday School teacher Lizzie Andrew Borden was guilty, there is no evidence directly linking her to the crime. A handle-less hatchet found by police in the cellar was presumed—but never proven—to be the murder weapon.

Lizzie, a 32-year-old spinster, reportedly discovered her 70-year-old father, Andrew J. Borden, lying dead on the settee in the sitting room near 11 a.m. on August 4, 1892. He had been struck 10 times with a hatchet or axe. The body of her 64-year-old stepmother, Abby Durfee Borden, was found bent over on her knees by the bed in the upstairs guest bedroom. She had been struck 18 times, according to the autopsy report.

Lizzie was arrested for the murders following a three-day inquest held August 9 to 11, 1892. A grand jury began hearing evidence in November, with Lizzie indicted for the crimes on December 2.

The "trial of the century" held June 5 to June 20, 1893 in the New Bedford Superior Court garnered nationwide media attention and interest worldwide, especially once the verdict came in: not guilty. The sensational crime would have been punishable by an equally grisly death—hanging on the gallows.

Lizzie and Emma were later estranged, but Lizzie continued to live in Fall River until her death on June 1, 1927 at age 67. She is buried next to her parents and sister in the family plot at Oak Grove Cemetery.

Sources

Following are some great places to read original documents and other background material about the Borden murders, along with a list of key places to visit. (Links were checked at the time of writing.)

Books

* *Lizzie Borden: Past & Present* by Leonard Rebello (1999, out of print)

* *The Lizzie Borden Sourcebook* by David Kent, Robert A. Flynn and Adolph Caso (2012)

Newspapers and Research

* "Enduring Mystery: The Life and Trials of Lizzie Borden" (2013). Six-day *Providence Journal* series, or search special reports: http://tinyurl.com/qx2u3vq

* *Herald News* crime chronology: http://www.heraldnews.com/news/20160803/timeline-day-of-borden-murders

* Library of Congress, period newspaper stories on the case: http://www.loc.gov/rr/news/topics/borden.html

* Tattered Fabric, Lizzie Borden blog, Faye Musselman: https://phayemuss.wordpress.com

* University of Amherst investigation into the Borden case: http://ccbit.cs.umass.edu/lizzie/intro/home.html

* University of Missouri, Kansas City School of Law. Crime scene photos, news accounts, transcript excerpts: http://law2.umkc.edu/faculty/projects/ftrials/lizzieborden/bordenhome.html

* Warps and Wefts, Lizzie Borden blog: http://lizziebordenwarpsandwefts.com

Places of Interest

* Fall River Historical Society: http://www.fallriverhistorical.org

* Lizzie Borden Bed & Breakfast/Museum, 230 2nd St., site of the original Borden home at 92 Second St. Maplecroft, the home Lizzie bought after the trial, is also opening as a B&B. https://lizzie-borden.com

* Oak Grove Cemetery, Fall River, MA. Borden family burial plot: http://friendsofoakgrovecemetery.org

* Lizzie Borden's dogs are buried at the Pine Ridge Pet Cemetery, Animal League of Boston, by the Dedham Animal Shelter, 55 Anna's Place, Dedham, Mass. http://www.arlboston.org/pine-ridge-pet-cemetery

TV Movies and Filmography

* The Legend of Lizzie Borden (1975) Elizabeth Montgomery, TV movie. Re-released on DVD.

* Lizzie Borden Had An Axe (2004) Discovery Channel forensic investigation.

* Lizzie Borden Took An Axe (2014-15) Christina Ricci, Lifetime movie and mini-series.

* Lizzie, Chloë Sevigny, Kristen Stewart (2018)

Want Some Music To Read By?

* Cry - Johnnie Ray (1952); David Cassidy (1990)

* Just Playing With My Axe – Buddy Guy (1968)

* Lizzie Borden – The Chad Mitchell Trio (1962)

* Small Axe – Bob Marley & The Wailers (1973)

* We Bury the Hatchet – Garth Brooks (1991)

About the Author

Christine (C.A.) Verstraete is an award-winning journalist who enjoys writing fiction with a bit of a "scare."

Her short stories have been published in anthologies and publications including, *Descent into Darkness, Mystery Weekly, Sirens Call, Feast of the Dead: Hors D'Oeuvres; 100 Doors to Madness;* and in *Timeshares, Steampunk'd, and Hot & Steamy: Tales of Steampunk Romance*, DAW Books.

Learn more at her website, www.cverstraete.com, and blog, http://girlzombieauthors.blogspot.com

Works by C.A. Verstraete

Lizzie Borden, Zombie Hunter

Lizzie Borden, Zombie Hunter 2: The Axe Will Fall

The Haunting of Dr. Bowen,
A Mystery Set in Lizzie Borden's Fall River

Changes, A GIRL Z Prequel Story

~ * * * ~

Bonus! Excerpt from,
Lizzie Borden, Zombie Hunter 2: The Axe Will Fall!

When her sister Emma becomes a pawn in the growing war against the undead, Lizzie's only choice is to pick up her axe again. But can she overcome her personal demons and the rampaging monsters, no matter the cost?

Chapter One

"We pray thee that innocence may be revealed and guilt exposed..."
—The Rev. M.C. Julien, opening prayer,
Trial of Lizzie Borden, June 5, 1893

Fall River, Massachusetts—October, 1893

L izzie Borden sprang awake, startled by a sound she never expected, or wanted to hear again—a low, eerie keen that made her skin crawl and the long, straight hairs on her neck curl up into tight ringlets.

"No, no!" She jumped out of bed and ran to the window, her heart pounding in fear. "Please, don't let it be!"

The chaotic scene on the street below filled her with disbelief and horror. No matter which direction she looked, she saw pure evil—groups of the undead she'd truly thought were gone forever. They'd been vanquished—or so she'd been told. Who had lied?

Then she had another unexpected, but this time much more pleasant, shock—seeing her former self-defense instructor Pierre Moret. As the monsters shambled closer, he stood a moment as if in contemplation before closing the wrought iron gate. He waved for her to come down and disappeared out of view by the front door.

Why is he here? Why now?

The ghastly roars and growls outside quickly made her realize it didn't matter. Her panic rising, Lizzie threw off her nightwear and slipped on one of the old pair of bloomers she'd worn in previous fights. For some reason, she'd kept the costume in her armoire, though she'd expected to never, ever, be doing this again.

So much for that, she thought. *Or had I really believed it was over?*

She shoved her feet into sturdy black shoes, her worry level rising higher than the smoke spewing from the stacks of the numerous textile plants down by the river. Were these new masses of undead? Or worse—had those who'd been infected and hidden away secretly at home by family members managed to escape?

The questions dogged her as she ran down the polished oak staircase, a litany of muttered protests on her lips. "No, no, how can this be happening? Dearest Lord, how?"

A pounding on the front door made her move faster. "Lizzie, hurry, please, let me in," Pierre called.

"Coming, I'm coming."

She twisted the shiny gold lock and pulled the heavy oak door open. Her nose wrinkled at the sudden stench of rot and death that fouled the air. Pierre rushed in, pushed the door shut, and turned to embrace her. To her surprise, it felt like she'd seen him only yesterday instead of months ago.

"Pierre! I didn't expect you."

"Obviously, though I'm glad to see you had your fighting dress at the ready."

The low moans from outside made further conversation impossible. She moved closer to the door and peered out the window, her heart pounding as she viewed the motley mob of ghouls clamoring at the gate. She counted eight, ten, fifteen of the decayed monsters and saw more approaching.

The bastion of quiet she'd enjoyed in the past few months since moving to the more prestigious section known as "The Hill" had been replaced by bedlam. She watched a group of men run into the street swinging axes, garden tools, and almost anything they could get, at the approaching foes. She turned away and wrung her hands, not daring to look at Pierre when he gave a snort of disgust.

"Why did you lead them here?" she asked. "Why? I don't want to deal with it."

"You think I do? A thank you might be more in order since I wanted to make sure you were safe. Sorry to say, they're up and down not only this street, but the whole area. We have no choice but to help."

"No, no, I-I can't do it. I can't." She inhaled sharply when Pierre reached out and spun her around.

He tucked his finger under her chin and raised her head. "Look at me. You can't, or you won't?"

"No, I can't." She bit her lip and shook her head harder. "I can't do it."

Her resistance faded as he pulled her near. She breathed in his masculine scent and the lingering musky, ambergris shaving lotion on his skin, wishing this was any other time, any other place.

The horrific sounds of the undead made Lizzie's skin crawl. Her first impulse, to let him and others take care of things, did battle with her innate sense of duty. She peered out the window again, relishing the satisfaction of seeing others out in the streets now, men with guns, women with garden tools. Even the neighbors who had turned their back on her were out doing their part to keep the monsters at bay.

Let them handle it, she thought.

Still, her feelings of obligation niggled at her. Yes, she'd trained for this. She had fought this fight before. She couldn't let others do all the work for her.

With a deep sigh, Lizzie pushed herself from Pierre's embrace and regarded him. "I guess I have no choice about getting involved, do I? I have to do it, for Emma, if nothing else."

"Neither do I. I trained you. I'll be right there with you and will help you any way I can. You know that. Should I ask how is your sister faring?"

"The same, nothing has changed."

She went to the hall closet and took out a large leather satchel. It clanked with the sound of metal on metal. She sorted through the bag, pulling out a hatchet, a bat, and several small knives.

"Have you been practicing? Keeping in condition?"

She gave a small laugh. "Somewhat… Well, a little. I stopped going downstairs to practice or use the equipment since the noise bothers Emma too much. So, I do what I can up here. I've been doing my basic exercises and practice my throwing out in the carriage house. It's not ideal, but it'll suffice."

"If only others had been as careful and prepared, we wouldn't be in the mess we are again."

She snorted. "Possibly. Too many people kept their infected family members at home without sufficient preparations—"

"Or really knowing what they were dealing with," Pierre said.

"Agreed. The awful cycle continues. I truly thought it had ended."

"Yes, so did I."

Pinning her hair into a tighter bun at the back of her head, Lizzie pulled the multi-pocketed apron she'd refashioned for her own use from the satchel and tied it around her waist. She slipped the knives and other tools into the pockets.

Pierre gave her an appraising look. "Well done. I see you haven't forgotten anything."

She took a deep breath and steeled herself. "Some things you never forget, ever, no matter how much you might wish it. Are you ready?"

"When it comes to you, always."

A frown on her lips, Lizzie opened the door and rushed out, hatchet in hand. The picturesque street, lined with well-kept homes, now resembled a waking nightmare. Mobs of the monsters stumbled up and back on the road, and the sidewalks. Some strayed closer to the front walks, their rotted limbs gouged by misguided attempts to claw past iron spiked gates, or reach through long, spiky bushes. The frantic yells of people coming to the fight, weapons in hand, mixed with the bone-chilling laments of the creatures.

Pierre lunged ahead. He stopped, whacked one creature in the head with his short sword, and ended another's un-life with a fatal blow. The head rolled away, tracing a bloody path through the piles of dead leaves.

Lizzie followed him through the gate, her grip tightening on the hatchet. *UNHHH. ARGGH.* The monstrous sounds made her think again of their earlier battle. She prayed this one would be shorter, and far less disastrous. The thought was enough to make her hesitate as the horrors of the past year came rushing back—*her father's gruesome face … her stepmother Abby's monstrous stare … the terror and loneliness of being arrested … the shame and horror of standing trial for their murders.*

She shook herself out of the memory. The hatchet held high, she charged at the first monster that turned her way. The ghoul shuffled closer, mouth open in a fixed grimace, a hungry shriek on its half-decayed lips. She slammed the hatchet into the creature's head, crushing the skull with a loud crack and a splatter of black goo. Its undead life gone, the ghoul fell at her feet in a grisly pile. A parade of insects skittered from the remains.

—Continued in *Lizzie Borden, Zombie Hunter 2*

Bonus! Excerpt from,
The Haunting of Dr. Bowen

Gruesome deaths haunt the industrial city of Fall River, Massachusetts.

Can Dr. Bowen discover who, or what, is shattering the peace before Fall River runs red? Or will he be the next victim?

Prologue

"Never did I say to anyone that she had died of fright. My first thought, when I was standing in the door, was that she had fainted."
—Testimony of Dr. Seabury W. Bowen,
Trial of Lizzie Borden, June 8, 1893

"Why won't anyone believe me? Why, Phoebe, why?"

Dr. Seabury Bowen shoved back the shock of white hair hanging over his forehead and wiped a wrinkled hand across his stubbled chin.

His appearance, like his surroundings, could stand a bit of major housekeeping, not that he cared a whit.

"Here, it's here somewhere," he mumbled.

The old man rummaged among the giant pile of documents, books, and what-not littering the large walnut desk in his study. Several minutes later, and after the search through dozens of loose papers, he saw the faded red book lying beneath a tottering pile. He pulled at it, sending the rest of the stack falling like so much unwanted garbage.

The good doctor, but a shadow of his once- robust self, flipped the pages. He stared at the offending journal entry before setting the book aside with a heartrending sob.

Chapter One

"I saw the form of Mr. Borden lying on the lounge at the left of the sitting-room door. His face was very badly cut, apparently with a sharp instrument; his face was covered with blood."

—Testimony of Dr. Seabury W. Bowen,
Trial of Lizzie Borden, June 8, 1893

The man reached toward him with long, lean fingers. Dr. Seabury Bowen blinked and tried to make out the features of the unknown figure standing in the corner. The unexpected visitor had a broad, dark face and what looked like a band across his forehead. Bowen stretched out his arm in turn and jumped when their fingers touched, the jolt surging through him like the electricity he knew would soon replace all the gas lights.

"Seabury, dear, are you all right?" His wife, Phoebe, sounded concerned. "What's wrong?"

Bowen breathed hard. He bolted upright and held a hand on his chest, trying to catch his breath. Still stunned, he gazed about the room, disturbed at the odd shapes until he recognized familiar things... the bureau, the armoire, the paintings on his bedroom walls. He swallowed and nodded.

"Ye-yes. I-I'm fine. A bad dream, that's all it was. Just a dream."

"A bad dream? Dear, you're breathing so hard, your heart must be pounding like a drum in Mr. Sousa's band! Are you sure you're fine?"

The doctor took his wife's hand and kissed it, relieved to feel his heartbeat return to normal. He had to admit his reaction worried him for a minute, too. "I'm fine now, Phoebe. Really, it's all right. Go back to sleep. I'm too wrought up to rest. I think I'll go downstairs and read awhile."

He gave her a loving smile before he rose and slipped on his robe, his thoughts in a whirl. To tell the truth, these dreams, or hallucinations, or whatever they were, appeared to be getting stronger and more frequent. Not that he'd tell her, of course. It made Bowen wonder if he was losing touch with his faculties, something he'd never dare mention. Nor did he want to even entertain the thought, but he did. *Am I going mad? Am I?*

The doctor mulled over the idea as he tiptoed down the stairs. A cup of coffee sounded good. If he were truthful, he'd admit that these strange visions or hallucinations had begun that ghastly morning two years ago.

After his neighbor Miss Lizzie's frantic call at his back door, he'd grabbed his worn leather medical bag and rushed with her to the adjacent Borden home, not sure what he would find. Despite the horrors he encountered, by instinct he'd switched to professional mode, making sure the Borden sisters weren't harmed. Of course, nothing could, or would, help the horribly butchered Mr. Borden. Then they discovered Mrs. Borden's body, and all hell broke loose.

He put the iron coffee pot on the burner and turned the flame on high. While the coffee warmed, he pondered how many lives had changed that day, his included. He'd tended to many terrible accidents and injuries over the course of his nearly thirty years serving the medical needs of the families of Fall River, but this had affected him the most.

Maybe it was the proximity of his own home, and the underlying fears he naturally had about the safety of his wife and daughter. No matter what, it was enough to make him decide to retire sooner than he'd planned. It made him try to forget those other strange incidents, too. Not that he could.

"How can I ever forget?" he wondered. "How?"

271

Indeed, the odd occurrence was etched on his mind as much as anything else that fateful morning. He recalled how he'd glanced up a moment after checking Mr. Borden's body. In that instant, he'd caught what looked like a dark shadow lingering near the door of the sitting room. He'd stopped and almost cried out in alarm when the odd thumping sounds started. He remembered his panic, and the questions he'd had: Was the killer there? Was someone trying to break in?

A quick glance around told him no one else seemed to hear it. But he did. THUMP. THUMP. THUMP. He listened, hand on his chest, and realized the thumping wasn't his heart, though it was pounding hard. No, it was inside the house, and sounded like... a drum?

* * *

Bowen shook himself out of the memory, taking care as he poured the coffee with trembling hands before making his way to the study. Setting the cup down, he turned the jet on the gas lights and burrowed among the haphazard piles of journals and papers covering most every inch of the worn, walnut desk in search of a certain book. He spotted the faded red leather cover in the pile, picked it up, and flipped it open to the first page. It was dated the year 1892.

The pages contained his records of house calls and patient interactions, his observations and actions scribbled in a somewhat legible, far from neat handwriting. The entries varied in length, some a paragraph or more, others only a short line or two.

His thumb caressed the page marked August 4. He wasn't surprised when he turned the page to find no more than a couple words entered, the rest of the day's events far too terrible to mention. Not that he needed to write anything down. It was still etched in his memory.

Or maybe he'd realized it best to not repeat anything else in writing, especially in light of the arrest of Miss Lizzie, and the unfolding farce of putting someone of her gender and social standing on trial for such horrific murders. He'd been called to testify at the trial, of course, though he had nothing much to say beyond his professional observations.

But deep down inside he wondered yet again at his mental state when he reviewed what he'd written. Two words, only two, covered the page: darkness, drumming. That aspect of the day still made no logical sense to him.

He closed the journal, regret filling him. What he didn't know about that day—the why and how— haunted him still. But what he did know, and had felt certain of when he looked at the agitated face of the youngest Borden daughter, Lizzie, and the sour, disapproving face of her elder sister, Emma, was this—neither of them had been at fault.

He stared at the book and rubbed his finger over the textured leather cover. Again, not for the first or last time, his thoughts returned to the day of the murders. Nothing had changed his mind about his initial impressions. Nothing.

A noise at the door pulled him out of the memory. He gazed at his wife standing in the doorway, her forehead creased with worry.

"Dear, are you sure you're all right? I'm concerned about you."

Bowen put the journal down, knowing he should ease her worry, and walked to the door. "Dearest, I'm fine." He took her hands. "Since we're both awake, let's go have something to eat. I'll make you some toast, how's that?"

She chuckled and shook her head. "Now Seabury, you sit. How about I make us some eggs to go with that toast?"

In the kitchen, he got out the ingredients, glad to be doing something. But try as he might, he couldn't get away from the one thing that still bothered him. He fought to stay silent, but had to ask: "Phoebe dear, do you think I'm being haunted?"

He speculated that maybe he'd gone too far in asking when she stopped in mid-beating of the eggs and turned her wide blue eyes on him. "Haunted? Seabury, whatever do you mean?"

Now I've done it, he thought, and wished he'd kept his mouth shut. "You know about the dream I had this morning and that moment at the cemetery, at the Borden funeral, remember?"

She looked at him, confused at first. "Oh, now I remember. You looked like you'd seen something, but you said everything was good." She paused. "It wasn't, was it?"

He shook his head. "No. I mean beyond the terrible situation, of course."

A sad affair it had been, made even sadder once the Borden sisters learned there would be no burial, and their parents' bodies would be held for evidence. Necessary he knew. Unthinkable just the same. Then he'd glanced at the gravestones across the way—and for the first time in his married life, he'd told his wife a lie.

"I couldn't tell you," he admitted. "I-I didn't want to worry you. It was already upsetting enough with what was happening at the funeral."

He felt emboldened at the encouraging smile she offered. She'd never been anything but understanding and supportive.

"I think I saw the man from my dream." His voice was soft. "I first saw a shadow in the Borden house the morning of the murders. Then at the funeral I noticed a tall, dark-skinned man standing behind a tree out beyond the gravestones. You could hardly see him, he blended so well with the color of the tree trunk."

"Who was he?"

"I don't know. It doesn't make sense. I still can't figure it out. You touched me on the arm and asked what was wrong, remember?"

She nodded.

His smile wavered as he continued. "And when I looked back, whoever the man was, he was gone. He simply disappeared, if he had even been there."

His answer made Phoebe shake her head as she resumed her breakfast preparations. "I think we were all a bit upset that day. Whoever it was, he left. I wouldn't make much of it, dear."

Maybe she was right. Leave it to his always practical wife to see the sense of things. Whoever it was, the man had gone without any notice, the same way he arrived. But it still seemed rather strange.

The conversation faded as the two of them had breakfast in companionable silence, Bowen trying to bury the memory in the back of his thoughts. Something still bothered him about it, though. Just what he wasn't sure. The idea eluded him.

He chewed on the thought as he put the dishes in the sink and decided to do more research in his study. Maybe the answer was somewhere among the towering piles of books and papers he'd insisted on keeping these many years. If not, whatever had he saved them for?

Or maybe, just maybe, this was all the musing of a madman. Maybe he was as mad as a hatter. The thought depressed him.

"Seabury? You're still not thinking on all that, are you?"

He hated to worry his wife, but at this point it felt wrong to keep everything to himself.

"Something bad's going to happen again, Phoebe," he muttered. "I feel it. It's like an ache in my bones."

"It's the rheumatism, dear. Don't worry so much. You need to stop being your own doctor and use that salve Dr. Dolan gave you."

He shook his head. "I suppose you're right. I think I'll go read awhile in the study."

"That's a good idea, dear. Get your mind on some other things. Don't forget there's a freshly washed quilt on the back of the settee."

Having gotten up so early, Bowen laughed at his wife's knowing remark that he'd end up taking a nap before he did anything else. "No wonder we got married. Whatever would I do without you?"

Like he'd done every day before he'd left for work, Bowen told his wife he loved her and went to his study. Getting some sleep sounded attractive, especially if it came without any bad dreams. He shut the door, a silent plea on his lips. "Let them stay away, at least for an hour.

—Continued in *The Haunting of Dr. Bowen*

* For more details, visit the author's website,
www.cverstraete.com

Chapter Six

Q. You saw where the face was bleeding?
A. Yes, sir.
Q. Did you see the blood on the floor?
A. No, sir.
—Lizzie Borden at inquest, August 9-11, 1892

T he two of them made their way to the gate, their footsteps quiet and sure. She glanced at her companion, wondering at his composure. *Surely his heart is pounding as hard as mine?*

Her nerves on edge, Lizzie licked her lips and picked at invisible lint on the front of her coat. As if he knew how she felt, John switched the small lantern to his other hand and gripped her fingers tight. She didn't resist since, despite his warning, she did indeed have to fight off a strong, and growing, urge to flee.

A man dressed in dark clothing, a shovel in his hands, joined them, falling into step beside John. He greeted her with a quick nod and leaned close to her companion, his head barely topping John's broad shoulders as the two of them began whispering. Lizzie strained to hear what he said, though what she could make out made absolutely no sense to her logical mind.

"John, glad you're back. It's been a dreadful night," the man remarked, his voice low. "As dreadful as any. I fear the situation's worsening."

"But it's still being managed?" John asked.

"Yes, but barely," the man responded. "One of the other men came back from town a while ago, said there was some kind of problem, and well, you know what happened tonight." He glanced at her. "Beggin' your pardon, Miss."

Her eyebrows rose. Problem, what problem?

He turned back to John and continued, his voice low. "We tried to get there first and take care of things, but somehow one of the captains didn't get the message before the marshal heard about it. I'm afraid things will just have to play out now, like any other case. But they'll do their best to keep the real truth out of the papers and out of the courtroom, we hope."

Lizzie's feet tangled with each other. She stumbled, leaning heavily against John as she weighed the smaller man's words. Papers… Courtroom… *He means me! I'm going to jail!*

Everything went dark.

Moments later, Lizzie blinked and gazed about, surprised to find herself held tight in John's arms. Her eyes met his. Her face warmed at the intimate embrace, while oddly enough in such a moment, part of her wished for it to never end.

She cleared her throat and tried to steady herself. "Please, forgive me. I don't know what happened. I must've blacked out." Then she remembered. "Is-is it true? Am I going to be arrested?"

The dimple in John's cheek deepened as he smirked. "I never thought I'd need to carry the smelling salts with me. Pardon me, I don't mean to make light of this. Most likely you will be arrested, but please, don't worry. As you'll soon realize, we have most everything under control. This last chain of events was, uh, quite unexpected, though. Your father—"

That stopped her cold. "Father? What did he—?"

Her question got lost in the sudden eruption of terrible yells and high-pitched screams. A horrific growl made her jump. *Oh, heavens! What was that sound?*

"There! There!" a man yelled. "Don't let it get past you! Stop him!"

Her heart slammed against her ribs, and her palms became slick, as she struggled to see down the road where the noises and yells had come from. John's body tensed. His hands clenched, he peered in the direction of the disturbance.

Lizzie's hair practically uncurled as another high-pitched scream erupted.

"Stop him! Oh, God, get it away!"

Metal on metal clashed. The sounds of a struggle drifted their way. John's companion hoisted his shovel and took off on a run down the gravel-lined path. "I'll be back," he yelled. "I have to help!"

Seeing his worried expression, Lizzie laid her hand on John's arm. "Go on. Go if they need your help. I can manage."

"No, I can't leave you. They can take care of it. You'd best go over—"

Almost too late, he saw another man heading their way. "John! John, we need your help, hurry! There are too many of them!"

The look of alarm on John's face told Lizzie all she needed to know. "Go on, really. I can wait here. Go, I'm fine."

John looked torn on whether to go, or stay. There was another scream. The look of pain on his face alarmed her. She hurriedly looked around and picked up a big rock. "Go, I'll use this. No one will get near me."

Her cavewoman imitation made him chuckle, but the moment quickly passed as someone yelled, "John, look out! They're coming your way!"

His expression turned serious. Setting the lantern down and pushing his jacket aside, he pulled a large revolver from a leather holster at his side. He then rushed over, grabbed a long metal poker leaning against the iron fence, and shoved the smooth end at her. Her hands went clammy as she grasped the tool tight in both hands.

"No matter what, just stab and move, stab and move," he warned. "Keep your distance so they don't get too close. And if I fall, run. Under no circumstances are you to help me. The others will do that." He reached out and gripped her shoulders. "Whatever happens, stay away from me. Do you understand?"

She nodded, not sure what he really meant. *Did he mean for me to leave him to die? How can I ever do such a thing?* She gasped and staggered back at sight of the creatures, the *things*, coming her way. *What is that?*

Whatever had happened to Father and Mrs. Borden, it was nothing like this. This was a scene from the lowest level of hell, right out of *Dante's Inferno*. The man stumbling toward her—at least what was left of him—shambled along on feet mottled with dark blotches of decay ringed with white spots. Lizzie gagged at the stench that drifted her way, but dared not look away.

No, not a man any longer, she decided. The creature shuffled along, one foot covered with writhing, wiggling things dragged behind the other at a weird angle. Its clothes hung in tatters, and looked like they'd been dug out of some hole—*not hole, grave*, her mind whispered—after months or years of rot and ruin.

Unknown things—*insects, bugs infesting the dead*, she thought, crawled and slithered across its ugly face. The mouth turned up in an awful grimace. The decayed, broken teeth chomped inside the gruesome orifice. Her eyes widened as the monster continued to move toward them, things she dared not think about shimmying beneath the surface of its gray, rotted skin.

Her panic bloomed, yet she stood and stared, unable to move, her feet rooted to the spot. *No! This isn't happening. Not happening. Not happening.*

The creature gave a low, horrible moan and struggled toward her, one foot sliding, followed by the other. It came closer, ever closer, staggering forward even as it left behind a trail of gore, and bits of broken flesh, and…

Lizzie looked away and tried to breathe. *The smell! Oh, it's awful!* She coughed and gagged at the musty stench of earth mixed with a yeasty odor. Beneath that, a touch of something nastier lingered—the smell of decay and death.

Then another of the ghastly creatures caught her eye. It, too, staggered along on broken feet behind the first, its body a torn, rotted, movable feast for bugs and other horrid creatures. It stumbled along, heading right for them despite its lack of sight, its eye sockets dark, empty. Wait, no; not empty. Cringing, she stared at things small and white, wriggling there. Lizzie began to whimper.

A yell broke her from her horrified trance. "Lizzie! Liz, move! Move back!"

John reached over and pushed her behind him before he pulled back the revolver's hammer, aimed, and fired. CRACK! She shook as the shot rent the air. The first monster's head caved in and exploded in a grisly spray of black gore and ghastly parts.

John made sure she stayed hidden behind him—*I have no intention of going anywhere*, she thought—as he again cocked the gun and aimed. BLAM!

The second undead creature's body crumpled into a shaking, writhing pile, and then it, too, stopped moving. Lizzie hid her face in John's coat as a surreal trail of black bugs and wiggling, white insects scurried forth from the now truly dead in search of a new host.

The sounds of fighting and yelling somewhere down the lane stopped them both cold. A hideous scream made her catch her breath and almost bolt. "Look out! NO-NOOOO!"

Heart pounding, she looked every which way. The bloodcurdling scream had her bouncing on her toes, ready to get as far away from there as she could. She fought off the urge and held firm, fearing that if she took off, she would never stop running.

Chapter Seven

Q. Is there anything else besides that that would lead, in your opinion so far as you can remember, to the finding of instruments in the cellar with blood on them?
A. I know of nothing else that was done.
—Lizzie Borden at inquest, August 9-11, 1892

The air filled with heart-wrenching screams and ear-piercing growls. Lizzie whirled around and shrieked as one of the creatures jumped on one of the workers. Like an animal, the thing ripped and bit at the poor man who tried fighting it off to no avail. His screams soon faded in the viciousness of the attack. Lizzie screeched as never before as the creature continued ripping apart the now dead man in a frenzy of blood and gore.

"John! Please stop that *thing*. Please, stop it!"

John ran past her with a yell and aimed his gun. "Got it." A minute later, the creature's horrid moans and groans quieted as one bullet, then two, stilled it, and made sure the unfortunate man never joined its ranks.

Lizzie staggered and leaned against a tree in an attempt to ease her vertigo and erase the horrors flashing in her mind. She had to get hold of herself, and fast.

"Liz, get ready!" He fired another shot at one of the ghouls suddenly bearing down on them. "Hit it! Swing!"

Grunts and roars filled the air as he engaged in keeping two others away, leaving Lizzie on her own. She tightened the grip on the poker and, to her horror, found herself facing a particularly gruesome specimen. The ghoul barely looked human anymore, although it had been male. Its face and jaw were bloodied and decayed, the enlarged mouth

41

showing rows of rotted teeth. It lunged at her with a low moan, the clawed hands, minus several fingers, reaching for her. She gagged at the awful, rotten stench.

Lizzie hesitated, not convinced she could do this. With no other choice, she raised the poker over her head, let loose a terrifying scream, and swung. WHAM! The monster let out a nightmarish groan as the poker hit the side of its face, pulling the skin down in a horrific parody of peeling wallpaper. Her terror turned to silent prayer. *Oh God, please help me, please. Make it stop!*

The ghoul shuffled closer. Lizzie swung the poker again, this time hitting it in the head where she should. A memory of Abby's gruesome face flashed in her mind. *No! Don't! I can't think of her!* WHACK! The creature stumbled, yet kept moving. She hit it again and again until finally, the creature crumpled to the ground in a gory, ghoulish mess.

The poker fell from her shaking fingers. She shuddered, feeling colder than she'd ever felt as the realization hit her: I have killed. Again.

Despite her decision to be strong no matter what, the whole of the day's events took its toll. Her legs began to quiver like they would buckle under her weight. Her head swam, the images floating around in a swirl of red and black. She grabbed at John, desperate to keep herself upright and awake. "John!"

He held on to her, trying to keep her on her feet. "Lizzie, are you all right?"

"I-I d-d-don't know." The tremors hit like she'd held on to a big block of ice for hours—or been touched by *them*.

"Here, let me get you to the carriage and under the blanket."

She took a few staggering steps and stumbled. John bent down and scooped her into his arms like she weighed nothing. In moments they sat in his carriage, her body bundled under the heavy wool, plaid blanket.

Despite it being so hot earlier, the air had a slight chill, or maybe it was just her. She gasped amid the shivers. "Did-did I get infected by something? I'm so-so cold!"

Even in the odd purplish glow of the moon, she saw his panic. His face turned a sickening shade of gray. "Lizzie! Did they harm you?" He began to inspect the uncovered parts of her body, taking special note of her neck and arms. "Are you sure that you don't have any scratches or bite marks? Did anyone break the skin or make a mark on you today? Anyone?"

What he meant was clear. She thought back to cleaning herself off earlier in the day, and changing her dress the first time. There had been blood... A lot of blood. She shook her head and tried to erase the ghastly memories. "No, there was nothing."

His eyes held hers. "This is important. Are you one hundred percent certain?"

"Yes, I am sure. Quite positive."

"Very well then, here." He held out a small silver flask. "Take a good swig and I'll get you home."

This time, she showed no hesitation. She did as he ordered, coughing slightly as the whiskey made its way down her parched throat. It warmed her inside. Beginning to feel better, she pushed down the blanket.

Maybe it was the whiskey, though even in the few times she'd sampled alcohol she felt able to handle far more than that demure little sip. Maybe it was the situation and the events of the day that emboldened her. Nothing mattered. Life as she once knew it was gone, probably forever.

When John leaned over to adjust the blanket, Lizzie boldly kept her eyes on his. She gasped, unconsciously licked her lips, and dared move in closer. He stared down at her, his eyes darkening before he quickly pulled away, putting distance between them.

He cleared his throat. "I had best get you home now. Andrew will wonder if I am taking his client away from him."

Lizzie rested her hand on his arm, as certain of anything as she'd ever been. "No, Mr. Jennings is my attorney. You're a friend, and someone I'd like to know better. Please, I don't want to be alone right now."

"Are you certain?

She nodded. "Yes. I think not much else matters. Everything is different now. From now on, my life is never going to be the same."

They looked at each other, and when he hesitated, she moved closer. When their lips met, Lizzie had never felt so alive. To her regret, they separated a few seconds later, leaving her filled with longing.

He took her hand and kissed it, sending shivers up her back, before taking the reins and urging the horse to go. It felt like only minutes had passed as the horse clip-clopped at a brisk pace down the dimly lit streets to his well-kept brick home on the "Hill." This was where she had always thought her family should live, given Father's public standing and his being on several bank boards, but she quickly pushed those thoughts aside. None of that mattered anymore.

She had no time to admire the rows of stately homes lined with fine green lawns and full trees, which formed a lush canopy over the street and darkened houses. Others would think her hard, heartless, and worse, she knew, if they saw the two of them together as John carefully guided the carriage into the shaded garden and yard. He told her to wait a moment and jumped out to make sure the horse was cared for by the stable boy. Minutes later, he returned and guided her to the house.

Once inside, he became the gracious host. He offered a drink and other refreshments, but when he helped remove her coat, Lizzie impulsively turned toward him. She boldly made it clear she wanted him to do much more.

She'd been courted before, mostly by much older men, usually Father's business associates, men who did nothing but annoy her with their fumbling attempts to steal a kiss or an embrace. She'd been quick to ward off their misguided efforts to get their hands on either her chastity, or Father's money. At age thirty-two, she'd always expected to remain a spinster.

Now, Lizzie decided if she was going to spend the rest of her life in jail, or worse—*best to not think of such things*—she wanted to experience everything possible first. The offer of drinks forgotten, they did just that.

Chapter Eight

A. I don't know what I have said. I have answered so many questions and I am so confused I don't know one thing from another. I am telling you just as nearly as I know how.
—Lizzie Borden at inquest, August 9-11, 1892

Later, as she sat beside John on the settee and sipped a glass of wine, Lizzie felt no shame or regret about being alone with him, even at the risk of her reputation being ruined. There was simply too much else going on. Nor did she feel bad about her role in the night's attack, and said so.

"I was thinking about what happened," she said. "It was shocking, but I realized I'm glad I could help. Really glad. If I can stop any of those horrid creatures from attacking anyone else, then I want to. I have no intention of simply standing on the sidelines and watching. I hope you don't think badly of me."

John cleared his throat. "Badly? No, never. You did well."

"Then you think I can accompany you again?"

He held up a hand. "We shall see. First things first. We have your situation to be most concerned about. I'll let your sister Emma know of the Society so she understands what's going on. We have to remain strictly professional after this in case I'm needed to serve in a legal capacity, but I suspect Andrew may want me to be available on a consulting basis instead. If, or when, you're arrested, we don't want your name to come to anyone's attention for any other reason outside of the trial, or be linked to our work. You understand we cannot allow that to happen."

"I understand." She sighed and pulled from his embrace. "Then you think they'll arrest me?"

He nodded. "I'm afraid it's likely. We should leave soon."

Emboldened, she leaned in to kiss him. "Then we'd better not waste more time."

Seated again in the carriage, they made their way quietly to her house via the back roads, each lost in their own thoughts. Lizzie dreaded the public display most, and the way people would view her if she were arrested. Since the murders, she'd already noticed the curious glances, the sidelong stares, the whispers… and she suspected it would get much worse before long. Local gossip had never interested her, but she'd never been in such a position before. She sat back and let out a breath. It was a lot to consider.

And, truth be told, now that she'd found John, she mostly did not—or could not—think of parting from him. Maybe their relationship had ended even before it really began, but she hoped not. Her mind swirled as she considered the impossible—*what if I'm convicted? What if I have to go to jail? Is my life over?*

And worse… the ultimate punishment. Lizzie began to hyperventilate at the thought, the panic choking her. *What-what if they find me guilty? Would they—could they—hang me?*

John brought the carriage to a stop in a shaded corner, just out of view of the house. His hand on hers stopped her inner turmoil for a minute. She tried to focus on him, on his fingers wrapped around hers.

"Lizzie, are you all right? Calm yourself. Take a deep breath, that's it. Now another."

47

She did as he suggested. The panic began to subside. "Yes, I-I think so. I was just thinking, what if…" She bit back a sob. She couldn't say more.

He squeezed her hand in reassurance. "Don't. We'll know in time. Focus on the positive, on the present. Let's only think of good for the future, shall we?"

That he said "we" made her feel much better, a tad hopeful even. Her analytical mind soon took over, however. *I must be mad! If I'm charged, and even if I'm declared not guilty, how would it look for him to consort with someone like me—an accused killer?* She gasped as the reality of that hit her. It would be professional suicide for him!

She gave a weak smile and took another cleansing breath as he patted her hand again. Either way, she realized, the options were few. Maybe it sounded wanton, scandalous even, but if their future relationship went no further than an occasional stolen moment together… She paused and thought about it. *Yes, I can accept that.*

"John, I wanted to say—"

He reached out and pulled her close in a tight embrace, kissing her neck lightly. "Before you say anything, know that I'll be thinking of you. I'll be working behind the scenes for your welfare," he whispered in her ear. "I'm hoping for the best of outcomes for you, for us."

"Yes." She agreed and slipped from the carriage into the shadows. "I'll be thinking of you also." Then she remembered and ran back to the carriage. "Wait! You never told me what you meant about Father? About his not working with you?"

A confused look came over his face for a moment. "I almost forgot. Well, I guess you should know. I don't want you to stay out here too long. I'll make it quick." He sighed, and then began, his tone serious. "Your father is, sorry, was, such an influential member of the business community, we

48

felt it important to ask him for his help. We thought there may come a time, if we needed any financial or other backing, he could be an important asset."

She nodded. "That makes sense. And?"

"He turned us down. Said he had no time, and I quote, 'for secret societies, and people with nothing better to do but chase nonexistent monsters.' His exact words. So, we left it at that, and hoped he'd keep our inquiries to himself. I told him that even if he doubted our veracity, it was of the utmost importance nothing be said of us, or our meeting."

"What did he say?"

John shook his head. "He said he had no intention of sharing such balderdash, and stormed off. I must have visited him on a bad day. You'd better get inside. I'll talk to you soon."

"I hope so," she added, saying goodbye with a half-hearted wave.

Watching the carriage drive off, she headed unseen into the backyard, certain that even the most stalwart of nosy neighbors wouldn't be spying out their windows. She went inside, a whispered prayer on her lips that the police hadn't been back to check on her whereabouts, either. She hoped to have at least a little time to digest the probability of her arrest first.

John's words troubled her. Her father could be stubborn, even a bit prickly at times. Yet when it came to business, if he saw any kind of advantage he'd never been the type to let an opportunity slip by.

The whole idea sounded odd; almost far-fetched. She thought her father would've changed his mind if he could present himself as someone helpful. Maybe it might've given him the chance to ingratiate himself with other businessmen and community members he hadn't worked with before. Apparently not, but something still felt wrong. What could Father have been thinking?

A darker thought occurred to her; a possibility that she would never have considered, but for recent events. *Could it be true? Was her father up to something that conflicted with the Society's plans?*

Taking off her coat, she slipped her hand into the pocket and felt the package still resting there. Her curiosity mounted as she went to the kitchen, lit the lamp, and pulled it across the scarred wooden table. Picking up a knife, she slit the string wrapped around the package and unfolded the heavy white paper. Inside sat a plain, flat wooden container. It had no description or label. Nothing was written on the inside of the packaging, either.

Being extra careful, she grasped the box and slowly pulled it open. She stared at the contents, surprised, but also a little disappointed. That's all it is? Just a key. A plain, utilitarian key. Picking it up, she noted the lack of any kind of imprint or name. What would it open? Maybe a small chest? A desk? A secret door?

Not sure what to think, Lizzie slipped the key back into the box, then rewrapped and retied it. Looking for something to write with, she spotted a pencil on the table and scribbled a message on the paper, just in case: *Emma, give to John.* For a second she considered putting the package back in her coat pocket. *No, no, that won't do*, she realized. *If—or when—I'm arrested, they'll find the box and confiscate it.* Then we'll never know what it opens. She suspected it needed to remain in the possession of someone who was aware of the bizarre events that had occurred here at home.

Where to put it? She went to the hall closet and spied Emma's favorite black cloak. *Yes, perfect!* She hurriedly stuffed the package deep in the inner pocket and hoped for the best. It seemed important for Emma to find it in case she had no chance to pass it on herself.

Heading upstairs to her room, she tried to block out the horrible images in her mind. How could such ghastly, monstrous things be real? How? Her head began to spin. Taking deep breaths, she clung to the rail and tried not to fall.

A few seconds later, she plopped down on the stair and waited for the vertigo to pass, but this time she couldn't stop the tears. Her head in her hands, she tried to regain her composure, hating the feeling of helplessness that flooded in. Her life had not been exactly idyllic, but for the most part, she'd been comfortable.

Still, she had hoped, and longed, to be more in control, and have fewer restrictions on her life. With neither she nor Emma expecting to be married anytime soon, at least not in the near future, the two of them had discussed taking the liberating step of living together in a small house of their own. Father owned enough properties around town that they thought one of them surely would be a suitable place for two spinster women living together.

Lizzie rose and trudged up the stairs, bemoaning the loss of her family life, maybe even the loss of her future. Anger stirred in her breast. *Why did this have to happen? Why did it happen to me? Why, why?*

She felt herself begin to unravel and grabbed the handrail for support. *Steady, now steady. I have to keep myself in order. I must.* The sigh she released came from the depths of her soul. *I have to stay strong. I have to—for Emma. But can I?*

Chapter Nine

Q. Did you give to the officer the same skirt you had on the day of the tragedy?

A. Yes, sir.

Q. Do you know whether there was any blood on the skirt?

A. No, sir.

—Lizzie Borden at inquest, August 9-11, 1892

August 6, 1892

"There she is! She-devil! Monster!"

Tears stung Lizzie's eyes as she peeked beyond the edge of the curtains at the growing mob gathered in front of the house. It had begun with a few curious onlookers. She expected the crowds to grow larger and surlier by the time they left for Father and Mrs. Borden's burials.

Emma walked over and squeezed Lizzie's shoulder before pulling her sister away from the window. She yanked down the shade with a mumbled curse. "Liz, don't listen to them. They don't know what they're talking about."

Lizzie let Emma draw her back into the kitchen and tried to blot out the slurs, though they still pierced her like fishing barbs. Part of her couldn't dismiss the hateful words so easily. "I know, I know, but…"

"You have to let go of it," Emma advised. "You have to stay strong. You can't let it eat at you."

Further discussion would have to wait as someone knocked at the back door. Emma motioned her to stay put and hurried to see who it was. Lizzie tensed, hoping it wasn't another one of those pesky reporters. They'd gotten bolder, and even more egregious, in their speculations in recent days. Lucky for them, Mr. Jennings handled most of the press inquiries, making it easier to withstand, at least most days.

Every now and then one boldly appeared at the door, seeking some lie they could print. Just the other day Lizzie spotted a shocking example Emma had tried to hide, the rag trumpeting the preposterous, most scandalous idea that she'd killed their parents because of anger over a love child. John, and his fellow Society members, fortunately did have friends in the press, and in higher places. He told her nothing had been said about the horrible creatures, or the fight at the cemetery because of that. No one had to tell her that the current preoccupation with her was likely the real reason, but at least it took attention away from their cause. But how long could that last?

A greeting from their older neighbor, Dr. Seabury Bowen, his face serious but kindly as he stepped in, halted her woolgathering. The well- dressed gentleman tipped his hat. "Thank you, Miss Emma. I contacted the marshal about this group out front. He said he would send out police to clear the walks, and send them on their way."

"Thank you, Doctor," Emma responded. "It really is getting out of hand, I think."

"Very well." He cleared his throat. "If you don't mind, I would like a few moments with your sister."

Dr. Bowen dipped his head at her in greeting as Emma left them alone. "Miss Borden? I wanted to check on you, and see how you were holding up. How are you doing?"

Lizzie feared her attempt to act cheerful failed to go over well. "I confess it's getting more difficult. I feel like I'm drowning. By the hour, it becomes harder and harder to bear."

He set his worn, black doctor's bag on the table, asking without words for permission to look her over. She agreed with a nod. He peered at her eyes, and felt her pulse. During his examination he said nothing, but gave the occasional grunt or a muttered, Mmm-hmm.

"Well." He finally stepped back and began rummaging in his bag. "Are you eating? Getting enough sleep?"

She shook her head to both.

"Hmm, given your situation, I'm giving you medication to relax, so you can get some rest."

The doctor drew out a syringe and small vial from his bag, and filled it. Dabbing her skin with an alcohol-saturated cotton compress, he inserted the needle into her arm. When he was done, he instructed her to hold the cotton in place for a moment.

"The morphine will help you feel calmer. I will be back to give you more as needed."

Lizzie sat stunned for a moment, thoughts of all the terrible stories she'd read in the newspaper about morphine fiends going through her mind. One of the papers just last week had a story about a man who'd committed suicide because of his drug use.

"Doctor, is it safe? I don't want to become—"

He patted her hand and cut her off with a wave. "There now. Don't be concerned. You leave the worrying to me. A small amount won't hurt you."

She supposed he was right, his words making her feel better. "Thank you, Doctor. The-the burials will be later."

"Yes, I will be there. Good day for now."

To his credit, the doctor never seemed to pass judgment, or treat her as anything but a patient, and a neighbor he had known for years, which helped immensely. Within minutes of his leaving, Lizzie leaned back in the chair and gave in to the dreamy feeling. Her whole body relaxed as the drug took effect. She nearly fell into a doze right there at the kitchen table but for Emma's interruption.

"Lizzie? Are you awake?"

Lizzie stirred, her movements slow and deliberate as she lifted her head. It almost felt like treading water, or fighting against an unseen current. "Mmm, yes, the doctor gave me something to relax." The clank of tea cups prompted her to rise, but the motion went no further than her thoughts. "Ah, I think I'll sit here a while."

"Yes, sit there. I'll get you some tea, and then we need to work on an advertisement for the newspaper. We should provide a reward, so it'll be taken seriously. How much should we offer? Is two thousand dollars enough?"

Emma's words made Lizzie look up. Neither of them dared voice their thoughts aloud—that no one would ever catch the real killer. No, not her, but whoever had passed that dreadful illness, or whatever it was, on to Father and Mrs. Borden.

Lizzie sighed, closed, and then barely opened her eyes as she slid the pen and paper across the table to Emma. Her words sounded slurred, even to her. "No, make it five thousand," she answered. "Have Mr. Jennings handle the inquiries."

Emma nodded and read back what she'd written: "A Reward of Five Thousand Dollars is Offered for the Arrest of the Man or Person Responsible for the Deaths of Mr. and Mrs. Andrew Borden. Contact Mr. Andrew Jennings…"

Lizzie nodded her approval, though it felt more and more like she was being sucked down in quicksand. She stumbled to her feet, her legs wobbled like jelly. "Emma, I need to lie down for a while. Can you help me to the staircase?"

A Verstraete

The way Emma tsk-tsked made the walk to the stairs feel like a miles-long trek. "The doctor should have made sure you ate something first. I will tell him that."

All Lizzie could do was nod. She grabbed the banister, hanging on as she slowly made her way upstairs. "I just need to lie down," she mumbled.

"I'll wake you in a half-hour and make sure you get some food in you before everyone arrives," Emma said.

Emma's words swirled in her mind as Lizzie fell into a deep sleep... wanted for the killings... murders... murderess...

She sighed and sat up an hour later, not sure whether she could stand the judgmental stares of others. Would she be able to hold up under the increasing pressure? Emma's call from downstairs interrupted her musing. Stumbling to the door, she called back, "Coming. I'll be down in a minute."

A quick rinse of her face, a light dab of rouge to her pale cheeks, and a change of clothing made her look, if not feel, better. She smoothed back her hair, preparing herself mentally. *All right. I'm ready.*

She still felt a bit dreamy and out of touch, but also a bit on edge. It would likely take hours for her to feel fully like herself. She considered putting a little of Father's whiskey in her tea, but thought better of it. *From now on, I'd best watch myself. If someone notices my imbibing, what is that but further proof of my defective character? Surely, that would be taken as a sign of my guilt once I am arrested.*

She couldn't help envisioning the horrid news headline that would add the words fake temperance supporter and fraud to her growing list of supposed sins. The idea hurt. Yes, she'd best rely only on the doctor's treatments.

Downstairs, she seated herself at the kitchen table, her hands worrying the edge of the tablecloth.

"Lizzie, are you feeling better? Did you sleep? You still seem nervous."

"I feel fine. I slept a bit."

Emma looked skeptical and set the steaming cup in front of her. Lizzie ignored her and leaned in for a whiff of the fresh, lemony scent. Her stomach growled in response.

"I made some sandwiches. You really should eat a little."

Taking a big gulp, Lizzie relished the honeyed tea, glad for the warmth and the sweetness. Her hunger kicked in. She bit into the cucumber and cream cheese sandwiches with appreciation. The crispness of the cucumbers and the sweetness of the cream cheese made her realize she was truly hungry. She nibbled the sandwiches quickly, not caring that she was eating so fast.

"Mmm, Emma, thank you, these are divine. Oh, and if you notice Dr. Bowen before I do, please tell him I need to see him, would you?"

Emma raised an eyebrow but didn't say anything, for which Lizzie was glad, what with everything else already on her mind. She wondered what would happen next. She followed Emma into the hall to get their hats before asking something both of them must've thought about. "Emma? Do you think those monsters will start coming around more and more?"

Her lips in a firm line, Emma went into the parlor and peeked out the curtain before coming back to report. "I would hope not, but brace yourself. I think the real problem we have is with everyone else. Quite a mob is assembled outside."

"Still? The doctor mentioned he'd ask the marshal to send the police to chase them off."

Emma frowned and stepped back, taking a moment to peer into the mirror and adjust her hat before answering,

"Hmm, did he? Well, the police have pushed the people back. They're holding them away from the direct front of the house at least. I guess that's the most they intend to do. It should be over soon. The pastor said he'll be quick."

Minutes later, immediate family members, including her uncle, aunt, and Mrs. Borden's relations, arrived and walked past the assembled onlookers as quickly as they could. The sour looks on their faces told Lizzie they considered the assembled mob an affront. She bit back a rude comment about it being a temporary inconvenience for them, but remained silent. There was nothing anyone could do about it. Breathing deep, Lizzie readied herself as best she could. It was time to bury Father and Mrs. Borden.

She held back a sniffle and took her place in the parlor. True to his word, the pastor kept his eulogy to a few words. He praised Father's community service and selfless giving, and Mrs. Borden's helpfulness and role as a good wife, before offering a prayer for their souls.

The eulogy over, the relatives rushed out the door to their carriages. Lizzie hung back, hoping to spare her relations further embarrassment if any of the crowd saw her and began hurling insults.

The rumble of voices outside made it hard to ignore what was going on. *Unbelievable.* There had to be at least a hundred or more people out there now. "Where are the police?" she murmured in irritation.

"I heard they're handling the *intruders* and keeping them confined to the other streets," Emma whispered. "It wouldn't be safe, otherwise."

Lizzie nodded as Emma hurried outside to their waiting carriage and seeing Dr. Bowen, motioned him to go in. He entered, hurriedly put down his bag, and looked Lizzie over before bringing out his supplies.

"I think you'll need this, but I'm giving you a much smaller dose than I did earlier," he told her. "I'll come back again the next few afternoons to see you."

"Thank you," she whispered, suddenly feeling weepy. "You are being so kind."

What she left unsaid was her surprise at his willingness to treat her, especially when he had been among the first at the bloody scene to see the bodies. He likely had heard or already been told what the police thought, but he said nothing. Or maybe he held a differing opinion. She dared not ask.

The doctor cleared his throat and packed up his bag when he was done. "I will see you to your carriage."

Her appearance started a ripple of mumbles and taunts from the crowd of onlookers. A quick glance and Lizzie saw a few sympathetic faces in the crowd, mostly the women. She looked away and stared at the walk. The doctor gripped her elbow and gave it a squeeze, hurrying her along. He tightened the pressure slightly to keep her focused. Once she was seated in her carriage, he rushed off to his own as Emma carefully pulled the curtains around the side windows against prying eyes.

No one spoke during the short drive to the cemetery. Emma appeared pensive, while Lizzie tried to keep her thoughts, and mind, unfettered. She couldn't help but remember her outing with John and wondered what he was doing or if she would see him.

The ride remained mostly uneventful despite the crowds lining the roadway, making their arrival more nerve-wracking. She hadn't expected to see so many people about. The funeral director understood the need for strict privacy and closed the gates of the cemetery, restricting admittance to only officials and family. She felt a slight twinge of disappointment that John was nowhere in sight.

The director ushered everyone into the small chapel, apologizing for the police stationed at the door. He surprised her with his next words. "I am sorry, Miss Borden, but the police insisted on being here to keep watch. I am afraid the burial will have to be postponed until later, as the police requested the bodies be kept until their investigations are finished. We will hold the bodies here in the vault and will schedule a more public memorial service later if desired, and when we are able. I am terribly sorry."

Lizzie swayed and grabbed on to her sister. Emma held her arm tight and led her to one of the benches. "It'll be fine, Liz. We can manage," she whispered.

All Lizzie could do was nod. She held her head high, even if most of what was said during the shortened service went beyond her understanding—partly from grief and shock, partly from the drug's effects. Everything felt hazy and detached.

The pastor led them in prayer, and then it was over. The few close friends in attendance filed past the sisters to share their deep sorrow and condolences. Most of the family members remained quietly supportive. Lizzie didn't know how most of them really felt, or if they blamed her at all, though they remained polite. She expected to learn more as things progressed.

They trailed out of the chapel, Lizzie taking note of the police stationed at the cemetery gates to keep the small crowd at bay. A groan escaped her at sight of several newspapermen in the crowd scribbling on notepads. Jackals.

Lizzie hurried over to Emma, who stood talking with several friends. They nodded cordially, but made a hasty good-bye when Lizzie neared. There was nothing she could do but shrug at Emma's sad face to at least let her know their reactions came as no surprise.

Emma shook her head and squeezed Lizzie's hand. "Don't worry about them. I need a few minutes before we go, if you don't mind. Let the driver know I'll be there shortly."

"I understand," Lizzie told her. "Take your time."

She expected her sister needed a few minutes to sort out her feelings. Both of them certainly did.

Emma walked to one of the benches across the road, her shoulders drooping, and stared out at the gravestones. Lizzie watched her and sighed with regret. For the thousandth time she wished things had turned out differently.

Lifting her face to the sun's warmth gave Lizzie a small moment of respite. She stifled the impulse to remove her hat and shake her hair loose. *Wouldn't that shock everyone?* To her surprise, as the carriage neared, she turned and spotted a tall, familiar-looking man in the distance. John! It was a shame he didn't stop by the house earlier, but given the circumstances she understood.

As she watched, he stopped to talk with a shorter man carrying a shovel over his shoulder. She glanced quickly at the group by the gate, glad that no one paid much attention though she did see one of the reporters look in John's direction. A minute later, John hurried back to his carriage and the other man took off in another direction. She suspected the reason he rushed off was probably to make sure one of the newly undead, and unburied, remained unobserved by anyone in the unwelcome crowd lingering at the gate.

Lizzie waited for her own carriage to pull up. She paused near the entrance to the cemetery office building when the door opened. Out stepped the director, who gave her a grave look. It became evident why when he moved aside to let the stout, disapproving figure of Mayor John Coughlin pass by.

The mayor cleared his throat as he twirled a thick cigar between his fat fingers and walked in her direction, his eyes pinched in an unfriendly glare. Lizzie had no inkling what he wanted. Nor was she in the mood to talk. Despite her misgivings, she did the polite thing and waited, though it set her nerves on edge when he sidled next to her. Without a greeting or any words of compassion or condolences, he whispered, "Prepare yourself. An arrest is imminent."

Her face grew warm. She gazed at the ground. The mayor gave her another grim, disapproving look before he headed to his own carriage. Holding back the tears that threatened to burst forth, she ignored Emma's call and turned away once the mayor left. She jumped at Emma's light touch on her arm.

"Lizzie, are you unwell? Was that the mayor? Whatever did the grumpy old toad want?"

Lizzie tried to control her nervous laughter and sighed instead. "Oh, Emma, thank you for trying to brighten the moment. Yes, it was Mayor Coughlin. He thinks I'm guilty. He warned me that I'm going to be arrested."

Chapter Ten

Q. Can you give any suggestion as to what occupied her when she was up there, when she was struck dead?

A. I don't know of anything except she had some cotton cloth pillow cases up there and she said she was going to commence to work on them. That is all I know. And the sewing machine was up there.

—Lizzie Borden at inquest, August 9-11 1892

August 7, 1892

The fear of her imminent arrest turned Lizzie into a bundle of nerves. Since she slept little, given the added tension of hearing all those strange sounds and eerie moans outside, the next morning had her up earlier than usual for her cup of tea.

As she donned an apron, an alarming thought came to her—the dress! *I have to get rid of that dress I stupidly hung on to!* She went and grabbed it from the hall closet when a knock at the door startled her. Who could that be? It was too early for anyone to call. Of course, what did it matter? These days her life was anything but typical.

"Coming!" Lizzie hoped it wasn't a reporter or anyone else searching for information. She peeked out the parlor window, not only surprised, but glad, to see her friend, Alice Russell, standing there. To her dismay, the police guard had returned and stood watch by the street. She opened the door, too late realizing she still had the damaged dress in her hand. She crumpled it up and motioned Alice to quickly come inside.

Alice hurried in with a warm greeting. "Liz, I know it's early, but I wanted to see how you were doing. I'm so sorry

63

about everything, and about your parents, of course." Her eyes widened as she noticed the dress in Lizzie's hands, though she tried to cover her reaction with a smile.

Lizzie's heart fell. She wondered if the mounting hysteria, the whispered accusations, and the unfounded speculations about her character, had gotten to Alice, too. Someone she had considered a friend. "Thank you, Alice. Would you care for some tea?"

Alice shook her head. "No, no, I only wanted to stop in before I go to pick up some things at the market. What are you doing with that dress, dear?"

"This old thing? I was going to burn it. It has paint on it."

Alice's face went pale. "Lizzie, is that a good idea? Should you be doing that, with everything else going on?"

Lizzie felt no need to explain. She remained silent, tired of explaining already. Instead, having no desire to stand around gossiping, she went to the kitchen. Her patience fading, she tore at the dress, wondering what was keeping Alice. Probably snooping.

Alice walked into the kitchen a minute later and lowered her voice. "Lizzie, I wouldn't let anyone see you doing that."

Ignoring her, Lizzie made no comment. She dropped the rest of the torn material into a basket before turning all her attention to the tea preparations. Alice prattled on about who-knew-what as Lizzie filled the kettle and chopped lemons, taking her frustrations out on the fruit. Why doesn't she take the hint and leave?

Finally, Alice took a breath and made her apologies. "Well, I can see you're busy. I'd best leave now. I'll go out through here if you don't mind. Those police out there make me nervous. I don't see how you can tolerate it."

Lizzie wished her good-bye and swung the door shut. She knew Alice would likely report what she thought was happening to other members of their social circle. *Make that my former social circle.* With a silent curse, she grabbed the basket and shoved the torn pieces of the dress into the glowing embers of the kitchen stove.

The small measure of relief she got from throwing the dress away, and from seeing it char and flame, did nothing to ease her distress, but it had to be done. She paced back and forth, wrung her hands, and fretted. *I need to get out of here!* No formal arrest had been made—not yet—but she felt stifled. *How would the police react if I went for a walk? Will they prevent me from going out?*

She'd soon find out. She went to the hall closet, grabbed her cloak, and to her surprise simply stood there. Her boldness evaporated like a puddle on a hot day. *I can't do it. I can't. I don't need to give the neighbors more reasons to talk about me.*

A minute later, Emma thumped down the stairs, her face flushed, her hair still mussed from sleep. "Liz, what're you doing? Where are you going? Come, have some tea with me." She went in the kitchen and came back to the doorway a minute later, a piece of the torn dress in her hand. "What is this? I found it on the floor."

She glared at Emma, not sure what to say. *Is it going to haunt me forever?* Finally, she reached out and snatched the fabric from Emma's hand. "Never mind. It's nothing."

Emma stared at her. "Lizzie, what's wrong?"

"Wrong? Whatever could be wrong?"

What could be wrong except my friends are all abandoning me? The police are coming to arrest me. What in the world could be wrong?

Her hysteria churned to the surface, the words pouring from her in a torrent. "Tea? You want me to sit and have tea like some refined lady? Like any other day?" She knit her fingers together, pacing the floor back and forth, her voice growing louder. "Emma, they're going to arrest me! THEY THINK I'M A KILLER! I AM GOING TO JAIL! I'M GOING TO DIE!"

Neither the feel of Emma's comforting hands, nor her soothing words halted Lizzie's tears. All she could do was weep. A bang on the front door sent her into a whirlwind of panic.

"They're here" Lizzie cried out. "Oh, no, no! They're here to take me to jail!"

She spun about and tried to press herself deep into the closet, her fingers gripping Emma's cloak in a vain attempt to hide herself. She was finally losing it, and fast.

"Oh, no, no," Lizzie muttered. "I'm not here, no, no."

Lizzie paid no attention as Emma ran to open the door, a heartfelt greeting on her lips. "Mr. Fremont! Thank goodness you came over. You need to talk to Lizzie. She's getting hysterical!"

The sound of John's voice drew Lizzie from her hiding place. She stepped out of the closet, her arms full with Emma's cloak. The look of concern on John's face made her feel even more vulnerable. *I must look like a lunatic,* she realized. The garment fell from her arms to the floor in a heap as she began to sob. She wobbled and would have fallen, but for his strong arms holding her up.

"There, there, Lizzie, there now, let it out, yes, there you are." He held her tight and continued talking to her, his voice soothing, calming. "Yes, that's it. Now, do you feel better? Come and let's have a talk, shall we?"

Lizzie nodded and sniffled, wiping at her face with the handkerchief he offered as he led her to one of the cushioned chairs in the parlor. "Thank you, both of you, I-I'm fine now. Forgive me. I have no idea what got into me." Her cheeks warmed as she whisked a hand over her unkempt hair. "I-I must look a fright, like a crazy person."

Emma chuckled. "No more than usual, Lizzie." She glanced over and laughed.

Lizzie started to chuckle, too. "Very well, I guess you're right. John, have you heard anything?"

He shook his head, offering a reassuring smile. "No, nothing yet. I'm sorry. I know how stressful this is. The police are keeping their own counsel. The funeral director told me he heard what the mayor said to you. I must apologize for that, too."

"It was no fault of yours," Lizzie said. "It shocked me, I admit, but I guess his attitude isn't so unusual since he did business with Father and such. I suppose it's something I should get used to, correct?"

"Lizzie, not everyone thinks that way," Emma assured her.

"No, not everyone," John agreed. Lizzie shrugged. "I hope not."

Seeing the concerned look on Emma's face, Lizzie sought to reassure her sister as she rose and crossed the room. "Emma, no need to worry. I'll be fine. I'd better clean up my mess."

She bent to pick up Emma's cloak lying near the doorway. Her eyes widened in surprise when the package she'd forgotten about fell from the pocket with a thud.

"What is that?" Emma asked.

Lizzie hurriedly hung up the cloak before taking the package to her sister. "I forgot about this. I wanted to make sure you got it, in case…" Her words faded. "You know…"

Emma stared at it, puzzled as she read the scribbled message on the paper. "Maybe you should give it to John."

"You can look inside. It's nothing special. It only has a key in it."

Emma opened it and looked up in surprise. "What's so important about that? Did you wrap it like this?"

"No, I found it that way in Father's coat. He probably meant to give it to someone, or do something with it before…" She left the rest unsaid, unwilling to say more.

"It may be best if you hold on to it," Emma told John and passed the package over. "What do you think it opens?"

He turned the key over, looking at both sides before dropping it in an inner pocket of his coat. "Hmm, well, it looks like maybe it might work at one of these places." He held out a piece of paper. The unfolded page contained a handwritten list of at least ten addresses. "Andrew wanted you both to look at this, see what properties you can identify. He's trying to be sure all your father's holdings are accounted for."

Lizzie recognized some of the addresses right away, such as their house, and the small rental house she and Emma had Father buy back from them. Then there were a few other rental properties, a couple buildings in the business district, and warehouses located along the waterfront.

John brought out a large leather-bound volume from his briefcase. "I know someone in the city planning department who let me 'borrow' the town atlas. We can look up the properties and locations."

After an hour of peering at the maps, they whittled down the list. All the properties were identified and catalogued except for one—a property located near the Quequechan River.

"Some of the cotton mills around there closed up after the owners got caught embezzling," Lizzie recalled. "A few are still operating, though the conditions are just horrible. Members of the Ladies' Society at our church had been collecting food and clothing to help the immigrant mill workers' families."

John fingered the map, studying the area again. "Hmm. I represented a few clients from those mills, pro bono of course, when they tried striking for better conditions. The working conditions were truly horrendous. Some of those mills and warehouses are in not in the best parts of town."

"So what was Father doing here?" Emma asked.

"Good question." John rose and went to the door. "I guess we need to find out. Bring that book with you."

After talking outside with the police for a few minutes, he returned and told them to grab their cloaks. "I informed the police that I'm your attorney and the marshal knows you're in my company. As you're not under arrest, they'll leave us alone. We should go. We don't have a lot of time. I told one of the officers I trust to relay a message to a couple of our Society members to meet us there, just in case."

They left the business district and genteel homes behind them. The horse clip-clopped to the bottom of the Hill toward the waterfront where another world waited. Here stood the real backbone of Fall River—the mills and warehouses where the city's goods came into existence from the sweat, labor, and yes, tears of hard-working immigrants who had found a tarnished, shabbier version of the American dream.

Many of the once well-presented homes in the ensuing blocks had been subdivided into small flats now crowded with too many people. Dirty curtains flapped out of broken window panes and open windows. Ugly gray grime coated the glass, keeping the sunlight at bay. Previously pristine lawns had been trampled into dirt dotted with scraggly clumps of brownish grass. Debris clung to the broken-down fences. It skittered along the road like errant ghosts. Front doors hung crooked because of missing and broken hinges.

The whole area felt dingy, and forgotten. Lizzie shivered in response.

John directed the horse to the side of the road, where he stopped to study the map again. He looked around, pointing in front of him. "You wouldn't know it from all the weeds and overgrowth up ahead, but it looks like that's the road we want, right alongside the river. There are a few old warehouses here. I thought most of these were closed down. Never knew any were still in use. You ladies feel ready for this?"

"Fine," Emma said. "Are you all right, Lizzie?"

The threat of rain, or more likely the thought of needing something to keep away other nasty vermin, made Lizzie grab her parasol. "Yes, I think so."

The road got bumpier, jostling them from side to side. Lizzie hung on to the sides of the carriage, her irritation growing. "I could get a smoother ride in the big wheel that's coming to Chicago next year," she griped. The newspapers had called Mr. Ferris's invention one of the anticipated highlights of the upcoming World's Columbian Exposition being held in the Windy City. *Oh, how I'd love to see that!*

She sighed, knowing such a trip would probably never happen. Her nose wrinkled at the fishy scent in the air—and then she smelled it. As the carriage bumped along, something riper, raunchier, became more and more noticeable. She and Emma glanced at each other. Even John began to cough.

He stopped the carriage in front of a two-story building, its brick mottled and worn, and helped everyone out. He paused to soothe the horse, which snorted and pawed the earth. Its nostrils flared as the rotten scent in the air grew stronger. "There, there, easy." He patted the horse's head and pulled the blinders around its eyes so it wouldn't spook, before tying the reins to a sturdy tree.

Lizzie and Emma stepped carefully over stones, and through the wild growth of weeds that grasped at their clothing with greedy fingers.

The building looked unused and abandoned. Then Lizzie heard what sounded like low, spooky hums. No, wait. It sounded like-like... She gulped. Moans? "What-what is that?"

Lizzie gazed at the warehouse towering over them, the unwashed windows on the upper floor giving no hint to what lay hidden inside.

"How in the world can we find out what's in there?" she asked, puzzled.

Even at his full height of near six-feet, John couldn't reach the windows without a ladder or a perch. "We need something I can stand on. See anything?"

They hunted around until finally Emma motioned to the pile of garbage and refuse partially hidden behind the bushes. "Lizzie, take these crates. They look sturdy enough."

They picked up the crates and stacked them under the window. After inspecting them for rot, or loose boards, and seeing none, John stood on the pile, lifting himself up on his toes. He grabbed the concrete ledge under the window, hooked the tips of his shoes into the mortar-free gaps between the bricks, and managed to boost himself up. Now able to reach the window, he rubbed at the years of grime and soot with his handkerchief then cursed. He leaped down and shook his head.

"What?" Lizzie cried. "What is it? Please, I have to see! John, please help me up."

"Prepare yourself," he warned. "It's not a pretty sight."

With him bracing her, Lizzie managed to pull herself up and peek into the spot he'd cleaned on the window. "Oh, oh my, what are those? What are they doing there?"

She struggled to keep her balance and accidentally banged her elbow on the window. It cracked, sending down a shower of glass chips, prompting a louder chorus of moans from the captive creatures within. In response, the crowd of gray-skinned creatures raised their heads and looked up with filmy eyes. They gave horrid, low groans. Each one writhed and moved as best they could in the limited space, their diseased hands reaching for her.

"We have to go, we have to go now," Lizzie cried. "They saw me. They know we're out here!"

Emma stared at her. "What are you talking about?"

Lizzie urged John to help her sister so she could see for herself. Bracing her body against the wall, Emma stared in the window and gasped. "God help us. What did Father have going on here?"

Chapter Eleven

Q. Now, Miss Russell, did you see any blood upon her clothing?
A. No, sir.
Q. A speck of it?
A. No, sir.
Q. Or was her hair disturbed?
A. I don't think it was. I think I should have noticed it if it was disordered.

—Testimony of Alice Russell,
Trial of Lizzie Borden, June 8, 1893

"Hurry, Emma, hurry! Run!"
Lizzie urged her sister on. She scrambled through the weeds and overgrowth, unable to get to the carriage fast enough. John loped ahead and untied the reins, talking to the horse in a low whisper as he did.

To Lizzie's relief, the horse calmed and stopped its pawing and snorting, though the situation still had her just as frantic. "I'm glad you have a way with horses, but can we please leave? I'd rather not stay around too long."

"He's trained for the Society's needs," John explained, helping them into the carriage. "He's used to loud noises and gunfire, but odd smells still do get him a little agitated at times."

Lizzie didn't relax until John flicked the reins and directed the horse back to the road. She preferred they get Emma home. Lizzie already regretted her sister being there, and saw no need in getting her more involved than she already was. What sounded like cries and yells in the

73

distance caught her ear, interrupting her picking unwelcome weeds off her dress.

"Wait, did you hear that?" Lizzie asked. "Someone's yelling. It sounds like it's coming from back there, by the warehouse."

Emma's face went white. "Who is it? Who else is there?"

Whoever it was yelled again. John stopped the horse and listened. A moment later, he pulled the carriage closer to the edge of the road and jumped out. He made sure to tie the horse's reins to a sturdy branch, then soothed the horse again before directing them out. Lizzie stared as he pulled a revolver from beneath his coat.

"A couple of our members should have arrived already," he said. "I hope nothing's happened." He cocked the hammer and handed the gun to her. "Ever shoot?"

"Me? No. What am I going to do with this?" She held the Colt, her hands shaking, surprised at how heavy it felt.

"Shoot something if it comes near you. I should give you some lessons. For now, use both hands, like this." He held the gun in front of him and demonstrated how. "Hold it steady, aim up as high as you can. Aim for the creatures' foreheads. Remember, each time you shoot you have to pull the hammer back, like this. Hold it tight when you pull the trigger." He showed her the process. "Understand?"

She nodded, hoping she remembered everything.

"You have six shots." He gazed at her. "Do your best. Emma, get that poker from the floor of the carriage. Keep it close. If you miss with your first swing, stab them with it. Just don't let them get close to you. I think you should be all right."

Lizzie kept her doubts to herself. A high-pitched scream, and an eerie moan nearby, made her feel even less confident, if possible, about his assessment. Emma shrank closer after grabbing the poker, her grip tight like she was holding a bat.

"What's going on?" Emma asked. "What was that?"

A man ran toward them, waving to get their attention. "John, hurry! Something's happened. They're out!"

"Out?" Lizzie stumbled as Emma grabbed on to her. "They? Those creatures are out of the building?"

The horse whinnied and pawed the ground again until John talked to it in a low voice. "Emma, stand here. He'll stay calm with someone next to him. You can rub his neck. Go ahead."

Emma moved closer and brushed her hand across the animal's velvety neck. The horse quivered and snorted as another scream sounded.

"Quick. Lizzie, watch out! Be careful with that gun. I need to see what's going on." He yanked her arm. "Do you hear me?"

"Huh?" She looked around wildly before finally focusing on him. "Y-yes. I have it, I have it. Go-go!"

The horrible sounds of fighting—men yelling, unknown objects banging, gunfire, and the nightmarish moans of the warehouse's former captives—filled the air like an orchestra playing the wrong notes.

Growing more nervous, Lizzie watched John rush ahead and then turn back to join the fray as a group of men and several creatures suddenly appeared on the road across from them. Two of the men tried to fight off the decayed beings. The creatures lunged and grasped with diseased hands, showing an amazing amount of strength for having been locked away for who knew how long. Lizzie thought they should've been weak and ravenous by now. *Well, of course they're ravenous*, she thought, and made a face. Ugh.

Growls and snarls filled the air. As much as Lizzie had no desire to get involved, she felt terrible doing nothing.

She'd just taken a step forward, thinking of trying to help, when a rustling in the bushes behind them got her attention.

"Liz!" Emma screamed. The horse shrieked.

Lizzie spun around with a gasp as one of the creatures clad in holey pants, its jacket torn, dragged itself through the scraggly brush. The spiky twigs left gouges and deep, black furrows on the creature's mangled limbs, the marks outlined with scraggly pieces of torn flesh. Lizzie coughed and gagged as a horrid scent of cesspool rot, decay, and a mixture of other nasty things wafted her way on the shifting breeze.

The ghoul moaned and staggered toward them, dragging one fleshless foot after the other. Lizzie shivered at the scraping sound of bone against rock. The creature wobbled and wove back and forth, steadily making its horrific way toward her. The horse stomped and snorted again in panic. Its sides quivered as it began to step backward.

"Emma, keep the horse steady!" Lizzie yelled.

Content her sister had the horse under control, Lizzie fumbled with the gun. She tried to remember John's quick instructions. *Steady. Pull the hammer back. Aim. Pull the trigger.* "Oh, dear God, please help me," she murmured. "Help me."

She pointed the gun's muzzle, her hands shaking like an old drunkard's. The snarl of the creature as it shambled closer made Lizzie's heart leap in her chest. *Can I do it?* She glanced at Emma's white face. *I have to. I have no other choice.*

Taking a deep breath, Lizzie calmed herself. Her arms held out straight, she followed John's directions, aimed, and pulled the trigger. BLAM! The thing lurched, and with a loud groan, fell to the ground. The blast made Lizzie stagger backward. It had badly pulled her arm, yet she felt a thrill of accomplishment. It worked. She'd done it!

Emma's yell made Lizzie forget her feeling of success. "Liz, it's getting up!"

The monster struggled to its feet, an ugly hole in its leg leaking black ooze. Lizzie was lucky to have hit it, but one wound didn't stop it. The creature growled louder and staggered toward them. Lizzie aimed, cocked the hammer, and pulled. BLAM! The creature gave one last low moan and crumpled to the ground. This time it remained still.

Seeing no movement, Lizzie stepped closer, noting the big hole just under the empty eye socket. The bullet had hit the brain, ending the creature's un-life for good. She watched the insects skitter away from the corpse and stepped back. A sense of sadness, relief, and even elation filled her at seeing the creature dead. She no longer felt that gut-wrenching repulsion. She didn't know whether this was a good sign or a bad sign.

"Are you all right?" John asked, coming back from the other side of the road. He stopped and peered at the corpse.

She nodded.

Hearing more noises, he quickly grabbed her gun, checked it, and reloaded. "How many did you fire?"

"Three. No, two."

He handed the gun back, his face grave. "Remember to keep track. You don't want to make a deadly mistake. I put in two more bullets."

An ugly roar filled the air. John yelled as several more of the gruesome monsters staggered from the brush. He pulled another gun from under his coat and fired at the group to his left.

Lizzie fumbled with the gun and finally got it set. She fired, her shot getting nowhere near the horrible creature crawling out of the bushes to her right. It raised claw-like hands at her—or rather stumps—since most of its fingers were gone. Dark, gaping holes leaked thick, nasty fluids.

She gagged and held her breath at the rotten stench hanging thick as fog in the air around her. Hands shaking, she pointed the gun again and fired. BLAM! Black gore erupted from a hole in the center of the monster's chest. It stumbled toward her. She stumbled backward in a panic.

Aiming higher, she cocked the hammer and fired. This time the blast hit dead-on. A hole appeared in the monster's right temple, sending bloody gore and brain matter spraying all over.

Ugh. Lizzie jumped back as it fell in a gory pile. She eyed the blood that had spattered her dress and arms, visions of Mrs. Borden's bloodied face flashing in her mind. *No, no. I can't think of that now.*

Shaking off the memory, she turned and checked on Emma, who had her hands full calming the horse. Lizzie gave her sister a sad smile. They'd made it.

Emma's scream jolted Lizzie from her wool-gathering. Almost too late, Lizzie whirled. She set the gun, aimed, and jumped aside as the monster lunged at her with only inches to spare. It shambled forward again and raked its gray arm at her as the shot went wild. She screamed as its cold, dead hand brushed against her side.

With no time to think, she pointed the gun. BLAM! This time the shot went true, hitting the hideous ghoul dead-center in its forehead. She stared at the bloody hole and felt nothing. *Maybe surprise has its merits after all*, Lizzie thought. *I must be getting jaded.*

More shots and shouting filled the air. Lizzie did a quick count. Realizing she only had two bullets left, she rushed to the carriage. "Emma, quick, untie it! Hurry, get in!"

The two of them jumped in, with Lizzie taking the reins. "We need to get the horse further down the road. Keep that poker ready. I only have two shots left."

To her relief, all fell silent. She turned at the sound of footsteps. "John?"

"It's over." He walked up to the carriage and took the gun back from her, signs of the fight evident in the streaks of blood across his cheeks and the smears on his clothing. He sighed and rubbed a hand across his weary face.

"We got all the creatures. Actually, not as many as we thought got out. Most of them are still chained inside. The ones that escaped are truly dead now, may they rest in peace."

His accounting made Lizzie grimace. "This is horrible. How many would you say got out?"

He shrugged and exhaled in relief. "I would say twenty-five, thirty?"

"Emma, stay here would you?" Lizzie asked and stepped out of the carriage. "I want to take a look. Or would you rather come along?"

Her sister made a sour face and shook her head. "No, I'll stay. I'm certainly not going anywhere else."

Lizzie turned and walked beside John down the path, the carnage increasingly evident. The decayed remains of body after body covered the hard ground. Even worse, now that the bodies were no longer reanimated, the decay seemed to accelerate. Already pieces of limbs had dropped off and lay next to the lifeless forms. The rotten flesh sloughed off like lizard skin. A mass of insects skittered off. She tried to block the disgusting images and analogies from her mind. It didn't work.

She coughed and covered her nose with a handkerchief John handed her. "Oh, the smell. It's truly revolting. Whatever are you going to do with them?"

Her question went unanswered for a moment as John directed a couple of men with heavy masks, shovels, and bags to begin the clean-up. He turned and took her elbow, leading her to the warehouse entrance.

"I'm very sorry, Liz, it's a beast of a job. The men will take all the remains to the county crematory. The medical examiner is a friend of ours."

A man dressed in a police uniform arrived and went to talk with the other fighters in John's group. Seeing him, Lizzie tried to keep her face hidden. She grasped at John's sleeve with crab-like fingers as she suddenly became lightheaded. "I-I can't breathe."

He leaned down and whispered to her, "Liz, relax. Take a deep breath. No need to panic, everything is fine. He's a friend of ours."

To her relief, he snaked an arm around her shoulders as she waited for the weakness to pass. It finally did. "Thank you. This is so unlike me. I've never been the frail, hothouse flower type."

"Never mind, no need to worry. I'm pretty worn down myself. I'd better unlock the door so the men can clear out the inside of the warehouse, then…" He paused in front of the worn, wooden door, his face confused. "Liz, look at this."

She stared at the lock he held in his hand—or rather pieces of the lock. "What in the world? It looks like it's been broken!"

"Indeed, it does," he muttered, his expression serious. "It looks fine, except the hasp appears to have been sawed through. Which I suspect is part of the reason for how the creatures got out."

Lizzie noted the steely look and growing anger on his handsome face. She couldn't blame him and felt much the same. "And the other reason?"

He shook his head.

She followed him in, listening to the creak of metal as he turned the valve on one of the kerosene lamps hanging on an iron hook jutting from the weathered brick wall. The scene of body after mangled body piled atop one another in a grisly tableau pulled straight from *Dante's Inferno* took on a ghastlier tone under the lamp's yellowish glow.

John took a few steps closer to the edge of the pile and covered his nose with his arm. He inspected the long link of old, rusty chains which kept one creature attached to the other. The end of the chain hooked to a crude wooden wheel in the center. Lizzie eyed the contraption, suspecting that somehow the creatures couldn't stand still, thus making the wheel turn while it kept its captives in a ghoulish merry-go-round of motion. Sadness filled her. *Oh, Father, what were you up to?*

John's face reflected her mood. Letting out a deep sigh, he wiped his hands and motioned her outside. She waited while he talked quietly with several of the men shoveling the remains out in front. The whole scene bothered her. How can they keep doing this? She sighed, almost overwhelmed with it all. She wondered what other surprises could occur.

True to form, the first came at her fast. John paused and held her hand. "Liz, I apologize. I have to take you and Emma home. I'm afraid there's much more going on here than I expected. I have to meet with the Society members to do some quick planning."

He grimaced and swore under his breath. "Not only was the door lock cut, but somebody sawed part of the chains keeping the creatures fixed to that wheel. That's the other reason, I fear. Those were no accidents. Someone definitely wanted to harm your father."

Chapter Twelve

The theories which were advanced by those who have been closely connected with the case agree on one thing, and that is that the murderer knew his ground and carried out his bloodthirsty plan with a speed and surety that indicated a well matured plot…

—*The Fall River Herald*, August 5, 1892

His words couldn't have startled her more.

Lizzie did feel a bit disappointed about going home with Emma instead of spending time alone with John, but that seemed trivial at the moment. She felt worse thinking her father might have done something to prompt someone to hate him so, thus endangering his wife and family. That completely boggled her mind.

"Then his being attacked, his getting infected, wasn't an accident." She pondered the thought as they reached the carriage. John helped Emma in and then her.

Emma's face went pale. "You—you mean Father?"

Lizzie nodded. "Yes, I'm afraid so."

John shook his head. "I'm sorry, Liz, Emma, I suspect not. The men will let me know more of the details once they've cleaned up and can better examine the warehouse, but it looks like someone planned this. Whatever your father was involved in, it seems to have been a nasty business all around."

Lizzie mulled over the situation as she handed John his driving gloves for the ride home. It would have taken some doing, some serious manipulating, she reasoned, for anyone to pull off such a thing. The person—or persons—responsible needed to not only know the infected were being kept here, but they had to know how to deal with them to avoid attack. And somehow, they had to fix it so the others wouldn't escape. An idea formulated in the back of her mind.

"I think we should go back in the warehouse," she suggested. "I want to look around Father's office. We might find something that can explain some of this."

"Good idea," John agreed and jumped to the ground, enthusiasm in his step. "I'll help you look so we can get out of here as soon as possible. Emma, are you coming?"

Her sister's hesitation before shaking her head no filled Lizzie with sadness. She hoped Emma hadn't lost all her nerve, but she decided to let her be for now. They'd have to talk about it, though.

She and John hurried inside. The stench alone was enough to make them move faster. The staleness and sour smells in the air also made her cough. She pressed a handkerchief over her mouth and nose as John walked ahead past the main workroom.

They headed down the narrow corridor and up the stairs leading to the back office. The small room, probably once a storeroom, took up the far end of the upper floor. Father must've liked this, she guessed, since the location allowed him to step outside and see what was going on by peering over the railing at the work area below. Lizzie pictured him standing there, a stern, unforgiving look on his face as he watched this whole eerie mechanism in use. A shiver hit her. It felt horribly, terribly wrong.

She was deep in thought when John whispered a warning.

"Liz, look at this." He pointed out the broken lock hanging from the heavy weathered door. "Don't move." He pulled the gun from inside his coat, crept forward, and

83

carefully pushed in the door, which gave a low creak as it swung further open.

As he waited, Lizzie decided there was no way she would let him leave her all alone. She picked up an old metal pole left lying on the worn wooden floor—possibly part of what the town night watchman had used to extinguish the candle lamps on the street before they switched to kerosene—thinking it might be of good use.

Creeping forward, she tiptoed behind John, who suddenly jumped back. "Liz, look out!"

"YAAA!" She yelled and stumbled backward, nearly hitting her head on the brick wall. To her shock, an aged but still spry male creature, skin a dark gray hue and mottled with disease, its head spotted with gouges and a few scraggly tufts of graying hair, sprang from inside the office. The air immediately became polluted with the distinctive odor of rotten eggs, bad meat, and other unmentionable smells. It lunged at John, who raised the gun but held his fire.

"Can't hit him, the angle's wrong," John yelled. "Liz, swing—move him back. Hurry!"

She took a breath and made a weak jab. It staggered the creature, at least getting his attention. The monster gazed at her with yellow eyes oozing streams of pus. It hissed like a snake, revealing a mouthful of rotted, black teeth. No one needed to tell her how namby-pamby her jab was, but it worked. It got the thing to back away from John. The way the ghoul hissed and dragged itself in John's direction, one rotted, decayed foot sliding after the other, made Lizzie forget everything else. She scurried away from it as fast as she could.

"Liz, get down—duck!"

She did. John aimed and fired, sending a bloody shower of brains, bone, and skin cascading down the brick wall and across the floorboards. The thing hit the floor with a

84

thump. Lizzie gagged, and hearing no other noises, rushed into the office.

Stack after stack of discarded papers met her eyes, souring her mood even more. She glanced at all of it, overcome, and exhausted. "I don't know how much we'll find. We'd better get out of here. I know I've had enough for one day."

"Make that two of us." He headed for the tall wooden cabinet overflowing with papers near the back brick wall. "I'll look into this pile."

She set the pole against the wall, sighed, and gazed at the other scattered stacks of debris, including worn leather straps, horse reins, and assorted supplies. It looked to have been here for at least a few years if not more. A thinner layer of dust covering the boxes on the desk made her think these might have been added to more recently. It looked like a good place to start.

The first two boxes held nothing but yellowed receipts and papers from a long-defunct wagon company. Another box held papers with her father's name and a business involving different kinds of carriage parts, also new to her. The discovery might have shocked her before, but not anymore.

She flung open one drawer, and then another, sending up a shower of dust which set her to sneezing. *Achoo!* She rubbed her fingers, trying to wipe off some of the dust, but only succeeded in making it worse. It was awful.

Papers. Sneeze. More paper. Sneeze. Receipts. Double sneeze.

"Lizzie, I hate to ask how you're managing over there?"

"I'm"—*Achoo!*—"fine. Ugh, this is… Oh."

"What is it?"

"I have no idea. The drawer is stuffed full of more paper."

85

She pulled the center drawer open further, dug inside, and held up a handful. Hmm, it looks like someone was doing a lot of figuring. She sifted through the papers. Her eyes widened as a pattern emerged. John came up next to her and peered over her shoulder.

"It's some sort of running tally, I think, like an order and price list." She flipped through several pages. "See? A three and a two hundred. Here's a one and a half—does that mean a time maybe?"

"Yes, I see. What else did you find?"

A small, black leather notebook taken from the bottom of the pile came next. She flipped through it. "Oh, my… It could be prices and I think purchases. It says one hundred and marked with a three. What was this for? There are names, too. Well, only initials. Do you see that?"

John shook his head and swore under his breath. "I suppose you can trace your father's business acquaintances from those."

"Perhaps, but if they live out of town we'll never know who they are."

A couple of faded pages fell to the floor from the back of the book. Lizzie bent down to pick them up, her eyes widening as she saw the contents. "Wait, the names… Harold S., James St. H. It appears several are partially spelled out."

She glanced at the other sheet before passing it to John. "It looks like some sort of insurance policy. It says, 'full value of one serviceable good owned by an AB.' You read the rest."

He scanned the page. "Hmm, uh-huh. Oh."

"What?"

He showed her what he'd found, pointing to the page with his grimy finger. "It clearly states that what he calls the 'serviceable goods'—and it specifies the gender and supposed age—are the owner's property, and it gives their estimated values."

The idea of what was going on here became disgustingly clearer. "It sounds like he was hiring those creatures out." She paused. "Like—like slaves."

Her thoughts whirled. As horrid as the undead appeared now, they'd once been people—someone's mother, father, sister, brother, friend. The Congregationalist Church teachings that she'd heard since childhood about respecting others made her indignant. *This is so wrong!* She gazed at the paper again and gasped. The initials A.B. again.

"Oh, Father," she whispered, voicing what was becoming an all-too-familiar refrain. "What have you done?"

John pointed out a line on one of the sheets. "Here, this has the initials of the persons who paid the fee. Two of the most frequently mentioned initials, and what could be the names, are written at the bottom of the page."

She stared at the blacked-out names, wondering how long it would take to decipher the writing—or if they even could. No matter what, she knew they had to try.

Chapter Thirteen

Fall River's Mystery - Clewes Followed Only to Come to Naught. Emma and Lizzie Borden Prostrated.

The daughters of the murdered Mr. and Mrs. Andrew Borden are beginning to realize the awfulness of the suspicion resting upon Miss Lizzie.

—Headlines, *The Bethlehem Times*, August 8, 1892

August 8-9, 1892

The latest news had each of them in their own thoughts on the way back home. Lizzie checked the small watch pinned on her bodice. It was already after midnight as John stopped the horse a few steps away from their front door. He climbed down and helped Emma out of the carriage before accompanying her to the front door.

"Well, goodnight then," she said.

He tipped his hat. "Always a pleasure, Miss Emma."

A minute later, a lamp glowed in the front parlor window. John stood at the side of the carriage and offered his hand to Lizzie, who shook her head. "I'd rather not go in just yet. I simply can't get that warehouse out of my mind."

He went to the driver's side and climbed back into his seat. "It does bring up a lot of questions. I'll talk to the Society members about it more. Maybe they have some insight or have heard something I haven't."

"Maybe." Lizzie nodded, wondering if she dared make a more personal suggestion.

He cleared his throat. "It might not be a good idea for us to sit out here too long. Someone may notice."

"Can we take a drive? I'm really not tired."

He took her hand and kissed it. "All right. Liz, you are a hard one to resist. I fear I'm taking advantage."

She gave him a saucy smile. "No more than I let you."

The horse's hooves made a rhythmic *clip-clop, clip-clop* through the empty streets. Lizzie's mood improved despite the discovery of some of her father's hidden activities. She knew more news was likely forthcoming. Like her looming troubles, she wanted to keep it as far in the future as possible. There was no reason to sulk and belabor her fate every moment. And truth be told, as wanton as it sounded, these stolen moments with John intrigued her much more.

The carriage pulled into the courtyard of his handsome brick house just in time for them to see someone at the side door.

"Stop!" John yelled. "Who's there, what do you want?"

A man dressed in a dark colored coat and pants turned and darted past, making the horse snort and stomp its feet. John jumped from the carriage and lunged at the intruder, but the man was too fast. John ended up lying in an awkward and embarrassing jumble on the street while the stranger ran off and disappeared.

Lizzie slid out of her seat and hurried to see if he needed help. "Are you hurt?"

He shook his head and stood. "No, only my pride. Whoever it was, someone younger and more agile I might add, he had the leap on me from the start." He rubbed his knee and took a quick look around before going over to unhook the horse from the carriage. "We'd better get inside before we attract more attention. Wait here. I might have to wake the groom to get the horse brushed and settled in."

89

She tried to keep out of view by the wall as John led the horse into the barn through one of the double doors. The air felt heavy. Each passing second made her more nervous. Minutes passed. What was taking so long?

Her fears became harder to dismiss when a distinct, unforgettable bad odor wafted her way. She turned in time to see the side barn door slowly creak open. Heart pounding, Lizzie retreated in the direction of the carriage. "John?"

The door swung open further, revealing not John, but a lanky young boy about twelve. His greasy black hair hung over what would've been a handsome face if the mouth hadn't been twisted into an ugly grimace. The boy-turned-undead-creature stared at her with filmy white eyes and groaned, shuffling much faster in her direction than the other creatures she'd encountered before.

"John!" She stumbled toward the carriage. Seeing nothing else at hand, she grabbed her umbrella. As the young creature staggered toward her, she held her breath. The strong, nearly overpowering scent of rot surrounding him soon had tears streaming down her face.

Her panic grew as she wrapped her hands around the umbrella like a club. Not the best of weapons, she knew, fearing the flimsy metal and fabric would break with the first pressure. She vacillated between swinging and stabbing at the undead boy, doing her best to keep it just out of reach. But for how long?

That he was so young made her hesitate, but as he closed in Lizzie saw no other choice. "John!" She swung, the umbrella hitting her attacker across the face and forcing it back. Her strike left a weepy gash. Thick, black fluids oozed across his cheek and dribbled down his chin. She grimaced at the ghastly sight.

UNNHHH-UNNNHHHH.

The young ghoul moaned louder as it resumed its forward pace and grabbed at her again. This time she knew better than to trust it. Holding the umbrella like a javelin, she pulled her arm back, and when the creature came at her, she aimed straight and struck. The umbrella's point pierced the center of its gray forehead with a sickening clunk. She jumped aside as the now truly dead boy pitched forward into a heap.

John finally ran from the barn, his face white. "Liz, are you all right?"

"Where were you?" she demanded. "I thought that ghoul got you. I was yelling for you."

"I'm so sorry, yes, I heard you, but the smell was all over the barn. The horse started going into a panic. I had to settle him down and be sure nothing else was lurking inside." He disappeared back inside the barn, emerging a minute later with a large horse blanket. Moving closer, he looked at the body before draping it with the blanket.

"Looks like you did a superb job on your own."

"I admit some of your fighting lessons really helped," she mentioned, hoping her voice wasn't trembling as much as her hands. "It took away my fear of being unsure of what to do."

"Good, I'm glad. We'd better get inside. I'll alert one of the Society members that I need a clean-up. They'll inspect the area as well and check that no other creatures are about."

John escorted her to the door and unlocked it. Lizzie slipped inside, surprised to see him reach in and take something from the mailbox. He stuck it in his pocket before coming in after her and locking the door.

She slipped out of her coat, noting the worried expression on his face. "Do you think your young groom had anything to do with that man we saw running away?"

"Young Henry?" He grew pensive as he hung their coats on the dark walnut umbrella stand taking up most of the space in the hall by the door. "I doubt it, not that I can say for sure. The sad thing is, no one will know of his death. I was told he was an orphan. The crew will take his body to be picked up by someone we know in the department. We have no other choice when something like this happens so the Society's work is not exposed."

Lizzie nodded, thinking it sad that the boy had no one to care about his life, or what had happened to him in death. Of course, not much made sense these days. A crinkle of paper drew her attention to whatever John had put in his pocket.

"Is something wrong?" she asked. "What is that?"

His voice husky, he enveloped her in his arms. "It can wait," he said, his mouth covering hers.

Lizzie went to freshen up while John rustled in the pantry for some cheese, along with glasses and a bottle of wine. Once she returned, he set out the refreshments and filled two glasses before joining her on the settee in the parlor.

She relished the feel of his strong arms around her, as well as the delightful fruity warmth as the excellent burgundy tickled her taste buds. It went down her throat like silk. She chuckled to herself at the sudden rush of guilt, while at the same time thinking how much she'd missed in her life until now. Then she remembered and sat straighter. "What was on that paper you took from the mailbox?"

He pulled the crumpled sheet from his pocket with a heavy sigh and unfolded it, taking what felt like forever to smooth out the creases and lines. Finally, after studying it again and shaking his head, he silently handed it to her.

Lizzie stared at it and gasped. Someone had scribbled one word in clumsy, dark letters: GUILTY!

"Wh-who?" she asked, unable to say more.

"Don't worry about it." He pulled her in close and kissed the side of her face. As he did that, she wondered if it was possible to keep the feel of his lips in her memory. She might need it.

He took the paper and put it back in his pocket. "You'll have the best representation we can get for you. What you need to think about first is there'll likely be an inquest. I'm advising you to tell the truth, but remember you cannot tell them *exactly* what you did so the work of the Society isn't revealed. So far, our group's members have been able to labor mostly unobserved. They've been able to take care of these Frankensteinish creatures, and with the help of officials, keep it from exploding into a full public emergency. We're working to keep that from happening, but we're not sure how long we can do that."

"It makes no sense. Why didn't I know about this?"

"You didn't know about what was going on before the change happened to your father and stepmother, did you?"

Lizzie shook her head. "Well, nooo."

"Those who find themselves in this situation often don't make it out unscathed, exacerbating the problem," he explained. "Until now, we've been successful in keeping this mostly controlled. Our hope is that we can keep it that way, despite your father being attacked. It pays to have important friends in various places. Remember that."

She nodded.

"Now," he continued, "you'll not be lying, as you honestly didn't know what was going on. You need to be prepared on how you'll answer certain questions. Let me show you."

To her surprise, he caught her off guard as he fired question after question at her about the events, her whereabouts, and what happened on the fateful morning of the murders. She answered as best she could, carefully telling him some of her actions that morning, like fixing tea, not feeling well enough to eat breakfast, and going out to the barn. She left out the most damning events and actions. A sweat broke out on her forehead. Her hands shook as she answered.

Finally, after what felt like hours if only minutes, he stopped the barrage of questions. "Good. You should do all right. Your answers are clear and concise. Remember to keep it brief. Only answer what you are asked. The way you're shaking, though, you might need something to keep you calm. We don't want you looking overly nervous or fidgety. The jurymen will surely take that as a positive sign of guilt."

"My neighbor, Dr. Bowen, gave me something to help me relax earlier," she mentioned, not saying what the "something" was. She wanted no misinterpretation.

"Very well, ask the doctor to continue treating you." He gave her another tight squeeze and a long kiss before urging her to her feet. "We had better get you home now."

Lizzie felt a small rush of shame at sneaking into the house while everyone already asleep, as she should be, but she pushed the guilt aside for the time being. Still, she had to try and get some rest to erase the fog of exhaustion from her mind.

She hurried inside and upstairs to her room where she threw on a sleeping gown before stretching out on the bed. Thoughts swirled in her mind as she tossed from one side to another in an attempt to get comfortable.

Sleep seemed unobtainable. It felt like only minutes had passed as she struggled to consciousness and tried to recognize the soft knock. Someone softly called her name.

"Y-yes?" Lizzie muttered. "Who's there?"

She opened her eyes at the sound of the door opening, and saw Emma standing there.

"Liz, are you awake? Get up, you need to get dressed."

Lizzie looked at her sister and yawned, not yet fully awake. "Mmm, what time is it?"

"You've been lying abed all day. It's already eleven. Mr. Jennings is waiting for you downstairs."

"Mr. Jen—" That jolted her into full awareness, like she'd put her hand on a hot stove. A tremor of foreboding stirred inside. "Why is he here?"

"Oh, Lizzie!" Emma cried, her voice quivering. She covered her face with her hands. "He's to take you to the police station. You have to testify at the inquest. He said they're going to call all of us for questioning."

Emma's gaze held hers. Lizzie rose and reached for her sister's hand. "It'll be fine, Emma, don't worry, it will. John told me all you have to do is tell the truth, but don't say anything about the odd events that happened. You don't know what happened to Father or Abby. Neither of us understand how they got in the condition they were in, correct?"

"Yes, but—"

"Listen to me," she advised. "He said all you need to do is truthfully describe all the other events of the morning. You had no idea what happened to them, as you had just returned from out of town. You saw Father's body lying on the settee and found Abby upstairs, already dead, isn't that right?"

"Yes, that is true," Emma agreed before heading to the door." You'd best hurry. Mr. Jennings said we need to be there in thirty minutes."

"I'll be down quickly. Oh, and Emma? Can you run over and ask Dr. Bowen to stop by? Thank you."

Her sister gave a sad half smile and left, a sign she'd best not dawdle. Lizzie put on her mourning clothes—a black gown, a black trimmed hat with netting she could pull over her face if needed, black stockings, and black gloves—the ensemble making her look as grim as her mood. She hoped it wasn't some kind of omen.

She waited for Emma to come in and hook her back dress buttons before smoothing her hair. Her appearance in order, Lizzie slowly made her way down the stairs alone, her shoulders aching like she carried a heavy weight. Despite that, she maintained her dignity and stood tall, taking care not to stoop or make herself appear any smaller.

She went down the stairs, then to the sitting room where Mr. Jennings waited. He greeted her, his face grim. "Miss Borden, are you ready? Mr. Fremont told me that he went over some of the possible questions with you. Remember this is an inquest, not a trial. Do you feel that you can answer the questions without reservation?"

The look in his eyes told her what he really meant was, *can I tell the truth but not the whole truth?*

"Yes, sir. Mr. Fremont practiced the questions with me he thought I'd need to answer." She gulped, the reality of the situation hitting her. Her legs wobbled a bit as she grabbed the back of a chair for support. "I think."

"Very well." Mr. Jennings cleared his throat. Lizzie wondered if she passed inspection.

"One warning," he added. "I have entered my objections and have been filing grievances, but I'm afraid you'll have to face the panel on your own. They won't

96

permit me to be present during questioning. The proceedings are closed to everyone."

Her loud gasp made him pause.

"Miss Borden, this is important. Are you certain you can do it?"

She sat down, trying to compose herself and gather her thoughts. This was a test, she realized. No one she knew would be present in the room. There would be no one she could gather strength from. She would be totally alone.

A knock on the door, and the entrance of Dr. Bowen, took her mind off the unknown for the moment. She had to admit feeling somewhat relieved at the doctor's well-timed visit. After extending his greetings, Mr. Jennings said he would wait for her outside and left. Dr. Bowen made his visit quick, urged her to eat something when she could, and wished her well before escorting her to the carriage waiting out front.

For the moment, only a few onlookers had gathered on the street—the crowds grew larger each day—though their stares still made her uneasy. The carriage's dark curtains afforded a bit of privacy as she and Mr. Jennings covered the short distance to the Central Police Station.

She tried to keep awake as the medicine took effect. Peeking around the curtain, she took in the crispness of the colors and the odd shadows lurking behind the trees. She knew the images for what they were—slight hallucinations brought on by the medication—and fought to stay focused. Hiding her yawns, she tried to sit straighter and act more alert. She felt like she could sleep forever.

All too soon, the carriage stopped in front of the Central Police Station. They hurried inside the stone building, dodging the questions of several eagle-eyed reporters perched like vultures near the front steps. Lizzie looked straight ahead, not daring to meet anyone else's eyes as she headed into the solemn upper courtroom for the proceedings. The closing of the heavy wooden door shook her to the core. She shivered slightly, but showed not a trace of emotion lest it be taken the wrong way. She whispered a prayer and steeled herself.

Judge Josiah C. Blaisdell of the Second District Court issued a stern warning about the questioning and explained the proceedings. Save for the stenographer, the marshal, and the deputy marshal, the room spread out empty around her. Lizzie gulped as District Attorney Hosea Knowlton stood and formally addressed the judge before turning to her.

And so it began.

Her mind worked overtime at the need to answer truthfully, as she knew the truth, while fighting off the effects of the medicine. The questions came one after the other like a flood.

"Do you know something about his real estate?" Knowlton asked, his face stern.

"About what?"

"His real estate, your father's," he responded, sounding a little annoyed.

She shrugged. "I know what real estate he owned, or at least part of it. I don't know whether I know it all or not."

That is the truth, she thought, *the existence of the warehouse bearing me out.*

The questioning went non-stop. She answered as best she could, though many of the questions sounded like repeats. Places, times, and events jumbled in her mind, but Lizzie thought she answered as correctly as possible under the circumstances. She was glad when her time to testify finally came to an end. Maggie, she learned later, endured a much deeper grilling than she had.

Lizzie walked out of the courtroom a bit shaky, grateful to see a friendly face as Mr. Jennings met her in the hall. He directed her out a back door to the carriage, which speedily took her home. They talked about the questions as best she recalled them, him giving her some advice but not saying much otherwise, which struck her as a bit odd. Still, she was too tired and weary to the bone to say anything, or think much of it.

"Keep on with what you are doing," he advised, giving a fatherly nod. "You're doing fine. Don't worry, this will be over soon.

The carriage stopped in front of the house to a crowd that had doubled in size since the morning. Lizzie held her head high and ignored the onlookers as Mr. Jennings helped her out of the carriage. Once inside, she heaved a sigh of relief. She was exhausted.

"It went well, I trust?" Emma asked, a look of concern on her face.

"As well as could be expected. Yes, I think so."

Emma held out a hand for her hat and coat. "You look completely worn out. I'll make you some tea. Then you should go upstairs and rest."

Lizzie did. Or at least her body did, as she wrestled in her dreams with faceless, horrid monsters and bodiless voices speaking legalese.

A chime from the clock in the hall woke Lizzie, who sat up surprised that she'd slept most of the next day and night away again. Yet she still felt like she needed another ten hours of sleep. Her mind uneasy, she gazed out the window, alarmed to see movement in the shadows of the trees across the street. She began to breathe harder as someone dressed in a proper jacket and trousers moved out of the shadows, revealing himself as one of *them*.

"Oh, no, go away!" she cried out. "Why can't you leave us alone?"

As if it knew she stood there, the well-dressed ghoul raised its claw-like hands and reached for her. A low, eerie moan filled the air. Lizzie moved to the side of the curtain, hopefully out of view, as two men sprang out of the darkness and overpowered the creature. She should be glad of their work, Lizzie knew, but it felt so hopeless. Could they really make a difference?

A small piece of paper on the edge of her dressing table caught her attention. She picked up the dingy white slip, recognizing her sister's scribbled handwriting. 'Liz,' Emma wrote, 'John came by. He said he had news. Mr. Jennings said you should be ready to return to court tomorrow. We both have to testify.'

The note fluttered from her hand to the floor. *I have to go back and do it again.*

A wave of shivering hit her. She hurried back to bed and crawled under the covers, a prayer on her lips that tomorrow would never come.

Chapter Fourteen

Q. Did you then know that he was dead?
A. No, sir.
Q. You saw him?
A. Yes, sir.
Q. You went into the room?
A. No, sir.
—Lizzie Borden at inquest, questioned by District Attorney
Hosea Knowlton, August 9-11, 1892

August 10, 1892

L izzie hung on as the carriage bumped and jerked over the ruts in this godforsaken place near the riverfront. "Where are we?"

John's silence, and the need to rush out so early when she still felt half asleep, only made her grow more irritable by the second. She blurted out her next question, knowing she probably sounded like a complaining Portuguese fisherman's wife.

"Maybe you could've checked whatever this is on your own and let us know the results. Or you might've taken Emma. You could've left me out of it since you insist on getting her involved in all this."

John shook his head, not answering, though the vein throbbing on the side of his temple told her the question had gotten under his skin. Her protests faded, even if her anger only grew.

The horse clip-clopped down the road clouded in pockets of fog. The London-type morning did nothing to improve her mood, instead making her think of that strange

101

Robert Louis Stevenson book about an evil Mr. Hyde lurking in the shadows, ready to jump out at them. She tried to push the thought away.

Thick, leafy tree branches and clumps of weeds hung over the path. The river itself looked dark and murky. Lizzie sniffed at the underlying musty smell of mold and decay hanging in the air. This forgotten path seemed even more ill-kempt than the one by Father's previously unknown warehouse.

"If you must know," John said, "we're on the other side of the river, precisely a couple miles down from your father's warehouse. It turns out there are quite a few of these forgotten buildings along the river paths. A lot of these places went out of business, or were abandoned—or so everyone thought."

He pulled the carriage to the side and stopped. "Take a look at that paper I gave you."

The paper's crinkle sounded unusually loud as Lizzie pulled it from her coat pocket. She flashed John a look of alarm.

"Don't worry. No one will hear us here."

Unfolding it, she stared at a neatly typewritten list of addresses and names. A few of the names seemed somewhat familiar. She wracked her brain, trying to think of where she might've seen them. Nothing came to her, but she vowed to have another look at Father's papers at home. Though it could be coincidental until they had absolute proof, she wondered if any matched the first set of names and initials on the papers from the warehouse.

John jumped down, hooked the horse's reins over a tree branch, and held out a hand to help her from the carriage. He then turned to Emma, who instead went to the horse and took the reins. "If neither of you mind, I think I should stay here and watch the horse. Just in case."

102

"Good idea," John said. "We should be back shortly."

Lizzie studied the paper as they walked. "Where did you get this?"

"I asked somebody I know in the assessor's office for addresses of unused, closed, or abandoned buildings by the river. This is what he came up with, though there may be others we overlooked."

A growing feeling of apprehension hit her as they trudged forward and pushed their way through the overgrown brush and weeds. She yanked her coat sleeve from a branch it snagged on and cursed the burrs that would have to be picked off later.

They remained silent and fought through the brush. Her mind jumped from wondering what they'd do, to questioning if all this was even worth it, and then to the most unexpected of thoughts—typewriting machines. Previously, she'd seen several officially dressed young women walking downtown clad in their crisp office suits and serious looking blouses with tied cravats. Lizzie had often thought it a preferable profession for a young woman if she could obtain the training. So, she'd promoted it as such to the ladies in the Women's Christian Temperance Union as a way to help young working and immigrant women improve their lot.

John's call of alarm broke into her woolgathering. "Liz, watch out!" He grabbed her arm and pulled her away from a deep rut in the road.

Lizzie took a breath, knowing she might have ended up with a serious sprain or broken a bone from a fall like that. "Thank you."

"Pay attention," he ordered, pointing ahead. "There's the side door. I think that bank of windows is part of the main workroom. Hopefully we find it empty."

The warehouse was drab and gray, the tired façade sporting pitted, broken bricks darkened to beige and black instead of the once bright pink and red hues. A thick coat of grime and decay, painted over time by nature's brush, covered the shoulder-height row of large windows. The whole place looked dejected and forlorn.

John edged to the windows where the dirt hadn't totally taken over, which provided a glimpse into the rundown interior. Time had stood still as wooden benches and tables became covered by piles of thick cobwebs. The floor disappeared beneath layers of dust. A couple machines and a giant fixture of some kind had collapsed under the weight of neglect.

Several worn boxes stacked under a broken table caught Lizzie's eye, as did the pieces of glass scattered on the floor. Her eye caught the partial word BOTT written on one box. Saddened, she followed John as he traipsed through the overgrowth to a smaller set of windows.

He stepped closer to the wall and peeked in one of the first windows. "Maybe the offices are here. Let's see if they look any different." He fell silent and then out a low whistle. "It appears they had a big problem."

"Yes, indeed." Lizzie agreed, wishing the macabre office scene could be erased from her mind, though she knew it could now never be unseen. Heavy wooden cabinets and desks had been overturned, their paper contents spilling out and across the floor like typewritten intestines. The room looked like a riot had taken place. And maybe it had, given the rotted remains of several of the undead lying on the floor and hanging over furniture.

Even worse, many of the now-skeletal remains sat perched behind their typewriting machines, still dressed in the raggedy remainders of their professional suits, all ready to do the day's work. It gave her an entirely different view of the job.

"Looks like the workers never had a chance," she shared, her voice sad.

They turned to leave but paused when something rustled in the bushes. John motioned her to be alert and brought up his gun. Unknown to him, she pulled the small revolver he'd given her previously from her jacket pocket and held it by her side, out of sight.

To her surprise, the creature that emerged from the overgrowth remained almost professionally presentable, if not for the hole in its cheek, the gashes on its arms, and a distinct rotten odor. It wasn't unusual except so far, Lizzie hadn't yet seen a she-creature like this one. Yes, *her*. Undeath doesn't discriminate, and while she was sure they existed, in her forays outside all she'd encountered so far had been male undead, with the exception of Mrs. Borden, of course.

"Careful," John warned.

She stared at the creature, even more stunned when it markedly increased its pace despite its one shoe on-one bare foot gait. In those few quickly passing seconds, it moved close enough that they met each other's gaze, her hazel eye staring at the she-creature's film-covered eye.

"LIZ, MOVE!"

John's yell broke Lizzie from her unusual fascination with the creature. It lunged. Lizzie jumped aside in the nick of time, and then she did the unexpected. Whirling around, she cocked the hammer, turned back, and took aim. Steadying herself, she fired. BLAM! The round hit perfectly in the she-creature's temple. It crumpled, and with a thud and a rattle of old bones, fell in a gory pile inches from Lizzie's feet.

"Ick." She gagged and kicked aside the creature's once fashionable shoe. She could feel another good griping session coming on. "I think I've had enough for today."

John stood there and gawked at her. "Well, damn. You've become quite the shot."

"As you can see, your instructions paid off. I still don't know why you brought me out here, though. Can we go now?"

He gave an exasperated sigh as he put away his own gun. "Damn it, Liz, look around."

His demeanor got her attention. She did as he suggested, carefully scrutinizing the wretched remains of the once human woman lying at her feet. Her eyes took in the worn-down building. Images of the office, its desks, contents, and equally wretched former workers, filled her thoughts.

She threw up her hands in exasperation, unclear what he wanted. "What? What am I looking...?" She paused as the different possibilities flashed through her mind. Then it hit her. "Wait, the typewriting machines. It's like the telephone at home. Father wanted nothing to do with any kind of 'modern tomfoolery' as he called it. There was not one of those machines in his office at that warehouse, was there?"

John nodded his encouragement. "Go on."

"Yet, yes, the desk was filled with handwritten notes and ledgers, but he also had typewritten letters and records. He had no intention of getting his own, but he still needed proper correspondence at times. When he did, he turned to someone else like...who owns the building here?"

Paper rustled as John took back the list and perused the names. "Looks like a Samuel Smith."

She nodded, warming to the subject. "Maybe Father contacted Mr. Smith, or someone else, for the needed correspondence. Somehow the two of them conspired to

106

put the creatures to doing other kinds of tasks in the factory. One day something happened and it backfired."

Lizzie pretended not to hear when John chimed in again with his ever-practical lawyerly side. "It sounds good in theory, but we need proof, solid proof," he cautioned.

"We have to go inside." She grabbed his arm. "We have to examine that pile of papers in there. We need to see if there is something, anything, that ties the two of them together."

John cleared his throat and pulled out his pocket watch, opening the burnished gold cover with a soft click. "Well, as much as I like your idea, and think you're right, we've run out of time. I'll have to come back, or have someone else do it. We need to get you home in a hurry. You have to be at the inquest," he glanced at his pocket watch, "in less than three hours, like it or not."

She sighed. "There is nothing to like about it. Nothing at all."

They hurried back to the carriage, where Emma fretted and worried. "What happened? I heard shooting. Are you all right?"

Lizzie gave a small smile and grasped her sister's hand. "Yes, yes, we're fine. We came upon one of those creatures, a female this time. She possibly worked for Father, doing his typewriting. I'll tell you about it on the way home."

As John turned the carriage, she showed Emma the list and shared her suspicions about the mass of papers they had left behind.

"Well, then." Emma shook her head and stared at John, then at Lizzie. "Once you're done testifying today, I should come back here and help pack up those papers. John can send someone to pick me up. I insist. Since you want help with the paperwork, then this is a good place for me to start."

107

No amount of arguing, Lizzie knew, would budge Emma once she'd made up her mind. It would have to do. But her glee at besting John quickly faded as he pulled the carriage in front of the house.

"Be forewarned," he said. "I'd think he might wait until the inquest is over, but if I know anything about Marshal Hilliard, he's prompt. He'll get some judge out of bed if necessary to get the proper papers for an arrest."

Chapter Fifteen

The Jurors for the said Commonwealth on their oath Present—
That Lizzie Andrew Borden of Fall River in the County of
Bristol…on the fourth day of August in the year eighteen hundred and
ninety-two, in and upon one Andrew Jackson Borden, feloniously,
willfully and of her malice aforethought, an assault did make…

—Murder Indictment,
Commonwealth vs. Lizzie Andrew Borden,
Commonwealth of Massachusetts, 1892

August 11, 1892

Lizzie spent the morning mumbling through the last of the inquest testimony, her nerves drawn so tight she feared she'd explode into a million little pieces. Afterward, she, Emma, and John sat in the parlor at home, everyone tense and silent. Waiting.

Lizzie had no idea if what she said had made any sense, especially after Doctor Bowen gave her another shot. She began to worry about his frequent visits, but suspected she need not give it much thought. After all, she wouldn't be getting such treatment when they sent her to jail. There, she acknowledged it—jail. She'd been avoiding the idea, not wanting to dwell on it.

The blare of the newly installed telephone made Lizzie jump from where she perched uncomfortably on the parlor chair. Emma reached over to grab her hand as John rose to answer. Lizzie felt near to choking at his grave demeanor.

"Yes, yes, I understand." John hung up the phone's clunky ear piece and turned, his face grim. "Marshal Hilliard is on his way. They're coming to arrest you."

Her deepest worry and fears had come to life. Lizzie's heart jumped, but then she simply got to her feet with a deep sigh, her mind in a dark cloud.

This was it.

She remained silent as Emma hurried her upstairs to change and mentally prepare. Emma pushed her around like a puppet, laying out her best black mourning dress and hat, before going to wait outside as she splashed cold water on her face and hurriedly changed into fresh undergarments. Lizzie stood, eyes closed, as Emma fastened the dress's back buttons. She pat a touch of pink rouge on Lizzie's pale face and smeared on some lip pomade.

"Lizzie, I'll be there for you, every step of the way," Emma assured her, taking Lizzie's hand in hers. "Don't worry, if…" She paused and continued, her voice breaking, "if the trial is set, know you have to but look up and see me sitting there. None of us will let you go through this alone."

Lizzie nodded and embraced Emma, words still failing her as she nervously picked up her reticule and checked that her hair was in place. After all, what could she really say?

A clatter downstairs told her they had arrived. Marshal Rufus B. Hilliard's sonorous voice floated to where she stood waiting in the upper hall. "I am here for Miss Lizzie Borden," he called out. "Miss Borden, please come downstairs."

Lizzie walked down the stairs, head held high, and stopped at the bottom of the steps where John and her attorney, Mr. Andrew Jennings, quickly moved to her side. Her voice strong and sure, she stated, "I am Lizzie Borden."

The marshal handed over the official arrest warrant, which the two lawyers quickly perused and explained to her. With a nod, Mr. Jennings handed it over for her to read. She gave it a cursory glance without really seeing the words. She already knew what it said, and needed no further instruction.

The men escorted her outside to the waiting carriage. Lizzie kept her head down, unable to look at the faces of the people once again gathered on the street, but not because she felt guilt. No, she felt shame and anger and sadness, and, yes, fear that it had come to this.

After her arrival at the police station, Lizzie waited in the matron's room until she was taken to the jail in neighboring Taunton to await the next stage of her trial. The ivy covering the stone jailhouse gave it an almost homey appearance. She was told there were but nine cells in the women's section at the southeastern end of the building, with five cells already occupied.

A stout, unsmiling matron led her down a long, dreary corridor lined with depressing, heavy iron bars, the air damp and cool from the stone walls. The lantern hanging on the wall and a small barred window at the back of the cell allowed barely more than a smidgen of light into the dim space. She was led to a cell much like the others, though the matron placed her in the unoccupied section, far from the other inhabitants. The hard cot and rock-hard pillow in her new home, if you could call it that, offered little comfort. She lay down in the seven-and-a- half-foot-wide space to await her fate and the next phase of her life.

The sun had already dipped behind the clouds by the time John arrived, his visit allowed as part of her legal representation. "How're you doing?" he asked, his voice concerned.

She shrugged and sat up. "All right, I suppose."

"Good, keep strong. This will be tough, but you can do it. Andrew is finalizing papers and getting ready for jury selection to begin. As for our other problem..."

Lizzie nodded, though with her mind already so full, she couldn't really focus on what he was saying. "What?"

A rustle of paper caught her attention. She watched him pull a large, bulging folder from his briefcase and set it next to her on the cot. "Here are the records we found with the names and the papers we scooped up from the other place we were at. I need you to go through them—"

"No, not now. I can't concentrate on anything. Emma can help you."

His voice low, John leaned in closer to explain. "Liz, your sister is working on something else, sorting through that huge stack of papers we found at your father's and Mr. Smith's warehouses. It's quite a bit to go through. Once she makes some sense of it, we can begin finding common denominators and see if there are any clues as to who's involved in what."

She ignored him, staring at a spot of dirt on the wall.

"Look at me." He reached out and grasped her hand, squeezing her fingers. "This is going to be a long haul. You need something to keep your mind focused. I need help. Please. We've come too far to simply let it all go. I think we're close to an answer. Please."

His pleadings made sense. Still reluctant, she nevertheless nodded her agreement and eyed the folder.

"Good." He lowered his voice before getting up. "I never wanted to say this, but things are getting bad. There are more surges of the undead. The members are having an urgent meeting tonight."

That got her thinking. "That's not good, is it?"

"No. We need more patrols. At least we have a few more officers helping us. We might have other possible leads, too. A couple businessmen in our group had close calls. Someone locked a few of those creatures in their warehouses overnight. They were almost attacked when they went to check on their inventory the next morning."

The news, as awful as it was, did perk her right up. "Then someone is getting desperate. We must be on to something."

John nodded and clapped his hands in excitement. "Yes! Now you see why it's so important you continue to work with me. We're also checking into their office staff to see if there is any connection there. A few of the men recently hired new office workers and—"

"Wait." She stared at him, eyes wide. "Women to handle the filing and the typewriting."

"Yes, go on."

"I recommended the typewriter courses to the leaders in the temperance union as a way to get working women out of the factories. Our church began a project, interviewing women who wanted to move into this field. We screened them and did a preliminary test to see if they had the potential skills and dexterity for it. If so, we paid for their course. We bought their machines for them if they were accepted into the school since they had to have their own equipment to be hired. It was pretty successful."

John pursed his lips as he thought. "Hmm, then maybe one of those women had access to the warehouses. They knew where the keys were. They might've known what kind of security was, or wasn't, there."

She saw where he was going with his reasoning. "The women were either threatened, or maybe their families were, for them to decide on providing such information. Or maybe they'd been mistreated, or released from their employment."

"It opens up a whole other avenue for us to look into," John added. "Do you remember the names of the women you recommended?"

"I think so. Emma will be a big help. She has access to the program records at the church. No one will think anything of her looking around."

John rose to his feet and straightened his coat. "Good, good. This sounds like something we'll get some answers from, and soon."

"One more thing," Lizzie added. "Tell Emma to look in her top bureau drawer. I saved a list of women who either dropped out of the project, failed, or were to come back at a later date. Perhaps one of them could've been angry enough to resort to other circumstances if they were contacted and persuaded."

"All right, then." John gave her hand a squeeze and sidled close to whisper in her ear. "I would much rather have you in my arms instead of saying goodbye like this, but we must be professional. Remember, the walls have eyes and ears."

A different matron glared at her before shutting the heavy cell door and escorting John out. Lizzie sat on the bed and stared at the drab, medicinal gray-green walls, feeling as alone as she had ever felt in her life. With the threat of tears pricking the backs of her eyelids, she took a deep breath. "Get yourself together," she muttered.

To keep her mind off her problems, at least for a while, she pulled over the bulging folder and began to pick through the voluminous contents. Bills of lading. Receipts for mortuary supplies. Wood, jars, bottles. Hmm, he bought a lot of bottles, she saw. The growing stack of bills piqued her interest. She pulled a pad of paper over and a pencil. Glass bottles, nearly three-inches tall, she wrote. For what? She considered it and made a note.

In spite of her dismal surroundings, Lizzie suspected John was right. It was a good idea to have something to occupy her thoughts for a time. She pulled the thin, scratchy blanket over her shoulders, stuffed the hard pillow behind her back, and tried to get somewhat comfortable as she leaned against the wall to read.

Soon, she yawned and set the papers aside, a bit disappointed that nothing beyond those bottles stood out so far in the stack of papers and bills she had sifted through. She thought of giving up for now, as she'd already been at it for a couple hours, when the light faded, leaving her sitting in an eerie dimness. Bedtime, even if it felt way too early for sleep. She sat in near darkness except for the ray of moonlight streaming in through the one small window on the cell's rear brick wall.

Her thoughts jumped around until she settled on an appealing mental image of a bare-chested John lying in bed, his hair tousled, when something slammed against the outer wall with a bang. BAM! She bolted from her near-dream state with a cry and sat up, fully aware again of her dismal surroundings. BAM! Something hit the outer wall of her cell again. BAM! Then the yells, taunts, and laughter began.

"Killer—murderer!" More laughter.

"Help, what's going on?" she cried out, her fear of being attacked in the dark growing. "Is anyone there?"

The silence mocked her. Lizzie tried to settle her nerves when something scraped down the hall. Mice?

Something scraped again.

Then she heard something else and her heart froze.

Chapter Sixteen

Fall River appears to be prolific in the way of hatchets...
—Ex-Governor George Robinson for the defense,
Trial of Lizzie Borden, July 20, 1893, *The Omaha Bee*

Lizzie pressed against the cold, damp wall next to the bed, listening, her heart pounding in fear. Then she recognized it—a distinctive shuffling, sliding sound. *Slide, scrape. Slide, scrape.* Her mouth went dry as the sounds grew louder, accentuated by a low, uneven moan.

Terror gripped her.

It was one thing to be outside, fighting off the undead creatures with others around to help. It was something else entirely to be stuck alone in a small, dark cell the size of a closet, waiting for a monster to attack without anything she could use to defend herself.

She jumped to her feet, her heart nearly jumping out of her chest, and cursed as the folder fell to the floor with a thud. The creature down the hall must have heard it, too, and increased its shuffling. *UNNNNNHHH.* Its long, low moan filled the air even as a horrific stench of spoiled eggs, decay, and rot drifted her way.

It's getting closer! Frantic, she scanned the room, looking for something to use as a weapon other than a plain old pencil. Given she was locked away behind sturdy iron bars, she had a good chance of remaining safe without the creature getting near her. Still, Lizzie felt quite like a mouse stuck in a trap.

Not sure what to do, she leaned against the door and peeked out, trying to see as best she could. To her horror, she felt the door move. It slowly opened with a low, eerie creak. OH DEAR LORD PLEASE, NO! It opened further. Oh, no! The matron had left the door unlocked!

The undead creature's moans increased. She realized she had minutes, if not seconds. She could stay here, take the chance that the creature wouldn't be able to get inside, but she hated the feeling of being a sitting duck.

Lizzie peeked through the bars again when she remembered the emergency axe. The jail had to have one in case of fire. It had to be somewhere at the end of the hall near the exit! Thank goodness she wasn't stuck in a center cell.

Holding her breath, she pushed the door open a little more, praying it didn't creak again. She had just enough room to peer to the right and saw the ghoul advancing. It shuffled on at a slow pace, intent on its deadly mission. Seeing it still four cells away, she knew this was her chance—maybe her only chance. She shoved the door fully open and lunged out.

UNNNNNHHH! The creature saw her and moaned, growing even more agitated. It tried to move faster, though it was still three cells away. Lizzie took in its gray body pocked with black holes, peeling hunks of dead skin hanging like rotted tree limbs, and pockets of black gook oozing from holes on its body. If that wasn't terrible enough, the nasty, rotten stench drifting her way provided more than enough motivation to get her moving. She ran in the opposite direction, frantically scanning the walls for the axe, another weapon… something to protect herself.

GRRRRRN.

The creature moaned again and shambled closer. Lizzie tried not to breathe in as the horrible rotten smell filled her nostrils. *Shuffle, slide.* It was two cells away now.

Lizzie ran to a battered old wooden desk at the end of the hall and frantically began searching the drawers, scattering papers and what-not. She grabbed the pair of scissors from beneath the mess.

The creature shuffled closer. *Shuffle, slide, shuffle, slide.* Now it was one cell away and moving steadily in her direction.

Panic squeezed her chest. "Oh please, God, please help me," she whispered. *Where was that axe?*

Ever more frantic, Lizzie scanned the floor and walls, sweat popping out on her forehead, when a shape sticking out on the upper wall near the exit caught her eye. She ran into the small alcove and looked up. Yes! Relief flooded her to see the emergency fire axe hanging from two hooks on the upper wall.

UNNNHH.

The low moans made her turn to check the ghoul's location. Lizzie gasped in shock. The monster stood only feet away and rounded the desk. Its body scraped against the wood, leaving horrible gobs of itself behind.

Her panic in full bloom, Lizzie jumped and tried to pull down the axe. It got stuck. Jumping up again, she stretched and reached. This time she did it. Her fingers wrapped around the axe tight, she yanked it from the hooks holding it to the wall.

Her feeling of triumph faded as a stench like dead, stagnant water enveloped her. Taking a firm grip on the axe handle, she ignored the sudden feeling of déjà vu, turned, and braced herself just in time. As if sensing its victory, the creature shuffled faster, dragging its bony feet across the paving stones with a sickening scrape.

Two feet… It kept coming. One foot…

Lizzie took a deep breath, moved into position, and swung like she was one of the Boston Beaneaters hoping to make a hit. WHAM! Home run! The axe glanced off the monster's head with a loud crack, hitting bone and jolting her arm like she'd slammed into a brick wall. To her relief, she hit it with the side of the axe head and didn't have to yank the blade free.

Hurrying, she wiped the gook from the side of her face and swung again. WHACK! Brain matter splattered the wall. She gagged, swung, and hit. WHACK.

She swung and hit again. WHACK. WHAM. WHACK.

The swings became automatic. She no longer saw the bloodied thing in front of her, the horror of it sending her into near hysterics. She kept at it, tears running down her cheeks, until she heard a voice call her name. The sound of running, and the jangle of cell door keys, broke into her hysterical fog. Giving one last cry, she let the axe fall from her gore-encrusted hands.

Stunned, Lizzie stumbled away from what was left of the creature, a gory pile of massacred, bloody pulp. Breathing heavily, she turned and leaned against the other wall, resting her head on the cool stone.

Someone touched her shoulder, making her jump. She looked up, surprised to see John there. "Liz! Are you all right?"

She took several deep breaths and let herself calm down before answering. "Yes, I'm fine."

"My God, what happened?"

"I wish I knew. After you left, the matron, a heavy woman I never saw before, left the door open. Then *that* came along." She pointed at the remains of the horrid intruder.

"At least you weren't hurt." John gripped her shoulder and led her down the hall, not to her cell as she expected, but to the shower room. There, the matron who first checked her in, handed her a towel and a set of new clothing.

John tried to reassure her. "I fully intend looking into this. The only matron on tonight was this woman, who was stationed on another cell block. I'll talk with the warden and ask him to put on extra guards. You shower and change, then the matron will take you to another cell on a more populated block so something like this doesn't happen again. Will you be all right?"

Lizzie nodded, wiped her hands, and gripped the clothes, her terror waning. She felt tired and numb. "Yes, thank you. I-I'll be fine."

"Very well. I'll see you in court tomorrow. Don't worry. You'll come to no more harm."

Not from them, she knew.

The thought stayed with her as she showered, dressed, and trudged with the matron down the hall to another cell block. She entered the new cell, relieved to see one thing familiar: the folder of papers waiting for her on the bed.

As the door shut behind her, this time the matron double-checked that it was locked. Lizzie knew all she had to fear now were the people who would be in court tomorrow, the ones in the jury box deciding whether she was a killer or innocent. Fit to live—or die.

Those she feared most would be issuing the verdict—guilty or not guilty. As if to accentuate the point, the silence filled with the eerie, non-human keens of the undead emerging outside. There could be no more fitting end to the night.

Chapter Seventeen

Those who saw Miss Borden for the first time were very much astonished. Her newspaper portraits have done her no justice at all. Some have made her out a hard and hideous fright, and others have flattered her. She is, in truth, a very plain-looking old maid.
—The Boston Daily Globe, June 5, 1893

L izzie held her head high as she rose and addressed the court to formally enter her plea. "Not guilty," she stated, her voice and conscience clear. "If you please, I will rely on my attorney, Mr. Andrew Jennings, to speak for me from now on."

With that, she sat down to the sound of pencils scratching across paper as the court artists faithfully replicated her every feature and article of clothing. As the reporters wrote about the least of her reactions during the legal proceedings, she took care to keep her face emotionless. She ducked her head to stare at her hands clasped firmly together in her lap. How long she could maintain such behavior was yet unknown, though she knew her very life depended on her looking calm—not like the prosecution's image of a crazed killer.

That didn't mean it came easy. She smoothed the front of her plain black brocade dress, a fashion some would call rather schoolmarmish; even old-fashioned. True, maybe, as she was never a slave to the latest fashion trends, though she did appreciate looking presentable. What she did resent was one newspaper's description of her as "a plain old maid" and detailing a look of wear on her face. Well, given what she was going through and the night's horrific encounter, she suspected anyone would look tired and far from their best.

Of course, this was only the start. Lizzie tried not to fret, especially as the daily barrage of newspaper reports and speculations kept on. Add to this the stress from the nightly noises of the other inmates housed near her, the taunts— *Chop-chop, Lizzie,* they'd yell—and the undead creatures parading outside the cell, and it all took its toll. Even the carriage ride to a larger cell in New Bedford, normally used for the ill and infirm, offered its stresses. She felt like a museum specimen, but remained stoic and outwardly calm. It all amounted to pretty good reasons for having perpetually dark circles under her eyes.

Interestingly, despite the jailhouse noises, the curious eyes peering at her window from outside, and the way some jail staff eyed her though they tried not to show it, Lizzie felt almost glad for the semi-privacy her cell offered after a day in court. At least she was away from the public and the newspaper writers' constant prying.

As she spent another grueling morning in court, listening to her attorneys haggle with the district attorney over appropriate jury choices and such, her mind wandered in illogical directions. At one point she wondered—would any women in the temperance union, or her church associations, sit on her jury if they could? What did they say about her as they talked with their husbands at home? Of course she'd seen enough cold stares and unfriendly faces to guess the answers to both questions. She decided not to dwell on that further lest she fall deeper into the black hole of melancholy beckoning her.

Back in her dreary cell, Lizzie walked aimlessly in a circle as exercise and tried fluffing the rock-hard pillow in an attempt to use up her nervous energy. Minutes later, the jingle of the matron's keys let her know she had a most-welcome visitor, likely John or Emma, the only two besides Mr. Jennings she could count on these days.

She stepped back and waited, hands folded primly in front, as the door swung open to the mood-lifting sight of her sister.

The matron relocked the door with her usual warning, "I'll be back in half an hour."

Lizzie reached out and gave Emma a hug. "It's so good to see you."

Of course, when she glanced over the courtroom each day, she saw Emma faithfully seated in the first row. But being able to converse with her sister and touch her, to feel like someone cared, was much different. To Lizzie, it felt wonderful to be in contact with someone who would offer cheery conversation, even if was often one-sided. It still helped to hear about some bit of news; anything, besides her grim situation.

Emma returned her hug and after a minute pulled back, waving the woven basket in front of her. "So, what do we have for today's special?"

Lizzie crossed the room in a few steps, patted the bed, and urged Emma to sit down. She eyed the basket with a big smile, followed by a grimace. "How about cranberry-apple-prune?"

She laughed and removed the cloth napkin cover from the basket, revealing a pile of nicely browned cookies. Even if she could eat just about anything at this point other than what passed for meals here, nothing equaled Emma's homemade oatmeal raisin cookies. She grabbed one and bit into it, savoring the sweetness and the chewy texture.

"Emma, these are wonderful, thank you. I never thought a cookie could taste so good. Do you have any news? Find anything of interest in the papers from the warehouse?"

"I have some names." Emma offered a paper covered with neatly written rows. "Well, they're mostly the initials and first names of persons I found in the papers. I also listed the activities or goods linked to them if it was included. Most involved office supplies or unspecified items."

Lizzie looked at what Emma had carefully recorded. Her hopeful feeling soon turned to disappointment. "Yes, I see here, SS, wooden crates. BC, shipping containers. Well, more initials, not much hope there, I fear, unless we can positively identify the person."

Letter after letter flew past her eyes. She saw nothing but initials, until she turned to the other side. "This looks more promising. Adelaide, typewriting." Lizzie glanced up at Emma. "No surname, no initial. Did you look at the class list I had in my drawer, or the potential applicants list from the church? Maybe there aren't many Adelaides who expressed interest."

Emma shook her head. "Not yet. I haven't had a chance. I hope to do it next if I can. With everything going on…"

Nothing more needed to be said, of course. Lizzie went back to the list. "Wait, here's one thing. Bottles, Samuel S. The other warehouse we were at…" She paused and tried to remember. "Yes, Samuel Smith. He was listed as the owner of that dreadful place. We'll have to look through the rest of the papers, see who else he's connected to. Father bought a lot of bottles, I see. I can't imagine why."

"He must have used these bottles for something particular at his business," Emma stated.

But what? Lizzie wondered. An image of all the papers and boxes in that abandoned warehouse, especially one box

124

with the word BOTT on it—*for bottles*, she realized—flit through her mind. The thought gnawed at her. She shrugged and pushed it away to figure out later. "I suppose."

Emma's departure left her with plenty of time to sit and think about her case, not that she wanted to do more of that. She shifted through the stack of papers half-heartedly, noting page after page of mundane supplies. The actions made her feel more discouraged and disheartened, not the kinds of sentiments that would help her get through this ordeal, she knew.

To her surprise, the jangle of keys announced another visitor. She stood and waited for the matron to open the cell door, her eyes widening in surprise to see John again so soon. He nodded to the matron. "Thank you. I should be done in about ten minutes."

Once the matron disappeared down the hall, Lizzie let all caution go and rushed to give him a hug. "I miss you."

To her chagrin, he gave her arm an almost brotherly squeeze and stepped away. *What was going on?* Her shock at his unexpected coldness left her almost breathless, but she forgot that as his next bit of news unnerved her even more.

He lowered his voice. "I'm sorry, Liz, I don't have much time. I wanted to let you know what's been happening before the matron returns. I suppose you have heard what seems like more disturbing sounds at night?"

She agreed and whispered back, "Yes, I do try to get used to it, but it does seem like there are more of them out there wandering around. I can usually hear them somewhere outside my window."

He shook his head and raked a hand through his hair. "We've observed a new pattern in the last week. Remember I said we think someone is keeping these monsters confined and letting them out?"

At her nod, he continued, "Our crews are seeing triple the number of creatures out on the streets during the day. We've doubled patrols, but the danger is spreading. A woman downtown just missed being attacked when one of the creatures lurched out of an alleyway. Two of the Society members intervened before it could do any harm. We told the woman we were police and the man was sick. A fortunate turn is she didn't get a good look at him."

"That is alarming." Lizzie gasped, fearing for Emma's safety. She wrung her hands, her worry levels rising. "Have they harmed anyone?"

John shrugged and went on. "We can't be sure. Police have been checking on several recent incidents of missing persons, but they can't say with certainty what happened. You may not view it as such, and I regret saying this, but the press is too busy with your trial to bother with much else."

Lizzie gave him a sour look. "Yes, how ironic."

He shrugged. "All I can say is any reports have mostly been ignored. The police did issue warnings about being alert, isolated attacks, and being aware of suspicious, ill persons roaming about. They were buried in the back section of the papers."

His face grew grave as he tapped on the bars for the matron's return. "I wanted you to know how bad it's getting out there." He lowered his voice. "I heard other rumors that someone is planning some kind of action, what exactly, we aren't sure. In the last few days, I've seen indications the police are closing ranks. They're ignoring our requests for more help. I think we're being shut out. Things will only get more difficult. I'm not sure how much longer we can hold out."

The sadness and genuine alarm on his face made Lizzie forget her own worries for a moment. She reached out and squeezed his arm. "That's terrible. I'm sorry, John, I really am. I wish there was something I could do."

"There is," he whispered, as the sound of footsteps announced the matron's return. "Keep digging in those papers. There has to be a clue in there somewhere as to who else is involved in this."

After he left, Lizzie ignored her sadness and tried to tamp down the anxiousness she felt at things getting worse. She paced up and back across the cell, going over the whole scenario in her mind, pondering Father's role in everything. He was at the center of all this. Of that she felt even more certain.

Determined to find something of value that would help them, Lizzie fanned out a handful of the papers taken from the Smith office-warehouse. *Maybe there's something in here we overlooked, or I haven't found yet*, she thought. First page, she found the same supplies ordered and signed by SS, with AB, for what she surmised to be Andrew Borden on the next line.

She set the paper aside, pleased if not happy that she had found something that potentially linked the two of them. A small AR Typewriting marked the bottom of the page. It could be the Adelaide she had spotted earlier, now with a last name initial perhaps? Maybe this could lead to further identification, too. That paper got set aside as well. The next two sheets offered more supply lists and little else. And so it went with the next few pages after that.

Soon, the tedium got to her. Tired of sorting and reading, she piled everything together in a neat stack and lay back, new paranoia setting in as she stared at her grim surroundings. Add to that the feeling of dejection as she went over John's apparent attempt to distance himself from her personally. At least that's what it had felt like to her.

A wave of melancholy flooded over her. Tears pricked the back of her eyelids as the awful truth filled her—if she were found guilty, she would either hang, or spend the rest of her life in a dirty hole like this. That is unless the creatures shuffling and moaning outside here, too, didn't get her first. She buried her head in the pillow and began to cry.

Chapter Eighteen

Counting from left to right with the face downwards, the wounds were as follows: 1. Was a glancing scalp wound two inches in length by one and 1/2 inches in width, situated 3 inches above left ear hole, cut from above downwards and did not penetrate the skull.

2. Was exactly on top of the skull one-inch long, penetrating into but not through the skull.

3. Was parallel to No. 2, one and 1/2 inches long, and penetrating through the skull.

—Autopsy of Abby D. Borden by W.A. Dolan,
Medical Examiner, August 11, 1892

The days went by in a blur, the routine ever the same. First it was the din from the few inmates in her vicinity waking followed by the clang of metal as the matron brought in the food trays filled with unappetizing dishes. Then came the odd, low moans outside her window each night. She sent up a silent prayer of thanks that Emma continued bringing in her most welcome basket of cookies as a treat each day.

As the weeks and months passed, Lizzie had stopped looking at the prison breakfast tray for sustenance, knowing it would be no different than the previous day's offering— cold, watery slop that passed for oatmeal. She dug out a couple oatmeal cookies instead and munched on those as she readied herself for another day in court.

Her morning toilette finished, she dressed, the gaunt figure in the small square of mirror on the wall barely recognizable. The months in confinement had clearly taken their toll, leaving her a shadow of her former robust self. Each passing hour she remained behind bars, her fate unknown, made it harder and harder for her to remain positive and keep up her hopes.

Taking a deep breath, Lizzie fortified herself with a whispered prayer as she followed the matron down the familiar path from her cell, down the long jail hallway, and out to the carriage for the ride to the courthouse. She walked into the always overcrowded courtroom, head high, not daring to meet the eyes of anyone assembled except Emma, who dipped her head slightly in a nod of encouragement.

As Lizzie made her way to the defendant's table she spotted an unexpected figure from the corner of her eye. Turning slightly, she took another peek, wobbling a bit in shock to find Mayor Coughlin sitting among the stoic group of police officials. He glared at her, his eyes hard and unforgiving, his face condemning. She quickly turned away and stumbled to her seat, rather unnerved. Her attorney Mr. Jennings caught the exchange and squeezed her hand as she sat down. She sincerely appreciated all his efforts and concern.

She had an inkling of how the mayor felt about her— even if she had no real understanding why—from their earlier encounter. But he'd stayed away from most of the proceedings up until now. She grew more uneasy about the upcoming verdict and testimonies. She wondered why the mayor felt he needed to make a personal appearance.

Her fears came to light early when she saw the tissue paper covering the mounds on the table. Her stomach clenched as Dr. William A. Dolan, the medical examiner who'd performed the autopsies on Father and Mrs. Borden, walked to the stand to testify.

Dressed in a well-cut dark suit, the serious-looking man wiped off his silver spectacles as he accepted the plaster skull cast from Mr. William H. Moody, one of the members of her defense team. Lizzie averted her eyes, focusing on her hands folded in her lap instead, as Mr. Moody earnestly began his questioning.

"How many wounds did you find on Mr. Borden's head?" Mr. Moody asked.

Dr. Dolan explained the portions of the skull cast he had marked in blue. "Ten on the fleshy part," he answered.

"What was the general condition of the skull regarding it being crushed?" Mr. Moody questioned again.

"The bone was crushed in about one-and-a-half inches in front of the ear, to probably one-and-a-half inches behind the ear," Dr. Dolan answered.

She grimaced and felt the blood rush from her face as Mr. Moody set the cast skull on the rail in front of the stenographer's table with a clunk.

"Now, Doctor, please explain the rest of the wounds," Mr. Moody said.

"The next wound was two-and-a-half inches above the eyebrow…"

The skull hit the wooden rail. Lizzie heard the axe fall again.

Images suddenly flashed in her mind—*Father coming at her, mouth wide and biting, his eyes white, unseeing, yet seeing…*

Lizzie clenched her hands tighter. She began to breathe harder, her heart pounding in fear.

The doctor's voice droned on as the horrible memories unfurled in rapid succession in her mind—Mrs. Borden's twisted, gray face…

Clunk.

Father, his face white, his breath fetid and stinking of death and decay and horror, standing over her…

Clunk.

An angry, disheveled Father, his face crazed, grabbing and clawing at her…

131

Clunk.

The clammy, horrible feeling of Father's cold, dead hands touching her…

Clunk.

As Mr. Moody moved in closer for more questioning, he brushed against the tissue covering the other evidence on the table. Lizzie's eyes widened as the sounds of the paper shifting and moving magnified ten-fold.

She watched in an almost slow motion kind of horror as the tissue slowly slid downward, unveiling the terribly mangled mounds it had previously hidden from curious eyes. The paper slipped to the floor revealing the actual broken, crushed skulls of her father and Mrs. Borden. The black, eyeless sockets stared at her as if in accusation.

With a whimper, Lizzie grabbed for the arm of the person sitting next to her. She plunged into a swirling pool of blood and biting teeth and darkness. Then she felt and heard nothing.

Chapter Nineteen

Q. Do you still say that the relations between your stepmother and your sister Lizzie were cordial?

A. The last two or three years they were very.

Q. Notwithstanding that she never used the term "Mother"?

A. Yes, sir.

—Testimony of Emma Borden, witness for the defense, Trial of Lizzie Borden, June 16, 1893

L izzie opened her eyes and stared into the kind face of Mr. Jennings, who helped her up and into her seat. Low murmurs buzzed around her like a swarm of bees.

He leaned down, offered her a glass of water, and whispered, "Are you all right, Liz? Do you need a break, or should we go on?"

She took another drink and breathed deep before answering. "Yes, I-I feel fine. I'll be all right. Thank you."

"Very well." He stood to his feet. "Your honor, the defendant says she is fine. The defense is ready to continue."

The lead counsel, Mr. George Robinson, a stout, mustached man of fine principle as well as a former governor of the state, took over most of the questioning, his manner precise and direct. More witnesses went to and from the witness stand like people getting on and off a merry-go- round. Lizzie brightened visibly and felt better when Emma took her turn as a witness for the defense. Emma smiled encouragingly on the way back to her seat.

Lizzie almost dozed off several times between the testimonies of some of the other witnesses, but bolted upright when an older woman suddenly caused a commotion after being asked to explain her comment further

"Why, I am talkin' about those there men who said they seen somebody runnin' down the street that mornin' with a giant cleaver under his arm," she said, her voice strong. "I'm wonderin' why nobody said anythin' about that yet. It was all over the papers."

Lizzie's heart lurched. Could the woman be talking about the Society? Had someone seen one of the members going after the undead? She took a quick peek at John who sat two rows behind her, a scowl on his face. He saw her and shook his head, letting her know that he saw no big problem or threat against the Society's work, at least by this.

He still looks rather unhappy, she thought, unable to stop wondering if maybe it was her he was reacting to instead. She turned to the front as the district attorney voiced his opinion.

"I object," Mr. Hosea M. Knowlton barked. "This has not been proven to be true by our investigations, and has been determined to be nothing but outright lies propagated by the newspapers to sell editions!"

"Counsel, approach please," the judge requested.

As the attorneys began an animated discussion in front of the judge's bench, Lizzie turned to look at John again only to find him intently listening to the whispers of a most attractive woman seated next to him. Inwardly, Lizzie fumed, unable to stop the sudden stab of jealousy at the two of them talking together. His companion's neatly coifed hair and lovely features, along with the fashionable cut of her soft mauve gown, only made Lizzie feel worse. She stared at the drab charcoal of her plain gown, feeling ugly and much older than her years.

Finally, the judge banged his gavel and ordered everyone back to their seats. "Members of the jury will please disregard the witness's last statement. Madam, you are dismissed. Gentlemen, call your next witness."

And so the trial continued.

Except for one quick glance at the twelve men seated in the jury box, a few who seemed to look at her sympathetically, Lizzie tuned the rest out. A dark cloud descended over her. She was numb and tired— utterly bone tired. Nothing anyone said now would change the outcome, her suspicion being that most of the jurymen had already made up their minds. Anything said from this moment on would either confirm their beliefs, or hopefully persuade them to change their minds if they truly thought her guilty.

Her thoughts had been so turned inward that she started when the judge gave his order. "The jury may be excused now to deliberate."

Her fate was cast.

Mr. Jennings offered an encouraging smile and patted her hand as they rose for the judge's exit. They sat back down and waited, the ticking courtroom clock sounding louder and louder by the minute. The air felt heavy as the minutes passed. Lizzie crossed and re-crossed her ankles, her fingers fidgeting with the silk tassels on her reticule.

She nervously took small sips of water. Seconds went by, then minutes. She gazed at the big black hands of the clock and began measuring the time in a quarter hour, a half hour, and then an hour.

Finally, one-and-a-half hours after the jury had retired, the members filed back in, their faces stern and emotionless. The clerk rose. "Miss Lizzie Borden, please stand."

She did, her heart slamming against her ribcage in fear. She could feel every eye in the room on her.

"Hold up your right hand," the clerk directed. "Look at the foreman. Foreman, look at the prisoner. Have you found a verdict?"

Her heart pounded in tandem with the passing of each second on the clock.

The foreman rose. "We have." He passed a paper to the court official who gazed at it and handed it back.

"What is your verdict?"

She dared not breathe.

The foreman looked at her, his gaze sure and steady. "We find the defendant, Miss Lizzie Borden… not guilty."

The courtroom broke into a pandemonium of yells and cries. Lizzie sank into her chair and leaned against the rail in front of her. Her face in her hands, she wept for the first time in public, letting out tears of joy and relief. *I'm free. I'm truly free!*

Finally, she composed herself. Wiping her face, she rose to convey her most heartfelt thanks to the diligent, hard-working members of her legal team. She looked behind her, wondering if John would come over to publicly offer his well wishes. To her disappointment, he nodded and mouthed his congratulations from a distance. He then headed to the door, his hand held familiarly against his lovely companion's back.

Lizzie felt betrayed and hurt, but let it go for the moment in the rush of good wishes and congratulations offered by a swell of supporters unknown to her until now. As Emma enveloped her in a hug, Lizzie fought back a new wave of tears and buried her head in her sister's arms. "Take me home," she told her. "I want to go home."

They finally parted from the crowd. Lizzie waited, this time not so patiently, as her attorneys finished all the details pertaining to her release. She turned and smiled, ready to thank another well-wisher who moved in beside her.

136

Instead, she found herself face to face with the stout, disapproving figure of Mayor Coughlin. Behind him stood a shorter man she'd never seen before.

She gasped in alarm and tried to move away, but couldn't go far. The two men squeezed in so close she began to choke on a stale mixture of cigar smoke, sweat, and the woodsy smell of someone's aftershave.

"Excuse me," she murmured, and fought off a wave of dizziness. "Please, I have to get out. Please, I need some air."

The mayor glared in the background as his partner leaned toward her, a menacing look on his face. "This is far from over," the man muttered. "It ain't good to be stickin' yer nose where it don't belong."

Chapter Twenty

Where is the Assassin?
—Headline, *Providence Journal*, June 21, 1893

"Who was that?" Emma asked as she herded Lizzie out to Mr. Jennings' conveyance for the welcome ride home. "Whatever did our old goat of a mayor want?"

"I have no idea," Lizzie answered on both counts. She got in and reached over to make sure the carriage's curtains covered the side windows. With a sigh, she leaned back in the seat. "I can't wait to get home."

The not-so-veiled threat from the mayor's mysterious companion did make her nervous, but she decided to forget both of them for a while. There was plenty of time to fret and worry until she found out more from John or one of the Society members. For now, she simply wanted to enjoy being in her own house again.

Once inside, Lizzie reveled in the familiar and comfortable surroundings. Unable to stop herself, she slid her fingers along every piece of furniture on her way to the kitchen, maybe to convince herself it had finally happened. *Home, I'm finally home!*

As Emma prepared a light repast for them of sweetened lemon tea and an array of delightful finger sandwiches, Lizzie allowed herself to begin planning what she would do with her life. Why, she could do anything now!

She reached out and squeezed her sister's hand as Emma set the table. "Emma, I can never, ever thank you enough for standing by me. Words aren't enough to tell you how grateful I am."

138

"You would've done the same for me. We have to help each other."

Lizzie nodded, took a big bite of one of the tiny creations filled with meat, or cream cheese and tomato, savoring the flavors. Wasting not a second, she quickly grabbed another. "Mmm, these sandwiches are wonderful. Of course, you could give me cardboard right now. I'd probably eat it and enjoy every single bite."

Emma laughed and jumped to her feet. "Oh, one more thing I almost forgot." She set down a plate of freshly baked cookies. "What kind of a celebration is it without oatmeal cookies?"

Lizzie grinned and began to laugh harder. "Well, if you don't mind, I think I've had enough oatmeal cookies to last a lifetime. Maybe we should have chocolate, ginger, or sugar cookies from now on."

The two of them laughed companionably as they finished lunch. She then headed upstairs for a soothing hot bath, slipped into her softest sleeping gown, and tucked into bed early. She planned to sleep away as many hours as possible no matter how many of the creatures moaned outside.

Lizzie stirred and finally woke late the next afternoon. She felt refreshed and ready to face the future. She stayed under the covers, her mind filled with plans. *I think it's time to move. With everything behind us, we can both enjoy nicer surroundings. I'm sure Emma would appreciate that. We need to put the bad memories here in the past and move on.*

As she dressed, Lizzie decided to ask Emma if she knew of any properties available up on the Hill. Surely, her sister would agree to her plan. Besides, they could certainly afford it.

Next, she thought of the trips she and Emma could take. She'd missed several shows like "Lady Windermere's Fan," which had received excellent reviews while playing in Boston. Being behind bars, she had been socially deprived for so long. *Oh, the things we can do now! I should ask Emma to go shopping. I can use something new to wear.* Her sister might like a cheerier, new gown, too, after all those months of somberness and mourning.

That thought prompted a most unwelcome memory of the beautifully dressed woman who had so thoroughly engaged John's attention. Was it too late for them? Given the time she had spent locked away, it seemed to be that way.

The thought of him moving on to someone else angered her. *Maybe I've simply been a fool. Perhaps I read more into the relationship than was even there.* Lizzie realized that given her inexperience with such situations, and her boldly throwing herself at him, it could be so. She sighed. *Maybe I clearly misjudged him.* She probably had gotten involved in a most unhealthy, one-sided, situation.

Lizzie pondered those thoughts as she rose and slipped into a lightweight day dress in a dusty rose color that brought out the pink in her cheeks, sans the tight-fitting corset. She hummed as she adjusted the more comfortable and looser fitting chemise. "I've been constricted enough," she muttered. "From now on I intend to do what I like, and dress how I like."

Going downstairs, she eyed the telephone hanging smartly on the hallway wall, a change she never regretted. Having their own telephone had certainly made it easier for her to contact Mr. Jennings or for Emma to make other calls. It also became necessary once the trial went on to ensure her and Emma's privacy.

Given the unfriendly behavior exhibited by most of the neighbors around her, Lizzie knew she had to keep her and Emma's lives as private as possible. No need to provide further fodder for gossip. Actually no one had any problems finding one thing or another about her to discuss on their own.

Lizzie also decided to contact one of the other Society members. She wanted to take a more active role in their work, no matter what John thought. She didn't know specifically what they'd been doing, but she knew it wasn't enough. Something more should've been done to vanquish those undead creatures by now.

She had an idea why that hadn't happened. Maybe she and John could discuss this, hopefully in more intimate surroundings—or not. Whatever the result, she thought, *I need to do this. I'll do it on my own, if necessary.*

As the day wore on, she realized that resuming her life wouldn't be so easy since others were not as willing to leave her alone, or to give her and Emma some privacy. As she sat downstairs in the parlor, she watched her sister angrily stomp to her feet and go to the front door again to shoo some intruder away from the front walk.

"I thought all the vultures would lose interest in me now that the trial is over," Lizzie muttered. "Will it ever end?"

Emma slammed the door after chasing the man away from the lawn. "I swear he was trying to peek in the windows! The nerve of people!"

Lizzie went around the dining room and front parlor, pulling down the shades and lighting a few lamps. She felt both angry and sad at the need to block the sunlight. Reporters still knocked on the door, or loitered about. The garish coverage and questions seemed to have no foreseeable end in sight. How long could this go on?

She stared at the headline in the day's newspaper and shook her head. With everything happening, she felt her argument for them taking up residence elsewhere becoming stronger.

"Emma, we really need to move."

"Where? It's not like you're that unrecognizable."

"Not far. I think we should move up to the Hill. We would no longer have people bothering us there. It's much more private." *And exclusive.*

Emma thought about it a minute and then nodded. "You may be right. I can contact Mr. Jennings for some real estate referrals, if you'd like?"

"Yes, please do. I can look in the papers and check if anything seems worth seeing, other than the headline."

Emma glanced at her in surprise and then laughed before she went to make her calls. The day began to look much brighter.

The anniversary of Father and Mrs. Borden's deaths two months later passed with her and Emma quietly remembering in the midst of boxes, bags, and packing materials. That John had not bothered to make time for them to talk other than a few moments on the telephone annoyed Lizzie, but she had other activities to keep her busy.

The charming, three-story Victorian they had moved to on the more fashionable French Street proved to be a balm to her frazzled nerves. Rich mahogany accents and the beautiful tin ceilings made the large rooms nice and cozy. She even had a selection of rich linen paper imported from France for one of the rooms. Six of the fourteen rooms had fireplaces, which she loved. Once it got colder, Lizzie looked forward to sitting in front of a fire with a cup of tea and a good book.

142

During the warmer months, she spent many an enjoyable hour sitting in the sunroom or on the porch, watching what went on outside from a safe distance. Even better, it had modern amenities like gas lights and a real bath. Oh, the joy!

Maybe the house was a little large for just the two of them, but with five bedrooms other than hers and Emma's, Lizzie relished having the space to house potential guests. Even if the furor over the trial didn't die down soon, she still intended to live her life fully by welcoming guests and friends, maybe even have a dinner party or two.

Another bonus—being higher up on the street did provide more protection against the creatures that continued to roam and shuffle along the roads all night, and as John had warned, increasingly by day. Emma had mentioned seeing a sudden scuffle near the library when she was out one day, and as she knew the telltale signs, she recognized it as a just-in-time intervention by a Society member.

She dared not tell Emma since she didn't want to alarm her, but not even the rigors of moving and unpacking made her sleep any better at night. She loved the new house and felt comfortable here, but bad dreams still plagued her.

After more hours spent tossing and turning, Lizzie rose and stood at the window, staring at the scene outside. To her surprise, she witnessed several of the creatures shambling slowly up and down the street.

Being higher up was a bonus, but the long-term still concerned her. In fact, it worried her. What if at some point one or more of those creatures do make it up the incline, right to their front door? As if to illustrate, five of the creatures nearly overtook two men whom she assumed to be Society members out on their regular patrol. It made her realize she could no longer sit idly by. She had to do something. Here was her chance!

Her mind made up, Lizzie changed into total black including the unconventional, but more practical, bloomers she'd sewn from one of her old dresses, which allowed her more freedom of movement. She quietly went downstairs, the black bag holding a few of her weapons slung over her shoulder. Heart thumping in anticipation, her palms wet, she slipped outside. Call her foolish given the many months of being unable to do any real physical activity, but she expected no real problem. In private, she had continued her exercises and done whatever possible to keep in fairly good condition. No matter what, she wanted—*no, needed*—to do this.

Her excitement mounting, Lizzie ran into the street, knowing her movement would attract unwelcome attention. It did. Two of the decayed creatures shuffling at the other end suddenly turned in her direction. *Good, let them come.*

They shambled closer and closer, giving her a whiff of rot and the sickly stench of death. She wrinkled her nose and grimaced, almost—but not quite—forgetting how bad the creatures smelled up close. Truth be told, it was something she would ever forget.

With low moans, they shuffled ever closer. Lizzie took in the nightmare-inducing creatures coming toward her. The first creature's eyeball dangled. Long white worms crawled in and out of the other empty eye socket. It made a disgusting rasping sound, its pocked and blackened tongue wriggling from between the decayed lips like a snake.

The other formerly male creature gazed at her from whitened eyes set in what was left of its head, the majority of the skull bashed and broken, exposing a darkened, rotted brain. Lizzie gagged and ignored the images of Father and Mrs. Borden that beckoned in the back of her mind.

144

Don't think of that. Pay attention!

She stood in the center of the street, waiting for them to draw near. The horrific scrape of foot bones against the brick roadway, coupled with their louder pants and moans like dogs excited about getting a bone, had no effect on her.

They shuffled near, three feet away, then two. Lizzie scurried backward, quickly pulling the wooden bat and silver knife from her bag. Arms riddled with rot, the hands with gaping black holes where the fingers had fallen off, reached for her. Mere inches remained between her and them. At the last second, the one with the half-skull shuffled to the one side, the other coming straight at her.

Ah, a smart one, she thought, and maneuvered herself into position just as fast. Her arm pulled back, she took aim and threw the heavy knife at the slightly smarter creature to her right. The weapon hit the center, exposed part of the brain with a *thunk*. It went down with a groan.

In seconds, the other one was nearly on her. It lunged with a growl. Lizzie jumped back with seconds to spare, and swung the bat. WHACK! It glanced off the ghoul's shoulder, sending pieces and slivers of bone sprinkling to the pavement like devil's snowflakes. WHACK! She hit again, taking note of her position as she turned and perfected her aim.

Visions flashed in her head. Her mind filled with rivers of blood and decayed, chomping teeth. WHACK! She struck out again, this time connecting with the target. The monster slumped to the ground in an ugly, stinking pile, what was left of its brain oozing out in a bloody, pulpy mass.

Her mind clear again, she looked down at what she'd done. Oddly enough, she felt nothing. *How calm and cool a killer I've become*, she thought. *So be it. It simply had to be done.*

That said, Lizzie grabbed the bat and wiped it with a cloth before tucking it in her bag. Reaching down, she pulled the blade from the creature's head. It released with a juicy, sucking sound. Keeping her wits, she wiped that off as well, threw the cloth on the ground, and turned to go back inside. Feeling rather pleased, she congratulated herself on seeing it through and doing the necessary, but horrible, tasks without turning into a puking, sniveling mess. *Good. I'm ready.*

With daylight only hours away, she cleaned up, changed, and settled into a chair in the parlor with a cup of tea. Her arms felt a little sore, but her outing had left her invigorated and enjoying a feeling of accomplishment. To tell the truth, as terrible as it sounded, she looked forward to doing it again. Most definitely.

After a short nap, she went to the kitchen and made a light breakfast. She poured hot tea in the cups just as Emma came down the stairs. "You're up early." She looked around. "Something smells good."

"Sit." Lizzie put a plate in front of her sister. "Just some sausage and eggs. Eat up. I want to show you something."

"No hints?" Emma smiled as she tucked into her food. "Mmm, this is good. You should cook more often."

Lizzie waited until Emma was mostly finished with her meal before she shared her news. "I went outside last night."

"Oh?"

"The creatures are on our street now. I saw them from the window."

That got Emma's attention. She set her fork down and stared. "They-they are? That isn't good."

"A pair of Society members held their own against five of the monsters, but they were almost overwhelmed despite

146

their efforts. I went down and took care of the other two creatures. I don't want you to take this wrong, but I have to admit it felt good. I felt like I was helping others, like I was doing something worthwhile again."

Emma eyed her for a moment before speaking. "I know how terrible it is, but it has to be done."

Lizzie nodded, glad her sister agreed. "Yes, and we—the two of us—are much better acquainted than most with the evils of these shuffling nightmares, except for longtime members of the Society, of course. I did some thinking. My church friends dropped me. I don't feel welcome anymore in my old circles. We could have moved anywhere else, but I thought, why should we? I was born here. I want to eventually die here. In the meantime, I want to help."

Emma nodded. "Yes, I understand. I think I'd like to help you also, if I can."

Her sister's words left Lizzie energized. "I hoped you would feel that way. I have something to show you. Come downstairs."

Unknown to Emma, between the unpacking and getting settled in, Lizzie had hired several men from the Society to transform the lower level into a space suited to their unique needs. She opened the door and turned up the lights. "Ready?"

Emma followed her down the steps. "I suppose. I admit you have me curious." She crossed her arms and looked around, her eyebrows raised. "Oh, my." She kept quiet and took it all in. "So, this is what all the building and pounding has been about? I tried coming down before to look, but the door was locked."

Lizzie flashed a smile at her. "I wanted it to be a surprise. I told the builders to not let anyone else in, even you."

"Well, it certainly is."

She watched Emma scrutinize the finished sitting room which held almost everything they needed, including a bookcase full of their favorite books, a table and chairs, and a comfortable settee. The real secret, however, lay behind the paneled wall.

"It looks nice." Emma looked around, still clearly perplexed. "It will be a good space to relax when it gets real hot. Or a good place to hide, you know…"

She did. "Yes, to hide from them. But there's much more to this room than us being comfortable and talking about whatever books we're reading."

Lizzie went to a small box near the back wall and pushed a button which caused the wood panel before them to slide open. Motioning Emma to follow, she walked into the small enclosed room fitted with all the accoutrements either of them needed to continue their physical training and preparation for fighting off the creatures. The room held several stuffed mannequins and punching bags for boxing and stabbing lessons. A table held an assortment of knives, throwing weapons, and other equipment. Soft padding covered part of the floor. Body outlines and circular maps decorated the main wall.

Emma pointed to the back of the room. "Interesting art. What are those for?"

"Watch." Lizzie walked over to the table, grabbed a small knife, and positioned herself. Taking aim, she let the knife fly. It hit and stuck at the throat area of the body outline. "I need to practice more. If that were a real undead creature, he would still be coming at me."

Emma muttered a soft, "Oh."

"So, do you still want to help me?" Lizzie asked. Emma gave a tepid nod.

"Look, I won't force you to do this if you'd rather not. I decided that, no matter what, I intend to make myself stronger and see this through. It's been going on far too long. It's time we find out who's behind this and see what they're truly up to. Whoever it is has a connection with Father and those creatures in the warehouse. Somehow this is all tied together. That's why I had this built. What do you say?"

"You sound so positive. I can't let you do this alone." Emma hesitated and finally nodded. "I want to help."

Lizzie motioned Emma to follow and hit the button again before turning to a switch under it. "Good. I already arranged for us to take special fighting lessons with one of the Society's members. Mr. Pierre Moret is an expert knife thrower and self-defense teacher. He will come here two or three days a week. Then, once we're ready, we'll join him and a few others in our own patrols. I have no intention of sitting around doing nothing but knitting or needlework."

With that, Lizzie hit the other switch. Emma's gasp made the moment even more poignant as the second paneled wall slid open, revealing a small space completely enclosed by the sturdy, shiny bars of a steel cage.

"We-we have our own jail cell?" Emma squeaked. "Liz, I thought you would've had enough of jail by now."

Her mouth fixed in a grim line, Lizzie shook her head. "As long as I live, I intend to never set foot behind bars again. This is our emergency holding cell. You know, just in case."

Emma grew thoughtful. "Yes, I understand."

Chapter Twenty-One

Many Points of Resemblance Found Between the Manchester and Borden Murders.
—Headline, *The Boston Daily Globe*, June 1, 1893

The two of them did a quick run-through of all the equipment, with Emma's halfway decent aim and accuracy coming as a welcome surprise. Even if she still questioned the need for the training room, Lizzie expected her sister to view it differently once she glimpsed more of what was going on outside the front door.

They went upstairs, where Lizzie grabbed a cool glass of lemonade. She stopped to peer out the front parlor window when something most unsettling caught her eye. "Emma, take a look at this."

None of the regularly occurring events surprised her anymore, but it still alarmed her all the same to see a man standing in the middle of the road madly swinging a cane. The man swung and when he missed, his attacker swung back with his arms in a wild, windmill motion. The assailant's choppy, uneven movements told Lizzie he was no longer human, but undead. The man swung again, this time connecting with the creature's head. The ghoul lurched and wobbled awkwardly in typical undead fashion.

Emma joined her, sucking in her breath in alarm. "Oh, no. We can't escape it, can we? Should we go out and help?"

Lizzie followed the battle for a minute, wondering the same thing, but the man seemed to be holding his own. "Wait a few minutes. He seems to have it under control."

As they watched, a wagon pulled up. Two other men jumped out and made a quick end of the undead attacker. Emma grew bored and went to the kitchen as the men loaded the body into the wagon and took off.

Lizzie stayed at the window a few more minutes. As the wagon passed by, she got a glimpse of the driver and his younger passenger. Neither of them looked like someone she'd seen in the Society, and she knew most everyone. Maybe they added a few new members, she mused.

Only when the wagon was almost past did she catch sight of the faded placard on the side of the wagon: *A.B. and C. Tonic, Good for Whatever Ails You.* She tried to read the rest, but only caught a few of the letters at the bottom of the sign as the wagon sped up.

These days you couldn't read a magazine or go to the druggist without being overrun with advertisements for new medicines. Tons of new tonics, elixirs and bitters aimed at treating or supposedly curing nearly every ailment sprang up overnight. No reason why this one should be any different, but as Emma called from the kitchen, for some reason, Lizzie tucked the name and slogan away in the back of her mind.

"Liz, did you hear? Did you want to look at some of those papers, or should we wait?"

"I guess we can look through the stack, if you like. There are several people whose backgrounds I really want us to look into also."

The room fell silent as Emma entered the room and stared at her.

"Oh? Who?"

"We need to find our typewriting source and then we have to locate Samuel Smith. I found his name on quite a few papers. It makes me think he had more going on than just ordering in supplies. What, I don't know. Then I think we seriously need to find out who that man was at the courthouse with the mayor.

She fell silent, not sure if sharing her experience was a good idea, but Emma needed to know. "I never told you. He threatened me."

Her statement made Emma almost drop the box in her hands. "What? You should have said something!"

Lizzie shrugged. "He approached me after the verdict. He said I should mind my own business. Whoever he is, he doesn't look the type to take no for an answer. Rather unwholesome. We need to find out what's going on."

"I agree. He could be dangerous."

Lizzie shook her head and frowned. "He unnerved me, I admit, but I figured we can't go complaining about people without first learning more about them. He seems of a different class. I have no idea how, or why, the mayor seems to know him. I would say it's to our advantage to first find out if anyone in the Society knows more about him."

Emma nodded and wiped a hand across her forehead. "That may be the best solution. I'm surprised you can think so clearly about this. I always want to jump right in. What about the mayor?"

That stumped Lizzie. She had no idea what to think about the city's leader. "His showing up in court the last day and his continuing reactions to me are most puzzling. As far as I know, he and Father weren't close personally. Maybe they were working together professionally beyond the usual bank boards and other business organizations Father was involved in. There must be some reason he doesn't seem to like me outside of his being angry that the jury decided in my favor."

"Hmm, well, most politicians have something secret going on, am I right?" Emma asked sarcastically. "We had no thought of anything out of the ordinary going on with

Father either, until we found that warehouse, not that I believe he was really involved in anything more than that. Do you?"

Lizzie shrugged. "Who knows what to think anymore?" She tapped her finger against the side of her face in thought. "The warehouse..." A shiver hit her. "That place disturbs me. I think we've hardly begun to learn what goes on there. Whatever it is involves Mr. Smith and our elusive office worker, Adelaide—and Father. I don't have the answers right now. But I will."

Emma set the box down, a determined look on her face. "Maybe you're right. We should do some checking around instead. The papers can wait." She paused. "Perhaps we should have someone from the Society go with us, you know, in case we need help. Why not call John?"

Her sister's expression couldn't seem more innocent, but Lizzie did wonder if this was Emma's way of getting her and John back in contact. Sneaky. She didn't want to share the details of their estrangement, but realized maybe Emma had a point. *I suppose the two of us do need to clear the air,* she thought. He'd yet made no effort to contact her, so she probably had to make the first move. That did annoy her, but she gave in. "All right. I'll call him while you get ready."

To her surprise, the conversation went better than expected. John seemed genuinely happy to hear from her, or else he should have pursued a livelihood on the stage. Ten minutes later, a knock on the door interrupted her musing. Emma grabbed the knob first and opened the door ahead of her.

"John! How good to see you. I'll leave you to Liz."

With that, to Lizzie's chagrin, Emma walked out ahead of her and climbed into John's carriage to wait. Lizzie waited for him to say or do something.

He smiled in greeting. "Liz, you're looking well."

153

He's being so standoffish, so formal, Lizzie thought. She supposed it shouldn't surprise her. *So be it. Well, I can act the same way.*

She nodded in greeting. "John, it's good to see you."

"Where are we off to? I have an appointment later this afternoon."

Lizzie tried not to sound perturbed at his seeming impatience. "We only need to go out for two or three hours. There are a couple addresses we need to visit." She handed him the paper.

He perused the addresses as she locked the door. "Very well. Who are you looking for?"

"I wanted to find out more about some of the women who took the typewriting courses," she said, allowing him to help her into the carriage's comfy padded seat. "Hopefully we can question those who dropped out, as well. Maybe we can locate our mysterious Adelaide."

He got into the front seat of the carriage and made a point of letting both of them know he hadn't been idle. Lizzie felt a little better knowing she wasn't entirely out of his thoughts, even if for another reason. Still, she had no need to grasp at crumbs.

"I had the Society secretary looking into some of the names, also," he added. "She hasn't found out anything yet."

She? Lizzie wondered, more surprised at the way her mind went in an entirely different direction than his lack of news. *Is she the pretty lady he sat with in the courtroom? Are they friends outside the office, too?*

"Thank you." Lizzie settled her skirts around her legs and gave herself a good, sharp pinch as a distraction from this self-destructive train of thought. *Stop it! It's none of my concern what he does, or who he's spending time with.* This wasn't something she needed to think of at the moment—and maybe never.

The horse trotted down the road, past the stately edifice of St. Mary's Church. The landscape gradually turned more timeworn the further they went. Patches of dirt replaced green spots of the well-manicured lawn. Bits of newspaper and refuse skittered along the street, or leapt into the air on the breeze. Her nose wrinkled at the strong odor of cooked cabbage, rotting garbage, and an under-layer of decay.

After several streets, John turned at the corner and stopped the carriage in front of a fading gray storefront, the façade missing chunks of wood. Lizzie climbed out and gave a curt "be back in a minute" to stop anyone from accompanying her. She felt the need to do this first interview alone.

Seeing no doorbell, she knocked, and getting no answer, tried the doorknob. The door opened into a plain, but clean, shop. Several sewing machines sat idle near the back wall. Piles of fabric cluttered the front counter. She couldn't determine whether the dressmaking shop had closed or was still in operation.

"Hello? Is anyone here?" Lizzie glanced at the list in her hand again, noting the name. "Mrs. Alves?"

Lizzie almost turned to leave when a little dark-haired lady, her olive complexion indicating her Portuguese ancestry, entered the room from a door in the back. The woman slowly walked forward in mincing steps which made Lizzie pause for a second. She let out her breath in relief when the woman responded.

"Hallo? Yes? I am Mrs. Alves," she answered in accented English. "You need sewing? I afraid shop closed. My last seamstress left. Younger girls all want to try that typewriting machine or work in business. They no want to

155

sew." She stopped and held out her hands, her fingers swollen at the joints. "I too old to sew now."

"Oh, I'm sorry to hear that." Lizzie decided to play along. "Did your seamstress move to another shop? I planned to get a new gown made."

"Which girl?" The woman stared at her from shrewd eyes.

Lizzie saw how the woman took in her attire, perhaps calculating how much she could make by providing a referral. Lizzie looked sheepish as she pulled a few small bills from her pocket. "I'm so sorry. I forgot her name. All I know her by is Adelaide."

The money disappeared in the blink of an eye into the voluminous folds of the woman's deep purple jacket. She eyed Lizzie, her mouth scrunched up as she gave the statement some thought. "Um, Adelaide, no, I know no one use that name. I did have girl named Adeline. That is close, yes? Perhaps she do work?"

Lizzie kept her thoughts to herself and nodded. She took the information on where the girl lived, though she wasn't sure close would do it. This girl likely wasn't the person they wanted, but she would look into it just the same. Offering her thanks, Lizzie walked out, the disappointment weighing her down. Of course, this was only the first stop. No sense in getting overly discouraged yet.

She got into the carriage, shaking her head at her companions' questioning looks. "No, I don't think it's her. The woman referred to a girl she called Adeline. But we can still find out more. The woman's English wasn't the best."

She handed John the address the woman had scribbled down. He nodded, clucked to the horse, and flicked the reins. "We're not too far away, but I must warn you, this isn't the best of areas. We may encounter more of the infected. I'm sure you read about the other murder in the newspapers?"

Lizzie knew her face must have telegraphed how she felt about the newspapers and their endless dragging out of her case for analysis or comment. She needed no further reminder of how her name had been brought up once again, given the similarity of a farm girl being killed by an unknown person or persons using an axe.

"Liz, sorry. I only mentioned it as a warning. The police are being tight-lipped, but we're suspecting one of these creatures was involved and the accused attacker wasn't a Society member. The papers aren't reporting on that element—yet."

His assessment proved to be an understatement. The horse clopped down the road, taking them near the river again. The streets became narrower, dirtier. Small buildings showed their age with falling plaster, gouged brick, and colors faded to shadows of their former, bright hues.

Lizzie coughed and held a handkerchief over her nose at the sudden strong odor of decay.

Emma did the same, her eyes watering. "Uh-oh. Does that mean there's—"

"Quick, there's no time to waste!" John yelled.

Chapter Twenty-Two

Q. This form, when you first saw it, was on the steps of the back door?

A. Yes, sir.

Q. Went down the rear steps? Around the back side of the house?

A. Yes, sir. Disappeared in the dark. I don't know where they went.

—Lizzie Borden at inquest, August 11, 1892

The horse screamed and tried to rear as John fought, and finally succeeded, in pulling the carriage to the side of the road. He jumped out and went to calm the animal. "Hurry, get out, get out! Emma, please stay and hold the reins. Liz, get ready!"

They jumped out, Emma clucking to the horse as it neighed and stomped. In desperation, she took off her scarf, covered its eyes, and held onto the reins as tightly as possible. The horse pawed the ground and whinnied, frightened by the ghastly stench that now enveloped the area.

A few feet ahead a sickening sight became visible—a trio of undead lurched into the road from behind a wall. Their appearance left Lizzie dumbfounded for a minute. The sight was unusual to say the least—an entire ghoul family, and of Portuguese ancestry at that. She shouldn't have been surprised, given the high percentage of immigrants who had settled in the river area, but she was.

The zombie father, his dark complexion pocked with decay spots and deep holes, still had thick, black hair except for the bashed-in side of his head. He stumbled and shuffled toward them with a sinister grimace. The woman,

158

his wife, Lizzie guessed, had her hair in a bun on top of her head. She wore a torn housedress, the front spotted with blood. A giant gash in the dress revealed a gaping hole in her stomach where, another ghoul perhaps, had taken part of her intestines, the rest hanging and swinging with each sliding step she took.

The child, a girl of about ten or so, appeared almost pretty at first glance, if not for the gruesome changes—she had a big brown eye, but the other one was missing. Decay spotted her arms, but left much of her light olive complexion unmarked. Black goo and a mass of moving, swarming insects atop her head spoiled the nearly waist-length strands of matted black hair. She stared in Lizzie's direction and gave a low growl, her personality no longer sweet and endearing.

Lizzie sighed, not sure if she could be the one to put the girl out of her ghoulish misery, but steeled herself, expecting the worst. John took the initiative, not waiting for them to attack. He leaped ahead, and pulling a long blade from beneath his coat, swung, hitting the father at the perfect angle. The undead man's head went flying, the body dropping in a smelly, gory pile.

The mother paid no attention to her lost mate, instead raising her arms and rushing at Lizzie with a loud growl and a moan. The little girl did the same, her actions and unwelcome grimace erasing the image of a little girl ready for school in her pink, now bloodstained, dress.

Lizzie paused, unable to stop the thought, *like mother, like daughter*. Echoing John's movements, she pulled the wooden bat from her bag. She took a huge step forward, reared back, swung—and missed. At the last second, the zombie family parted ways, mother going left, daughter veering right, leaving Lizzie as the potential entrée in the middle.

"John!" Lizzie yelled. "Help!"

He jumped over just in time and stabbed the undead mother in the back of the head, the blade thrusting all the way through her brain and jutting out her forehead in a burst of licorice black brains and matter. The little ghoul, seeing its mother fallen, stopped and gave a low, moaning howl. Whether it was in fear, or some tiny spark of recognition that she was now an orphan, made no difference. That few seconds gave Lizzie the time she needed. She swung the bat, catching the younger creature's head and crushing the skull. Its forehead split open like a ripe muskmelon with a loud crack. It fell in a bloody pile of faded pink frills and decay.

"Are you all right?" John asked, wiping his sword and putting it away.

"Yes, fine," Lizzie answered, doing the same to her bat. She took a deep breath, a feeling of sadness hitting her. Never would she expect this attack and kill to bother her any more than the others. Yet, seeing the little girl lying there like that would never make her feel any better.

A sense of regret filled her. Such a shame. This disease, or sickness, or whatever it was, must be taking a toll on families in the area.

Just last week Emma had relayed a story from one of the Society members about a friend's close encounter. "An unsavory-looking man lurched out of the doorway," she explained. "He was intoxicated at only the ninth hour. The man didn't understand what was really wrong before the Society members nabbed the ghoulish interloper. It surprises me that so many people don't pay attention to what happens around them."

Lizzie shrugged, the reason clear by painful personal experience—people only saw what they wanted and ignored the rest. She pushed aside the dark memories of her own tragedy and refocused her thoughts. "We need to go find that house and get out of here."

They ran to the carriage. Emma quickly jumped in beside her, there being no need to ask more questions, which made Lizzie thankful. The animal trotted down the rutted path, trees whipping scraggly branches at them as the carriage rolled past.

Finally, they reached the end of the road and made a narrow turn into what looked like a dead end. Lizzie saw the worry on John's face, the idea of being stuck here and surrounded making her heart skip a few beats as well.

"Wait a second, Liz," he said. "Let me turn the carriage around so we can bolt out of here if needed."

He directed the horse to turn. The carriage in place, he cautioned Emma to wait there.

"No, please stay here," Lizzie insisted. "I'd rather have someone with Emma."

To her surprise, he agreed. "All right, but hurry. I don't like the feel of this place."

Lizzie knew what he meant. It bothered her, too. She cautiously looked around, pausing to listen for any weird noises. It remained quiet. Still cautious, she poked the bat ahead of her into the opening to see if anything grabbed at it. When nothing happened, she parted the heavy foliage and went through. To her surprise, despite the foul odor in the air and the ramshackle look of the building hidden by the wild growth, whoever lived there took care of the property. Several rose bushes and a number of flowerpots had sprouted fragrant blooms.

She breathed in the heady scent of the flowers, appreciating the effort. The real reason for the fragrant growth soon became apparent: the floral perfumes made a perfect mask to the other odors. She went up the whitewashed steps and seeing no bell, rapped on the door with her fist. After a few minutes of waiting, she knocked again, relieved to finally hear footsteps and a voice inside.

"*Um momento,*" a woman called. "*Olá, quem está ali? Já vou!*"

The door opened, and Lizzie was greeted by a stout, cheery woman dressed in a plain, but clean, light blue wrapper. The woman peeked out and looked side to side before she motioned Lizzie to come inside.

"*Lamento muito*, my English little."

"Hello, excuse me. Someone sent me here from the dressmaker's shop."

The woman's smile grew wider. "Oh, yes, yes. I sew there. No more. I sew here, *minha casa.*"

"I was looking for a woman named Adelaide."

Her eyes brightened. "Yes, I Adeline. Yes. You want sew?"

Lizzie shook her head. "No, I'm looking for a woman named Adelaide." She emphasized the syllables, hoping the woman understood. "Ad-e-laide."

The woman smiled at her and nodded. "Adeline. *Minha filha*, Adelaide." The woman paused. "She goes to… *a escola, a máquina de escrever…*"

Lizzie shrugged and held out her hands. "I don't understand."

Adeline motioned at her and then began making an up and down motion, like she was banging or pounding with her fingers. Lizzie shrugged again.

"*Máquina de escrever.*" She motioned and held up a finger. "*Um momento.*"

She disappeared and left Lizzie standing there. A minute later the woman reappeared, a piece of paper and a photo frame in hand. Lizzie smiled as the woman held the frame out, showing her the photo of a lovely dark-haired girl, a younger version of the mother. "Adelaide." Then she showed her the typewritten page and pointed at the neatly typed lines.

At last, Lizzie nodded, unable to contain her excitement. Finally, she was getting somewhere! "Yes, yes, type, typewriting. Yes. Adelaide. She goes to school where?"

The woman took off again, returning a minute later with a card for a local business school offering typewriting courses. The business sounded slightly familiar, but Lizzie wasn't sure if it was one of the schools the church had worked with or not.

Lizzie nodded again and expressed her thanks. "Thank you so much. Thank you. I so appreciate this. Does your daughter come home soon?"

The woman gave her a perplexed look. "*Minha filha, sua casa…*"

Unsure what she meant, Lizzie pointed at the adjacent living room. "Here? Will your daughter come here?"

Adeline gazed at her a moment and then took the card from Lizzie's hand, grabbed a pen from the table behind her in the hall, and began writing. She smiled and offered the card back.

Lizzie eyed the address the woman had written, glad they'd finally managed to communicate somehow. "Thank you so much, thank you." She folded her hands together in gratitude and pointed at the flowers as she stepped outside. "I appreciate your help. Your flowers are beautiful. Lovely."

"Wait." Adeline motioned to her and pulled something from her pocket. She pressed the item into Lizzie's hand and squeezed her fingers around it. "*Para a senhora.* Not safe." With that, she gave a small wave and closed the door with a smile.

Lizzie ran back to the buggy where Emma and John sat nervously making small talk.

163

"Thank goodness," Emma declared and made room for her on the seat. "I almost thought we should get out and see if you were all right."

Opening her fingers, Lizzie showed them a shimmering crystal rosary the woman had given her before she passed the card to John. "I'm better than all right. That woman is very aware of what's going on. Her name is Adeline, but it is her daughter, Adelaide, that we need to talk with. She attends this business school to learn typewriting. Her mother gave me the address. Can we go there now?"

After studying the card, John handed it back, and clucked to the horse. "Why not? We can stop there on the way back to your house. Hopefully, we can finally get some decent answers."

Lizzie leaned back with a sigh. "I hope so. I really do hope so."

Chapter Twenty-Three

Q. You saw his face covered with blood?
A. Yes, sir.
—Lizzie Borden at inquest, June 9-11, 1892

Not even the bouncing over ruts, the smells, or the moans coming from ghouls hiding around the corners, could ruin Lizzie's much improved mood. She really felt like they were getting somewhere now.

She spoke too soon, it seemed. Her elation turned to anger when John refused to stop and take care of several ghouls loping their way.

"No, leave them. I saw several Society members on the other road. They'll get them."

To Lizzie, it felt wrong to leave the job to anyone else, selfish even. That thought irritated her even more. She realized his attitude made her decision much easier. *Maybe he's someone I don't want to associate with any longer.*

Emma must have sensed her growing anger and laid her hand on Lizzie's arm in caution.

Lizzie smiled at Emma, but she insisted on making her opinion known. "Very well, but I don't think we should leave any of them around, anywhere. It's simply not a good idea. Besides, didn't I hear that the Society's goal is to eradicate them?"

John opened his mouth and closed it abruptly, possibly thinking better of his answer. His face flushed, a sign she'd succeeded in annoying him, or had hit a sore spot. Maybe it was petty, but Lizzie rather enjoyed getting under his skin. Whether he decided to acknowledge their personal situation or not, she wasn't going to ignore things any longer. Nor did she intend to go away quietly.

Not that it really mattered. She ducked her head and smiled. *Now that my life is my own again, I'm ready for a change.* The image of their smart, well-muscled new instructor, Pierre Moret, came to mind. She and Emma both had learned quite a bit after only a few self-defense and fighting lessons in their training area. She felt stronger and much more confident.

That Pierre had a good sense of humor—*be honest, now, he's also a fine looking man*—only added to her enjoyment. She looked forward to the lessons, and yes, his company, thinking it one of the best ideas she'd had in quite a while.

Her woolgathering ended as John stopped the horse at the corner in front of a small brick building. The sign in front read Mrs. Thatcher's Business College. The black and gold line of script under it caught her eye: *Typewriting Our Specialty.* Perfect.

Lizzie gathered her wits about her and jumped out of the carriage, eager to get some answers. "Wait here. If I'm not back in ten minutes, you'd best come and check on me." John and Emma both nodded in response. Lizzie didn't have to explain that a delay likely meant she'd run into a bit of trouble of the undead variety.

The door opened onto a small reception area with a scuffed black-and-white tile floor. A giant testimonial touting the college's classes, along with letters from satisfied graduates and businessmen, nearly covered the dingy white wall. A young woman sat at a small desk in front, professionally dressed in a fitted white bodice, a crisp bow tied at her neck, and a black skirt. Most important, a shiny Remington typewriting machine rested on the desk at her side.

The young woman folded her hands primly, a welcoming smile on her face. "Hello, Miss. How may I assist you? Are you interested in learning about our current schedule of typewriting courses?"

Lizzie shook her head and guessed part of the young woman's payment must come from signing up new students. That she went unrecognized came as a big relief. It would certainly make her quest much easier.

"No, thank you. If possible, I would like to talk to one of your students, Adelaide—"

The woman cut her off. "Oh, yes, Miss Adelaide is now one of our newest instructors. Do you still want to speak to her?"

"Yes, I would." Lizzie watched the woman flip through a small directory of names. She had to ask. "I wondered if you had any other women named Adelaide in your classes?"

"Yes, I do believe we had several students named Adelaide sign up for instruction," the young woman answered. "Is there someone in particular you were looking for? Or perhaps the instructor can help you?"

Lizzie felt a glimmer of hope. Could she be this fortunate and find the information in only two stops? "Yes, I would still like to see the instructor if I could. The actual name of the person I was looking for was Adelaide—"

A loud bang and a scream made both her and the receptionist jump. The young woman dropped the directory she held. She leaped to her feet as another scream rent the air. "What is that?" she asked, her hands shaking. "What's going on?"

Lizzie's suspicions about the source grew as she listened carefully. Amid the noise she recognized the low, distinctive moans. "Quick, get out of here!" She yelled at the woman and shooed her from behind the desk. "Go! Get outside. Go, hurry!"

Instead, the young woman stood and stared, her eyes wide, her face pale. Fear and uncertainty held her in place. Lizzie knew they had little time. She grabbed the girl's hand and dragged her to the door, urging her to get away. "Go, go!"

The screams and ungodly moans became louder, coupled with the rapid approach of pounding feet. Lizzie hurried outside and frantically waved to John and Emma as a mob of young ladies bolted past her like a herd of spooked horses, their hair and clothing disheveled. Their hysteria and panic was palpable, spreading like wildfire.

Lizzie fought the urge to flee with them by taking several deep, calming breaths. She felt relieved to see nothing bloodied and no one mangled. So far, no one looked to have been bitten or attacked, though she knew the scene in the other room would be much different and likely, much worse.

John ran toward her, his sword at the ready. "What happened?"

"The classrooms! We have to go there."

He nodded, handing over the black bag she'd left behind in the carriage. A foolish thing to do, she realized.

"I know, I know. From now on I'll never leave my bag behind, no matter where I go."

Taking her dagger in hand, she threw the bag's long strap over her head and across her body, and tiptoed quietly toward the source of the noises. Growls, the sounds of shuffling feet, and the thud of furniture being shoved around told her and John what to expect as they slowly made their way to the first classroom. Ducking down, John peeked around the doorway and then held up five fingers. Once he got to three, she jumped into the room behind him.

The bloody sight before them almost made her turn and flee. Several of the undead crouched over the remains of a few of the more unlucky students who hadn't made it out in time. The creatures' grunts and gurgles filled the room as they pawed at the gory remains. The wet slurps and sloppy chewing turned her stomach. Blood splattered the walls and puddled on the floor. The stench of death, rot, and the cloying metallic scent of blood had Lizzie choking while trying to keep quiet at the same time. It didn't get much worse than this.

Suddenly, one of the monsters spotted them. It dropped the long, bloody rope of intestines it had been savoring with a wet plop. John lunged and attacked the approaching formerly male creature, its body tall; its face gaunt, gray, and gashed. Pockets of missing flesh on the monster's arms and chest revealed a glimpse of broken, mangled bones beneath. One swipe of John's sword and the undead ghoul's head bounced away in a ghastly arc, leaving a trail of black ooze behind. The body went limp in a pile of nasty smelling rot and still wriggling maggots.

He pointed behind her and attacked another creature that came at him. Lizzie turned in time and stabbed a huge undead man in the gut with her dagger, her action doing nothing more than opening a stream of black ooze that smelled worse than week-old meat. With a curse, she pulled back and tossed the gunk-covered weapon onto a table, intending to wipe it later. Panic and adrenaline coursed through her as she leaped back and pulled the wooden bat from her bag. She cursed to herself at how her dress wrapped about her legs and impeded her movement.

The bat held high overhead, she took a steadying breath, reared back, and swung. The bat hit the creature's head, splitting the skull with an explosion like lightning. The ghoul crumpled to the floor.

169

With not a second to waste, she hurriedly wiped the bat on an unbloodied part of the zombie's pants leg and put the weapon away. She grabbed the dagger and wiped it just as quickly on another part of the creature's ratty attire.

"Liz, c'mon, let's go!" He knocked down two more creatures in quick succession, including putting a rapid end to the last one. It had been stupidly shuffling back and forth in one area, stuck between the school's huge metal flag stand and a desk.

The room's quiet made Lizzie increasingly uneasy as she eyed the terrible carnage laid out before them. The dead women's untouched faces mocked them in their unspoiled beauty. Lizzie stared at the perfect complexion of a girl who looked about eighteen, sadness filling her at the future moments and joys that would never be experienced. She looked back at another young woman before she rushed to the doorway, no longer noticing the massacre. Instead, she saw the victims. It disgusted her. A sour taste filled her mouth.

John went ahead and stood at the door, listening. "I don't hear anything else. We have to go. We need to check the other rooms."

She nodded, "First, I need to look at the name tags first and make sure whether Adelaide is here or not."

"Fine. I'll see if your young woman is in the other room."

"Thank you." She sighed and let him go, her dread growing at the task before her. She made another grisly check of the unlucky few who hadn't made it. Her inner alarm told her to look once more behind the desks and the screen hiding assorted equipment from the main room. In the corner lay a young woman, scratched, bloodied and... Lizzie jumped back as the woman's legs began to twitch. "Forgive me," she whispered.

170

Taking a deep breath, she quickly stabbed the victim with her dagger, thus ending the young woman's venture into unlife-after-death. She wiped off the weapon and leaned down to read the name tag lying on the floor beside her, then gasped in shock. The tag read, A. Almeida, Instructor.

No! Was it Adelaide, the seamstress's daughter? Relief flooded her as she looked again and realized this dark-haired girl wasn't the same one in the photo she'd seen earlier. Thank goodness. Most victims remained unknown to her, but after seeing that woman's pride in her daughter, this would be the worst of blows for the mother to find her daughter's dreams turned into a nightmare. Lizzie was glad to not witness that, or have to be the one to end the girl's misery. She assumed, gladly, that the young woman had made it out safe and sound.

Her musing ended as John ran back into the room, his face grim. "Liz? All clear. I found two of them in the other room. Unfortunately, two girls were attacked and killed. The woman you wanted wasn't there. This is awful. I fear I'll never get used to this."

Her sigh matched his as they headed back to the reception area. "Nor I. I found one dead woman in back who was still twitching. I almost thought I'd found the young woman I wanted. Poor girl, but I'm still looking for the right one. Her name tag must have fallen off. Before we go, I want to look at the records. Maybe I'll find something useful."

"Very well. Take a few minutes before I alert the Society members as to what happened. They'll let the proper officials know."

Lizzie nodded sadly as she rummaged through the files in the wood desk in the front lobby. Bills, schedules, payments and other papers swept past her eyes in a whir of numbers and figures. Her fingers kept up a steady flicking through the pages until she got to the end, but nothing of use turned up. The other papers on the top of the desk weren't useful, either. She'd almost decided to give up when the directory the receptionist had dropped on the floor earlier caught her attention. Maybe this was something... She grabbed the book, flipped through the pages, and jotted down the addresses of several women with the name of Adelaide, though she wasn't feeling too hopeful.

The book back in place, she half-heartedly eyed the pages in the front when one line made her gasp. Wait a minute! A few handwritten entries had been added to the bottom of the page. Printed in a small, neat hand, the printed entry told of supplies ordered, but the last line had her heart pounding—a personal note. "Remember to pick up papers to type on Wednesday," followed by two initials, AR.

Her mind worked. She reread the entry. Could it be that the seamstress's daughter wasn't the person she wanted after all? These initials could be the same AR she'd seen in Samuel Smith's—and Father's—papers that they'd found at the warehouse. A huge smile lit her face as she saw the formal signature under the ornamental frontispiece of the book. There in a free-flowing script with neatly formed letters was the name she wanted: Property of Mrs. Adelaide Richards Thatcher, Mrs. Thatcher's Business College.

Apparently, the industrious and entrepreneurial Mrs. Thatcher not only had opened the business college for young women, but she'd made a nice little sum on the side typing papers and reports. She supplied a service to businesses and businessmen who neither wanted, nor needed, to employ a full-time typewriting service—like Father and Mr. Smith.

A further search among the files resulted in a master list with the personal details of employees, students, and teaching staff. The arrival of several Society members told her she'd best hurry. She wrote out the address and joined John, who was already tapping his foot with impatience at the door.

"How many places did you want to go yet?" he asked. "I don't have much have time before I have to get back to my office."

His impatience angered her. She thought about it a minute, and then gave him a cat-swallowed-the-canary smile. "Only one more stop and then we're through, for good. From now on, I'll manage on my own perfectly fine, without your help."

The shocked look on his face made her outburst worthwhile. Yes, she should've said that much sooner.

Chapter Twenty-Four

There is not a spot of blood, there is not a weapon that they have connected with her in any way, shape or fashion…
—Opening statement for the defense, A. J. Jennings, Trial of Lizzie Borden, June 15, 1893

As it so happened, the trip to Mrs. Thatcher's residence was on the way back to Lizzie and Emma's new home on French Street. John stopped the carriage in front of the stately brick manse only blocks from where she and Emma had moved. Lizzie suspected each of them had similar thoughts though Emma was the first to put it into words. "My, typewriting must pay well."

"Yes, so it seems," Lizzie added, "but our Mrs. Thatcher appears to be a most industrious person."

The accuracy of her observation only became obvious when they got out and went up the hewn stone steps to the highly polished oak door. A peek in the window revealed a massive crystal chandelier in the foyer, along with a giant carved fireplace and gleaming marble floor.

A petite woman dressed in a proper black and white maid's uniform answered the door. "Yes?"

"Hello, is Mrs. Thatcher available?"

"I am sorry, she is resting. May I ask who is inquiring?"

John stepped forward and offered his business card. "John Charles Fremont, attorney-at-law. We were just at the school and—"

Lizzie swallowed her retort at his pushiness as a strong voice from an adjacent room broke in. "It's all right, Anna.

Show them into the parlor, please, and bring in the tea, would you?"

The three of them followed the petite woman into a large room even more grand, if possible, than the foyer. Exquisite tapestries hanging at each end of the room competed for attention. Landscape wall murals in warm shades of green and brown made the visitor feel like they'd stepped into a formal garden. A lovely young woman, her peach silk gown glowing against her dark brunette locks, rose and greeted them.

"Please, be seated," the young woman said, dabbing a handkerchief at her eyes. "I am Adelaide Thatcher."

Lizzie fought to control her surprise at their hostess's youth. The lovely young wife had to be a late twenty something years, and if the stately portrait on the opposite wall was her husband, he had to be at least the age of Mr. Borden, if not older. She understandably looked as though she had been crying.

Everyone did as she asked, settling onto the silky sofa cushions.

"Thank you," Lizzie responded. "I am—"

"Yes, I know who you are," their hostess broke in. "I followed the trial."

The woman's admission surprised Lizzie, even if it shouldn't have.

To Mrs. Thatcher's credit, she remained ever the lady. She showed no emotion, or expressed any kind of opinion, on the trial's outcome. Mrs. Thatcher's demeanor appeared neither hostile nor threatening, so Lizzie felt it must be all right to continue her explanations since her hostess remained silent. Lizzie had no choice but to assume that a woman in her position would have already been informed of the full details of all that had happened at the school, as well.

"We just returned from your school," Lizzie explained, her words eliciting a sad sigh from the hostess and another sniffle. "I am so sorry. We wanted to share our condolences on the loss of some of your fine students."

Mrs. Thatcher nodded as she acknowledged the apology. "Yes, such a horrible, horrible tragedy. I don't understand where this came from. I sorrow for the families who will be suffering so." Her voice grew hard. "I certainly hope Marshal Hilliard and his staff are getting on top of this dreadful attack. I am sure Mr. Thatcher will be putting some pressure on those in charge to clean up this terrible mess. Mr. Fremont, I am indebted to you for your service and that of your membership."

"Thank you, Ma'am. We're here to help in any way we can."

Lizzie agreed wholeheartedly, pausing before returning to the subject. "Mrs. Thatcher, if I may mention, some time ago I worked with a program that helped young women enroll in typewriting courses as part of our church's outreach."

Lizzie's admission prompted a small smile from their hostess as she poured tea and offered her a cup. "Yes, I knew of your church program. It was a noble effort. I believe a few women did attend my college as a result of your program. Would you like milk or sugar?"

"Both, please, thank you."

"Mr. Fremont?"

"None for me, thank you."

The tea prepared, Mrs. Thatcher had Anna finish readying the other cups as she got to the point. "I'm sure you're wondering how I came to open the college, and have some other questions, I suspect."

Her eyes met Lizzie's. "My husband has had quite a bit of business success, and has been astute enough to invest in

176

several promising and growing companies," she explained. "He thinks highly of new ventures and has been quite taken with typewriting machines. He also approves of women being able to provide for themselves or their families, so he fully supported the idea of the typewriting school. I was one of those women who found themselves financially bereft after my father lost much of his investments as a result of the recession. The bankruptcy of the Philadelphia and Reading Railroad in February completely broke him. His heart failed, and he passed away shortly after that."

"I am so sorry." Lizzie apologized again, realizing how little attention she'd paid to such financial news, leaving most business dealings in the past to Father and his attorneys. Of course, she'd been quite preoccupied in the past year, as well.

"I will be frank, if you don't mind," their hostess continued. "Many have been rather harsh in judging me because of the age difference between me and my husband, but I was fortunate to have met him. I am saying that not only because he is a wonderful, caring man. I learned typewriting to help support my mother and younger sister after my father's passing. Before I met Mr. Thatcher I was doing quite well providing typewriting services to various businesses. We became acquainted through such contact, and as it turned out, he had done other business with my father before that."

Lizzie nodded, liking this woman for her strength while facing adversity. If circumstances were different, she suspected they might even have become friends. She toyed with her tea cup, unsure of how to bring up the subject of her own father delicately without offending her hostess.

Instead, Mrs. Thatcher attacked the subject without hesitation as she stood, signaling the visit was over.

"Now, please pardon my sudden ending of our meeting, but I'm afraid I have a situation to attend to at the school. I hadn't expected these horrors to hit so close to home. I am sure Mr. Thatcher will be taking new security measures after this. Mr. Fremont, please convey my heartfelt appreciation to your Society members for all their help." She held out a thick folder. "Miss Borden, I think you will find all the contracts and papers you need here. This is everything I typed for Mr. Borden and his contacts. And please accept my condolences as well. Anna will show you out."

Stunned, Lizzie murmured her thanks as the maid showed them to the door. Once outside, they hurried to the carriage, Lizzie barely able to contain her excitement as John helped her into the seat. "This may be it! I think we'll finally have some answers."

John tried to sound encouraging. "Perhaps, but don't get your hopes too high. So far, everyone has been pretty good at hiding their secrets."

I know he means Father, Lizzie mused. *But it won't be for long.*

She restrained from pawing through the pages lest something of importance got overlooked or misplaced. She and Emma needed to study the folder's contents in an orderly fashion so they could account for every single item. She squeezed the thick stack of papers tighter, wishing John would hurry so she could get home and find out exactly what they had.

After all these many months, is the answer right here in my hands? Will I finally learn the truth about what Father was really up to?

Chapter Twenty-Five

Q. At that time did you see a particle of blood on her dress?
A. No, sir
Q. Or her hands?
A. No, sir.
—Testimony of Adelaide Churchill,
Trial of Lizzie Borden, June 8, 1893

Finding Mrs. Thatcher made Lizzie think nothing else would, or could, surprise her at this point. She realized how wrong that assumption was after bidding John goodbye and joining Emma in the dining room for a couple hours of sifting through stacks of papers. The two of them made a good dent in the pile, unearthing mostly run-of-the-mill bills and correspondence, when Emma yawned and got to her feet.

"I have to say for a person who disliked and didn't need modern conveniences, Father sure approved of the typewriter."

Lizzie laughed and added, "as long as he didn't have to bring it home, or to his own office." She rose as well and took a good stretch before attempting to put the papers back in several folders. She sighed in exasperation as one stack fell and papers cascaded across the floor like a giant fan. "Sorry, clumsy me. I think these are making me ill and—" One paper at the bottom of the stack caught her eye. She pulled it out with a frown.

"What?" Emma asked and picked up the rest of the fallen papers.

"I-I have no idea. It has all these ingredients listed like—"

.A. Verstraete

"A recipe," Emma stated.

Lizzie stared at Emma in confusion. "Yes, or maybe it's a prescription, or some kind of list of pharmaceutical supplies." She read off the different items. "Let me see, Oil of Wintergreen, I think that works well for indigestion. Then we have Licorice Root, a familiar element. Oh, and Burdock, do you know what that is?"

Emma shook her head.

"There are some directions." Lizzie continued reading. "It says mix in water with a forty to forty-five percent concentration of alcohol. It also says to add three grams of opium per fluid ounce. It sounds like it'll knock out anything wrong with you, almost like when Dr. Bowen—" She trailed off, not wanting to revisit those unreal moments following the doctor's treatments. She was glad when they ended.

She went over the list, wondering what kind of ailments this might be intended for when Emma piped up.

"Wait, I know," Emma uttered, her voice rising in excitement. "Let me get something. I'll be back in a second."

Emma hurried from the room, leaving Lizzie wondering what she went to find. A few minutes later she came back and held out a bottle. "Here, read the label."

The familiar, stern face of Mrs. Lydia Pinkham graced the front of the tall bottle most of them had availed themselves of at one time or another. Lizzie knew she'd taken a couple doses when necessary to ease a headache and help her sleep.

The label featured the woman's face above the scripted title of Lydia Pinkham's Vegetable Compound, with the explanation, *is a positive cure for all those Painful Complaints and Weaknesses so Common to our best female population.*

180

"Yes, so? We have both taken this for headaches or other ailments."

"Yes, but would you say this," Emma pointed to the list in her hand, "sounds almost like the same kind of medicine?"

Reading the label made Lizzie think of all those other treatments, some with outrageous claims that they could even cure such heinous diseases as cancer, which she most sincerely doubted.

"I never thought much about all those soothing syrups and bitters and salts you can get at the druggist," she mentioned, trying to make the connection. "They're reasonably priced and often useful for headaches and such. Of course, there is a lot of 'quackery' as Father called it."

"I'd imagine the makers are quite successful, too," Emma added. "It most probably is a good sideline business for someone skilled in pharmaceuticals, or who is interested in such a field."

Emma's words stopped Lizzie cold. "What? A sideline, you say?"

For an unexplained reason, Lizzie thought of the sheer amount of advertisements she spotted most everywhere. Shops and magazines touted all kinds of new elixirs and tonics. There seemed to be more and more each day. *Wait, tonics.* An image came to mind. *That wagon!* The workers picking up the monsters from in front of the house. It had some kind of tonic advertisement on the side panel.

Something about that advertisement niggled at the back of her mind. *What was it?* Before Lizzie could put two and two together, the melodious chime of the doorbell caught her attention. With a sigh, she restacked the papers and helped Emma pick them up before her sister went to answer the door.

Emma came back with a visitor in tow. "Liz? It's Mr. Moret."

Lizzie greeted the instructor warmly, though she felt slightly annoyed that something important had indeed been overlooked. She tried to keep the thought firmly planted in the back of her mind, intending to revisit it later. Emma's retreat to the stairs made her glance over in surprise.

"Emma, you're not coming downstairs to practice?"

"If you both have no objections, I'd rather not today. I feel a bit tired. I think a nap is in order."

"All right then, you know where to find me if you need anything."

Lizzie chuckled to herself, thinking how scandalized many of the neighbors and church ladies would be at the idea of a woman keeping company—alone—with a handsome, young man like Pierre. At least living here, most of the neighbors paid her scant attention or said little, at least to her face. *Fine with me*, she thought. *Besides, in their eyes I've already done much worse.*

With those thoughts in mind, she led Pierre downstairs. "I'll go change and be back in a minute," she told him as he pushed the button, opening the training room.

"I'll be waiting," he answered.

His smile, Lizzie had to admit, dazzled her. It also set off warning bells. She paused a moment to watch him set up the equipment before hurrying into the tiny dressing room to change into her customized bloomers.

Maybe I should feign illness, too, she thought, but continued to change clothes. She enjoyed the interaction and the physical nature of their sessions too much to quit. She cautioned herself: *He's my instructor. Keep it professional. Stick to the lessons.* But as she stepped out of the room and met Pierre's gaze, Lizzie acknowledged she was lonely. Deeply and desperately lonely.

Chapter Twenty-Six

He began by declaring the defendant physically unable to commit the crime in the manner committed, and that aside from that it was only possible for a maniac-devil to do it.

—Opening statement for the defense,
Ex-Governor George Robinson, Trial of Lizzie Borden,
June 20, 1893, *The Omaha Daily Bee*

"Arghhhh!" Lizzie screamed and lunged. She attacked the sawdust- filled dummy with everything she had. The blade stuck dead-center in the space above the black spots she had painted on to give the formerly featureless face some eyes as a point of reference.

"Bravo, *Magnifique*!" Her instructor and fellow Society member Pierre Moret clapped his hands in admiration, his face alight with pleasure. "Liz, that was wonderful. Your aim and strength have improved tremendously. I'm so glad you listened to me about doing arm exercises with the dumbbells, even if it sounded strange. I can truly see an improvement."

She shook the wet curls off her forehead. With a smile, she removed the thick padded vest before taking a deep pull of cold water. "Thank you. I almost didn't believe you at first, but you were right. I can feel the difference in my arm and hand strength. It really has helped."

He returned her smile as he went to pull the blade from the target and handed it over. "Now, one more thing you need to practice is your thrust. Like so."

Putting one leg behind him, he stood in a lunge position and pulled his arm back before plunging it forward with all

183

his might. "You understand? Level your stance. I saw you wobble, which weakens your delivery. Put all your strength into the hand with the blade. Now you try."

He handed her the blade, his eyes dark and intent, as she positioned herself, pulled her arm back, and thrust the blade forward with a cry. "Arggh!"

"Good, good, much better." Drawing closer, he took her arm and showed her where to tighten her hold. "You're doing very well. Remember to keep your arm straight, like this."

He stood so close, Lizzie feared to turn her head, but she did. Her eyes met his and held, the seconds quietly ticking by. Her heart pounded harder as he leaned in, mere inches away, for the kiss that she knew was coming.

Ever since she and Pierre met, she had recognized the spark between them. As much as she tried to keep her mind on the lessons, as the days went on and they worked together, she couldn't help but notice that he cut a fine figure. She found herself admiring his agility and his muscular form, along with enjoying his wry sense of humor. To his credit, he never seemed the least bit curious, or judgmental, about her past. Yet, even if he was all business when it came to their lessons, Lizzie could see a growing interest in his eyes. And yes, she often wondered where it would lead.

She could easily have stepped back, or away, or stopped him with a word, but her feet felt glued to the floor. And in truth, Lizzie really didn't want to, at least not today. Today she was weak. With John no longer a part of her life, and after all the months of being judged and vilified, she longed to be appreciated. Truth be told, she was tired of being lonely and alone.

As their lips met, she gasped softly. She savored the feel of his mouth teasing and testing hers. His hand on her back pushed her closer to him. She felt her reservations fade with the realization that little separated them but his thin shirt, and her light cotton blouse and chemise, her electing most days to forgo a corset.

Just when Lizzie thought she would suffocate from the passion ignited between them, and what they might do next, her practical mind took over. She tried to focus, firmly putting her hands on his chest. Slowly, she broke free of their kiss, pushing herself out of his embrace.

"No," she muttered. "We'd better not."

He gazed at her, his hazel eyes dark, and reached out to caress her neck, willing her back into his arms. The brush of his fingers on her neck made her skin tingle. She felt herself weaken for a moment and almost gave in—almost. As much as she wanted to let things continue, she couldn't. Not right now. Silently cursing herself for her unexplained reticence, she shook her head.

"We-we can't—we shouldn't—do this." Lizzie made a feeble attempt to explain her decision, even if she didn't understand it. "I fear our lessons will suffer if we let ourselves become too personally involved. For now. Until... until all this is over."

He nodded, his eyes still dark with desire. "All right, for now."

With that, he grabbed a sword and challenged her to match wits and strength with him, but not before first pulling her close for one last, deep kiss that made her stumble in surprise once he let her go.

"*En garde*," he called out and got into position. Their swords met, the clang of metal on metal filling the air. They thrust and lunged and parried when movement near the stairs caught her eye. The pounding of footsteps and Emma's frantic cries stopped her cold.

"Lizzie, hurry! A bunch of those creatures are outside!"

Lizzie flung the weapons bag across her shoulder and added a couple more knives to the pockets inside. "How many? Is anyone else out there?"

Emma shrugged. "I lost count at ten. Yes, some of the Society members are trying to stop them, but only a few, and not nearly enough. I saw a couple of the neighbors come out, too. I felt sorry for them."

Lizzie raised her eyebrows at that. The neighbors most often ignored what went on outside their front doors, preferring instead to pretend that nothing unusual went on. Lizzie fell into that category as well, she knew, so if they had seen her taking such a shocking, unladylike action as fighting in the street, they simply turned away. They acted like they saw nothing. *They picked a bad time to quit being nosy*, she thought. It would be a horrible, and fatal, choice if they went out unprepared. Still, there wasn't a thing anyone could do for them.

Emma's comment drew a muttered curse from Pierre, who quickened his pace. He fastened two knives at his waist, slung a sword over his shoulder, and fastened a revolver at his side before heading for the stairs.

"Neither of you are to come out without a full supply of weapons," he warned. "That is why the unprepared should never get involved. It's far too dangerous. You both are ready, but be careful. See you outside."

That Emma wanted to get involved made Lizzie glad, but she suspected there had to be a better reason for her sister's interest. Then, as she turned, Lizzie saw the longing on Emma's face. It hit her like a brick. *How could I be so ignorant!* Until now she hadn't realized that Emma had any kind of romantic interest in their instructor given the ten-year age difference, but apparently she did. *How could I be so blind?*

Inwardly Lizzie cursed herself, also relieved that nothing other than that kiss had happened between her and Pierre. She decided to see how to get him and Emma together more often. If that didn't work out, she vowed to make sure her sister wasn't hurt, or feel rejected.

She finished gathering her tools, at the last strapping a knife to her waist. "Emma, are you ready?"

Her sister nodded, her face pale. "Yes."

"You can stay inside, you know. There's no need for you to go out there if you feel uncomfortable."

Emma's bottom lip quivered slightly, but she remained firm as they ran up the stairs. "No, I-I have to. I want to help."

"Very well, but stay close. You get in trouble, call out." Lizzie stopped at the front door and made her sister look at her. "Remember to attack and move. Whatever you do, don't get within grabbing distance. You only get one chance at this."

She gave her sister a trembling smile before pushing the door open. Lizzie almost pulled Emma back inside, but it was already too late. Their arrival drew the immediate attention of three extremely disgusting and ugly specimens, the rapid decay and rot on their faces having erased most traces of humanness.

The flapping pieces of clothing hanging from their legs and arms looked neither masculine nor feminine to Lizzie. Clumps of hair hung from the remaining grayish skin patches on their mostly bare skulls.

Decay had already eaten away the majority of their features leaving only gaping eye sockets and a hollow hole in the center where their noses had been. The holes now held a mass of nightmarish white worms wriggling inside. That the creatures turned and began moving in their direction as one made their eyeless appearance even creepier.

Her observations came to a halt as the first creature shuffled closer with a snarl. GRRRR! Lizzie jumped back and thrust her sword at it to make some room, catching the monster on its skeletal arm. The sword made a sickening scrape against its rotted arm bone.

"Emma! Get the other one." Lizzie motioned her to move aside. "Watch yourself. Don't let it get away!"

She thrust and danced, jabbed and jumped. The creature lunged, snarled, and chomped its mouth at her, the smell of rot wafting from between its few broken, blackened teeth. Out of the corner of her eye, Lizzie saw Emma jab at her evil pursuer. Her fighting skills proved to be adequate, but Lizzie had a bad feeling about how slowly her sister seemed to respond.

As if it sensed her momentary distraction, the creature in front of her moaned and swiped at her with its rotted fingers. Lizzie leaped out of the way and steadied herself. This had to end.

"Yiiiii!" She yelled and jumped forward, jabbing her sword through the ghoul's eye socket. Her action dislodged the squirming ball of worms, which dropped to the ground, the mass moving in a frenzy. The sword struck bone and then slid into the creature's soft, diseased brain mass. It released with a wet *slurrrp*. The spark of un-life faded, and the ghoul slumped to the ground, dying for the second, and final, time.

A grunt at her side alerted Lizzie to the second ghoul's impending attack. It clawed at her with the two remaining fingers left on its rotted left hand. Wasting no time, Lizzie pulled out the bat and swung. WHACK! The monster's skull exploded, sending pieces everywhere. The remaining rotted flesh folded in on itself like a piece of bad fruit as the fully dead body crumpled.

Lizzie had no time to savor her success, however, as Emma screamed. "Lizzie, help! Help me!"

In horror, Lizzie turned and ran to free her sister from a scene she knew would always haunt her—Emma wedged in a corner, swinging her sword at a steadily advancing group of creatures ugly enough to give her bad dreams for many sleepless nights to come.

Lizzie screamed to get their attention, to put their focus on her instead, but this time she failed. The garish group steadily closed in, keeping their empty eye sockets on the small figure bravely flailing away with her sword.

Her heart in her throat, Lizzie slashed at the other ghouls blocking her path. She stabbed and jabbed, making quick disposal of several more as she fought her way to get to Emma in time.

"Emma, keep fighting," Lizzie yelled. "Shoot them!"

"No gun! Lizzie, hurry, please hurry!"

Lizzie brought out her gun and aimed, but put it away a moment later. Given the close proximity, she couldn't chance hitting her sister. A quick glance told her she had a better chance of reaching Emma than Pierre, whom she saw fighting off a ghastly group near one of the neighbor's houses two doors away.

She slammed the bat into dead flesh. She swung and hit, sending the monsters crumbling and falling to bloody pieces to her left and right.

"Emma, keep fighting! Keep going!"

"Liz, help. I can't keep it up much longer. They're getting closer!"

With all her might, Lizzie fought and lunged. Her wild swings forged a path through the monsters. Only a few feet remained between her and Emma when Lizzie heard a terrible clatter of metal against stone. Emma cried out as the sword slipped from her hand, leaving her with only one weapon.

"No, No!" Lizzie screamed and pushed forward, shoving and swinging her bat like a madwoman. When the last few monsters dropped, she found herself inches away from a horrible creature. It looked barely human, its decomposed body mostly gore and decay. The rotted but still-moving remains came in closer, releasing a sickening aroma that made her wish she'd put cotton in her nostrils.

This was bad, but the scene beyond the crawling, snarling creature made Lizzie's heart stop. She held her breath at the sight of Emma's rich, deep brown hair, and the occasional tip of her bat, as she bravely swung at her last two attackers.

"Hang on, Emma, hang on!"

Whispering a silent prayer, Lizzie swung her own bat, hoping she could reach her sister in time.

Chapter Twenty-Seven

Q. See the gashes where his face was laid open?
A. No, sir.
Q. Nothing of that kind?
A. No, sir.
—Lizzie Borden at inquest, questioned by District Attorney
Hosea Knowlton, August 9-11, 1892

L izzie swung again—WHACK!—and cracked the head of the terribly putrefied creature nearest to her like a Brazil nut. What was left of its diseased brain spilled out in a black, oozing mess. She choked on the stench of death and rot, the odor worse than that of a skunk's decaying body lying on the side of the road.

Moving in closer, Lizzie came within swinging distance just as Emma screamed. The noise attracted two more undead, which came around the corner and moved in faster than Lizzie expected. Like one possessed, she swung like a wild woman against the horrific undead things encircling her.

"I'm close, Emma. Keep going, don't stop!"

Lizzie yelled and pulled out her dagger. Bat in one hand, the knife in the other, she stabbed one monster in the throat, grimacing at the flood of dead, black blood that oozed over the knife and onto her hand. Yet she couldn't stop. Lizzie stabbed and struck and jabbed.

Seeing her chance, she dropped the bat, got out the gun, and cocked it. Lizzie jammed it into the face of the other creature and pulled the trigger. *CRACK!* The thing reeled back and fell, the hole in its forehead telling her all she needed to know.

The gun re-cocked, she aimed, and fired again at one of the ghouls that had separated itself from the pack. It honed in on Emma, intent on taking her into its undead ranks. Now it fell truly dead. Finally, only two creatures remained between her and Emma.

"EMMA!"

Her yell got the creatures' attention like she'd hoped. The last two ghouls shuffled to one side, with Lizzie moving to the other. It was enough to give Emma room to get out of their reach and behind her.

ROWR! Both monsters went on the attack, fleshless arms raised, rotted hands reaching. As the undead duo lunged, Lizzie prayed for guidance, re-set the gun, aimed, and fired. BLAM! The bullet exploded the remaining pieces of one of the monster's rotted features into tiny bits. It rocked back and then fell in a gory mess at her feet. She whirled and plunged the dagger into the creature's eye as it jumped at her. It, too, fell with a final moan at her feet.

Lizzie let out a long sigh of relief as Emma emerged from behind her with a cry and fell into her arms. "Liz, Lizzie, I-I never thought I would make it." Her cries increased. "I-I want no more of this. I can't do it. I CAN'T!"

The street finally cleared, and with the last of the ghouls forever dead, Lizzie watched Pierre talking to the Society members who'd arrived for the clean-up. Sadly, she counted a couple neighbors' bodies among the fallen on the street. She waved and tried to get his attention. He loped over, a worried look on his face at the sight of Emma clinging to Lizzie's side like she'd never let go.

"Are you both all right?"

Lizzie gave a solemn nod and lowered her voice as Emma continued to cry in gulping sobs. "She's near hysterics. I'm taking her inside. We'll have to discuss things another time."

He reached over and squeezed her arm. "I understand. Have a good rest, both of you, and I'll check in with you tomorrow."

As he left, she spoke softly, urging her sister to come inside. "Emma, we should go in now, all right? I want to make you some tea, and we can get you into a hot bath. How does that sound?"

Emma mumbled as Lizzie led her inside and into the kitchen. Helping her into a chair, Lizzie quickly made two cups of strong black tea. Without hesitation, she added a good splash of whiskey to each of the cups. No question they both needed it.

The hot drink hit the spot. As Emma sipped and began to calm down, Lizzie gave her sister the once-over, her inner alarm clanging. She grabbed a wet cloth and wiped off most of the black gunk and blood that streaked Emma's face. She wiped Emma's hair, frowning at the spots of blood and fluids that dotted Emma's arms, blouse, and skirt. That was expected. Lizzie knew she looked as bad, if not worse, except for one difference—Emma's dress had several holes and tears in it. Her clothing had none.

Tears filled Lizzie's eyes at the thought of Emma getting harmed in all this. If anything happened to her...

She tried not to choke on the idea of what could've happened. Guilt flooded in. All those months Emma had been there for her, sitting in court, holding her up, keeping her spirits high when she faltered. Through the worst of it, Emma had never even had time to mourn the loss of Father and Mrs. Borden properly, all her focus being on Lizzie and the trial. Emma had been her main supporter—and she'd let her sister down.

A sob broke from Lizzie at the realization that she should've stopped Emma. No matter what, she should have insisted her sister stay inside the house where it was safe. Emma never, for any reason, should've gone into the fray, not under any circumstances!

"Oh, Emma, Emma." Lizzie tried to hold back the tears, but failed.

"I'm so sorry, Emma, I truly am sorry. I should've made you stay inside. You're not hurt, are you?"

Emma raised her tear and blood-streaked face, and smiled. "Hurt? No, I feel fine, jes' fine. I feel all right."

"Emma, your dress. It's ripped and torn. Are you sure you're not hurt anywhere?"

Perplexed, Emma shook her head and reached out to pat Lizzie's hand. "Nope. Only my dress is torn." She began to mumble again and then sighed. "They never touched me, they did not get me, no, not me."

"Are you sure?" She rose and went to refill their cups. "How about some more tea?"

Emma took a loud slurp and set the cup back down. "*Lis-che*, I am fine, so fine. Can I go to bed now? I feel tired, I could *ushhh* a nap."

Emma's slurring told Lizzie she'd better assist her sister in getting cleaned up while she could still walk. "Lean on me. Let me help you get changed and off to bed."

After Emma took a fast soak in the bath, Lizzie hurriedly washed herself off and changed into a clean dress. She then helped Emma wash her hair, braided it, and once she dressed, tucked her into bed. To Lizzie's immense relief, she saw no bloody spots or scratches anywhere on her. As she covered Emma and kissed her forehead, Lizzie knew they'd been extremely lucky—this time. Maybe next time they wouldn't be as fortunate.

As Emma fell into a deep sleep, Lizzie closed the door softly. She retired to the parlor and sipped her tea, enjoying the silence. From now on, she vowed to be more vigilant about keeping Emma safe. That was if her sister wanted anything to do with her at all anymore. She'd had the scare of her life. Lizzie wouldn't blame Emma if she decided against having anything to do with any of this anymore. Given today's events, that might be the answer to put both their minds at ease.

Too full of energy yet to sleep, she pulled over the pile of papers Mrs. Thatcher had given her, continuing where Emma had left off. Mostly she came across sheets of supplies, inventory, business letters, and more mundane papers.

Ready to stop, she yawned and turned over a few more pages when one of the letters in the pile caught her eye. In elegant and tasteful lettering, the top of the letter advertised *Borden and Almy, specialists in Crane's Patented Casket Burial Cases*, the business Father had operated with his former partner. The page contained a list of items ordered from a mortuary company, including cotton, gloves and a few tools, along with three-inch tall bottles, paper labels, and cement.

The list had her wondering, especially since she'd only known about Father selling the caskets, not the individual supplies. Nor had he done much in the undertaking end in recent years. Maybe he'd branched out into another auxiliary business. Why else would he need such items? Not that she seemed to know anything of what her father had been doing, of course.

The next letter made her even more curious. Typewritten on plain linen paper, the letter to Davis and

Hatch Spice Company in neighboring New Bedford included an order for ordinary ground spices like cinnamon and cloves, but the quantity made her take another look. Not twenty pounds, as she'd first thought, but—wait. Two hundred pounds? Why so much?

Cloves had a pleasant odor, she knew. Cinnamon, of course, also made a nice pomander. Both of them worked well perhaps for freshening the room the caskets sat in? Though she had no experience in such matters, she guessed it could help sales to ensure the room had no foul odors that could distract customers from their purchases. Otherwise, she had no idea how that fit into Father's business needs.

Lizzie yawned and stood to gather up the papers when she noticed the handwritten note on the bottom of the last page in the pile. The letter proved uninteresting. The note, however, had her mind searching for a plausible explanation.

In a firm, sprawling, and partly illegible hand, someone had added the question—Ask price, *gr—nd st—n—s. Deliver?* The center words had been written so fast the letters looked like a bunch of scribbles, not readable except by the writer. A dull throb in her forehead told her she'd already spent enough hours reading. Time to get away from this and rest her eyes. She gazed once more at the words, still unclear on the meaning. She decided to ask Emma to take a look once she woke. Maybe her sister could offer a fresh perspective, or do a better job at deciphering this than she had.

Rubbing her head again, she sighed and set the papers aside. At least she had no question about the identity of the note writer. The two initials couldn't be clearer: A.B. had to mean Andrew Borden, of course.

Father's secrets remained just that, but as Lizzie kept digging, with each little piece uncovered she knew the light

196

would soon fall on all his dealings. How it would affect her she didn't yet know. She'd had a difficult relationship with her father, a man who'd been overbearing at times, overly thrifty, and even stingy. But they had been closer once, as well, evidenced by the gold ring she'd given him years ago. It had remained on his finger until death.

If anything disturbing were found Lizzie guessed Emma would take it much harder than her. If at all possible, she vowed to soften the blow for her sister. That was one more thing she had to be diligent about.

Given the aftermath of the trial, plus the big changes in their lives, Lizzie still felt she owed Emma more than she had done. Through it all, Emma had stood by her. Her sister may be older, but Lizzie felt responsible for her, and to her.

With a sigh, Lizzie went up to bed. She hoped to catch at least a couple hours' rest despite her inner turmoil. Her heart felt heavy while her mind spun with more questions than answers.

Chapter Twenty-Eight

Q. Did you know that there was found… a hatchet and axe?
A. No, sir, I did not.
Q. Can you give any occasion for there being blood on them?
A. No, sir.
—Lizzie Borden at inquest, August 9-11 1892

A clatter of cups and kitchenware greeted Lizzie as she wandered into the kitchen the next morning and found Emma setting the table for breakfast. Her sister looked up and promptly dropped the floral china plate in her hand onto the floor, where it broke into several pieces.

"Oh, Emma, I'm so sorry. Did I startle you?"

"No." Emma tried to grab another plate, instead pushing a cup off the table edge. It, too, fell and broke with a crash.

"Emma, take it easy. Are you all right?"

She sighed. "Yes, no, I'm just a bit jumpy yet, I think."

"Please, take a minute. Now, breathe deep. Yes, again. There, better?"

Her sister nodded. "Yes, a little. I made Eggs Benedict. Oh, and what would Father want with grinding stones, of all things? Pour the tea, would you?"

The tea cup trembled in Lizzie's hand. She set it down before it, too, dropped and shattered. Her plan had been to tell Emma after breakfast about her findings. She'd wanted to ask Emma about the letter, or if she could decipher it, but it looked like the question was unnecessary.

"Wh-what? How did you know about that?"

Emma nodded at the letter and handwritten note on the table as she dished out the breakfast. "I saw that on the table where you left it. Those stones are massive. I have no clue what Father was making that he needed to buy such a thing, and order all those spices, too. It seems odd."

"It certainly is. I was going to ask what you thought. I couldn't make out those words for anything, what with the terrible writing. But I was pretty tired, too."

"Like with everything else, I suppose we'll know the answer soon enough." She tucked into her breakfast and urged Lizzie to do the same. "Eat while it's hot. We won't get any answers right away anyway."

"Right you are on that."

As they finished their meal, the thought of spending many more months ferreting out Father's secrets, and fighting off the undead creatures still shuffling around outside, weighed heavily on Lizzie. At least her fears of Emma never speaking to her again hadn't materialized. Happiness filled her at seeing her sister in good spirits. Best of all, she appeared healthy and unharmed, which gave Lizzie a most unexpected idea.

"I just had an interesting thought. What would you say about us having a party?"

"A party?"

"Yes, you know, have a few friends over for dinner and music. Enjoy a nice social evening here. We haven't invited anyone over since we moved. I think we both could use a night off. We deserve some relaxation."

Emma turned to the window and looked out. "I would think we have enough going on to keep us occupied."

She knew what Emma meant, of course, but the idea grew on her. Lizzie decided she couldn't take no for an answer. "Yes, but this is for only one night. I can invite our friends from the Society, the ulterior motive being they can keep an eye out for our uninvited, unwelcome, guests."

Emma answered with about the same enthusiasm Lizzie expected she'd get if she asked her sister to go fight monsters in the dark. At least Emma didn't totally pooh-pooh the suggestion.

"I suppose," Emma said. "Are you sure it's a good idea?"

"Positive. What can really go wrong?"

Lizzie felt uneasy as soon as the words left her lips, but decided she was just letting Emma get to her. "Our Society friends will be here on patrol. I would think Pierre would attend."

Emma only nodded and sipped her tea.

Her sister's lack of enthusiasm didn't dampen Lizzie's excitement. She thought maybe John and Mr. Jennings would come by, though she wasn't sure if that was a good idea or not. On second thought, she'd met some quite interesting theater people in recent months. The stage actress, Nance O'Neil, had tried to break the ice and draw her out with an invitation to one of her own shows. Lizzie decided maybe she needed to make new friends.

The party proved to be a great success, at least in Lizzie's opinion. Emma remained quiet afterward, but Lizzie credited it to her sister being tired and the change in their schedule, since they'd been up until the wee hours of the morning. The best thing, of course, was there hadn't been a creature to be found within shuffling or hearing distance of their front door. That, of course, was thanks to the diligence of Society members who'd kept a tight watch on the street. That might have been the best change.

As they sat in the parlor later that afternoon, Lizzie finally decided to broach the subject. "So, you haven't said much. Did you enjoy the party?"

"It was fine."

Emma's tone made Lizzie look up from the magazine she'd been reading. For whatever reason, Emma had been acting strangely. She'd been rather standoffish and quiet most of the day.

Lizzie had worried a little about the mix of people who'd been invited, but it proved fruitless since the guest list had dwindled considerably. It consisted of her, Emma, Pierre, several Society members, and some of her new theater friends. Old friends never bothered to even acknowledge her invitation, which is pretty much what Lizzie expected. John and others on her legal team stopped by to wish her well, but left quickly due to previous engagements, or so they'd claimed.

The real hurt fell on Emma, whom Lizzie felt never deserved being snubbed. Though none of her sister's friends, or even their cousins, chose to attend, Emma had seemed to take it in stride. Lizzie thought her sister had enjoyed herself. It had been a wonderful night mingling with such creative, fun, and humorous people like the most entertaining Miss O'Neil. The actress proved to be witty, charming, and the life of the party. To Lizzie's delight, Miss O'Neil invited her and Emma both to accompany a group of friends one weekend to the Columbian Exposition in Chicago. It sounded like a wonderful idea and looked to be a most fascinating event. She so wanted to see, and maybe even take a ride, on that new gigantic wheel built by Mr. Ferris.

Lizzie eyed her sister, wondering what was bothering her. "Emma? Is anything wrong?"

Emma shook her head. "No, not really."

201

"What is it then?"

"Nothing."

"Such a shame that none of your friends or our cousins could attend. They missed out."

"Never mind, Liz. That's all right. We did send the invitations on short notice."

Lizzie nodded, though she suspected that wasn't the problem. "That's my fault. I'm sorry I decided on this at the last minute. Maybe we can have just a dinner the next time. It was fun having the theater group here. What do you think?"

Emma raised an eyebrow. "Liz, should we really think of entertaining now with everything that's going on out there? And I'm not sure you can count much on show people. You know they're not always reliable."

Her sister's comment took Lizzie aback. She knew people in the theater and entertainment world were not considered by many in other social circles to be on the same social level. Not that any of that mattered to her anymore.

"Why, why, Emma," Lizzie sputtered. "I would say those people proved to be more reliable than our old friends, and even our family. After all, it's not like people here on the Hill or in the business district want anything to do with us, or, to be truthful, with me, unless they have a cause, or an event to solicit funds for. Am I right?"

Emma's face turned a deep scarlet.

Regret filled her. *Poor thing. I know she feels stuck between her loyalty to me and keeping some semblance of her old life, and trying to form a new one. It must be terribly hard for her.*

"I'm sorry, Emma. I didn't mean to make you feel bad."

Emma got to her feet, her face emotionless. "I'll be in my room. I think I'll pack and leave tomorrow. I want to visit my friends again in Fairhaven. I intend on spending a few days there."